Melkorka

The Thrall Prinsessa's saga

Alfreða Jonsdottir

Melkorka

The main characters are taken from the Icelandic Sagas. According to Laxardal Saga some of the events did happen but I have expanded on these events and on their lives which make them all a work of fiction. The characters not taken from the sagas are a total work of fiction.

Dedication

This book is decicated to my granddaughters
Charlotte and Emily

Melkorka

Index

Gaelic:

a stor = dear heart

Mæl Curcaig = Melkorka

Muirchertach = Mykjartan

Icelandic:

Dagmal = breakfast

eg þu elska = I love you

elskaminn = my dear

goða nott = good night

goði = chieftain

hellavitas = oh hell

Hoskuldstaðir = Hoskuld´s farm

Min = my

Nattmal = dinner

Pa = pai = peacock

Sonargolttr = winter soltice = Yule

Thrall = slave

Melkorka

Part I

Kidnapped

"They came out of the mist on an icy wind,

and froze the blood of weaker men."

Author unknown

Melkorka

Melkorka

Princess
Mæl Curcaig

Melkorka

Chapter 1 - Leinster, Ireland, 937 AD

The land was shrouded in an ominous cloud of dense fog that floated over the land – 'beware of dangers lurking nearby' it threatened. Through this floating grey mist Katie and I followed the footpath like ghosts walking through their own magical haze. This pathway was a short cut from the main castle which I had used on many occasions on my own. Usually there was laundry hanging on the clothes lines erected between the trees and with the wind that normally blew through this passageway it created a flapping sound, a comforting sound, of busyness. However this morning nothing was moving, the silence was sinister, threatening even. I was thankful for Katie's company. As I got closer to my destination shards of sunlight suddenly burst through the heavy fog. "Welcome sunshine," my voice dissolved into the mist which was suddenly twinkling with little firefly lights. The sun was desperately trying to peek through causing the moisture to twinkle like jewels as my salutations were carried off towards the struggling sun, to my beacon of hope, for a clear sky and to a glorious day of discovery.

Katie was one of the castle's servants, she accompanied me most of the way, then turned to the left towards the laundry door lugging a sack of my dirty linens. She bid me farewell as she disappeared into the mist. Chuckling out loud I skipped over the stone path trying to avoid the cracks much like I did as a child trying to avoid any bad luck. This whole day was going to be exciting – so much was happening. I headed straight towards the door at the end of the path as it was my starting point for my little adventure. Once through the door I knew it would be warm and inviting there – a safe refuse from this menacing silence.

"Good morning Cook" I called out as I entered the castle's kitchen, "it smells good in here as usual." I hung my damp cloak on a peg by the door then sat down at the heavy oak table still talking excitedly.

Melkorka

"This is the best time of day and your kitchen is the most comforting part of the castle. Did you see that thick fog out there? It felt magical and strangely threatening. Katie and I could just barely see the path. In truth, we could barely see each other, we looked like ghosts walking side by each. Although I did see that the sun was starting to work its' magic so I hope most of it has thinned out drastically by the time we are ready to go to the monastery."

"Yes I do know it is foggy and a good morning to you too m'lady, our lovely Princess Mæl Curcaig. You are always a breath of fresh air and as talkative as ever." Cook responded with a smile and a slight curtsy. "The good Lord has blessed you this morning and the fog will surely lift, it is nice to see that you are starting the day with such a positive attitude."

 She placed a steaming bowl of porridge on the table in front of me with a thick slice of freshly made bread smothered in butter. Devouring the warm bread first, I managed to tell cook between bites how much I loved her bread. Next I faced my porridge in complete silence. My mind was racing with ideas about dressing my hair, I needed the right hair style to go with my new grownup gown. All this anticipation of tonight's party kept me silent which was unusual, I admit, plus my new gown had just arrived last night and it was all I could think about. Cream coloured lace ruffles, that cost a king's ransom, dressed the edge of the sleeves and around the lower than normal neckline. The dress itself was the most beautiful turquoise blue. Suddenly I had this urgent need to tell Cook about my dress so I broke my silence exclaiming,

"Cook, I finally have a dress that will make me look more like an adult. Father has agreed that I can have my hair up too. Mor has found someone who is an expert at dressing hair and I have my mother's pearls to wind into the braids -- the creaminess of the pearls will match the lace on my dress. I am so nervous but excited at the same time. Tonight, just before dinner, I get to meet my future husband for the first time! As a princess I must look the part, don't you think?"

Melkorka

Cook responded breathlessly as she heaved a bag of flour onto her work space. "Yes m'lady, I am well aware of your special night tonight, you have talked of nothing else since you arrived. Two days ago, wasn't it? Also, I am the one cooking all those special dishes for tonight's celebration, remember."

"Yes, of course Cook, I did know that, it's just that I am so excited, maybe even a little scared if truth be told."

"Of course, m'lady, I understand and have no fear, you are a princess through and through, there is no need for a fancy dress to state that fact. Now take your time eating as we want most of this mist to lift off before your little journey."

Niall, cook's husband, should be here soon, I thought to myself. I am going on a little adventure with him, to Kilcullen Monastery and if it is too foggy he may not agree to let me go. He always picks up the beer order for this castle, Dun Ailinne and since today is the spring festival he will need to pick up than normal. My family and I came to this castle two days ago to attend the festival, we never miss it but today is extra special. The Northern O'Neill family will arrive later today to formalize my marriage contract with their son Liam.

"Cook, I understand that a troop of soldiers will have to escort us home as this beer order is such a valuable cargo. Is this true?"

"Yes m'lady. Why else do you think Niall agreed to let you tag along! The precious kegs of beer and you yourself being almost as valuable, the troop is a necessary precaution."

'Dun Ailinne, God I love coming here.' It is an imposing place, a royal castle and an ancient seat of the kings of Leinster. My grandfather lives here, he is the High King of Tara and the spring festival was always an exciting time to visit. The beer is the most important part of this celebration and will be eagerly awaited by all, young and old. This famous brew is made by the monks and Kilcullen Monastery is located

but a few short miles from here. I always enjoy going there but today –
'ahh today -- is special.'

"Niall better not change his mind about me tagging along," I exclaimed
under my breath as I stabbed my spoon into the middle of the porridge.
'Darn – I forgot the cream and honey' and proceeded to heap lots of the
sticky sweetess on top, stirred it well, then poured plenty of fresh cream
into the mix.

My nursemaid, Mor, was just telling me yesterday that I had always
been such a precocious child, but that now I had grown into a mature
young woman. How did she say it again?

*'Overnight m'lady, you have become this dazzling mature young lady, a
magical change!'* with her hand over her mouth in mock surprise.

My lovable nanny knows I am already fifteen summers, a good age for a
marriage contract. My father has been busy negotiating it since our
feast of the birth of Christ last winter. Sometimes I think Mor doesn't
want me to grow up, I think she would have me live like a child forever if
she could. I do think these marriage negotiations were the driving force
behind me shedding my immaturity. Under my father's scrutinizing eyes
I have had to act more like a grown-up recently, unable to run off to
discover things or get dirty. Childhood was such fun, I will miss it but
that is for children now, not for me. All my life I was groomed to be
married off to someone important so these talks came as no surprise.
*'Yes, childhood was a safe haven and now I must step out of that world
and into the world of adults. A scary reality, yes, but also a new
adventure. '*

My father and his powerful allies chose to work out a marriage
agreement with the O'Neil family from Galway, a family which would
bolster his power base and hopefully impress grandfather -- the High
King -- his father-in-law. My father is Muirchertech Cochall Craicinn
MacNeill, King of Alech, Leinster, a powerful king and my marriage will
help secure his control over the areas he rules. His rule is always

challenged by other petty Irish kings, trying to take over parts of his holdings. Ireland is ruled by many different tribes and these rival kings often encourage small uprisings of father's people, telling them that they are badly mistreated by him – convincing the peasants that they would treat them more as equals. Father, in turn, tries to convince them that these other kings or rebels as he calls them, are lying, these so called kings would not treat them any different than he does. He is not often successful, even though he is right – maybe it is the way he approaches his people? He can be rather arrogant with his peasants.

Also, in the past there were raids by those fierce Northmen. Father wants to be prepared to fight them off and has plans to fend them off, some of which were already in place. These raids are quite rare now but he needs this powerful family's support to suppress all uprisings and raids, whether Irish or Norse. The most important goal father says, as a king, is to secure peace over his lands. He is banking on this expanded control through an alliance with the O'Neills of the north and my marriage to the younger son. Father claims there is an ancient line to our families making us distantly related. Straightening my posture to sit more upright like a princess should, I sliced through all the rambling thoughts racing around in my head and deduced silently to myself,

'I understand more than you realize father. I also know that you want to be next in line to become the High King. You covet the Kingship of Tara, the highest title in all of Ireland – the title grandfather now holds but I think he is ornery enough to outlive all of us.'

Father does not always get along with the *'old man'* as he refers to him in private. Father also knows that the *'old man''* does not care much for him so he is hoping that this deal will help improve their relationship, at least for a while. When father has had a lot to drink he becomes loud and boastful, my brothers and I have often overheard his conversations with his new wife, Siobhan, our stepmother, whom we all despise. We generally know exactly what father is thinking and what he is planning next.

Melkorka

'Hmmm...' I mulled to myself, *'I wonder if grandfather has a nickname for you, father?'*

Last year father had organized a large army with the help of the O'Neill clan and with over one thousand Irish men, they forced the ruling Vikings out of Dublin. It was quite a *'coup de force'* for him and I was very proud of him. This expulsion of the Dublin Vikings put him in the good books with *'the old man'* last year. Although -- only temporarily

Grandfather's wife Emer, my grandmother, is really the only one related to the O'Neills. They are a very powerful dynasty and many of our Irish kings or queens claim to be related to them -- somehow. Father tried to explain it all to me but it was just too confusing to remember all those ancient names. This O'Neill family control all the northern lands, the largest holdings of any clan in Ireland and grandfather was the one who urged father to make this marriage contract with one of their sons. He has always wanted a stronger connection with the famous O'Neills from the north. I do understand that I am just a pawn in their ambitious plans. Oh well – I am only a woman!

Cook disturbed my thoughts as she took away the bowl. "You have been in another world since you arrived this morning m'lady. You have done nothing but mumble into your food."

I jumped at her voice in my ear. Fearing I may have mumbled something that she had overheard. I admonished her with my princess airs.

"Oh, I was just thinking about the marriage discussions. The negotiations are progressing rapidly towards a final settlement. There are just a few minor issues to sort out, so it has been absorbing my thoughts lately."

She arched her eyebrows as if to say, *'who are you?'*

Then I relaxed and smiled at her remembering she was just teasing me and admitted to her that I was really looking forward to this short escape with her husband, to enjoy my short lived freedom and go to Kilcullan Monastery, a place I delight in visiting.

"Cook, it may be a long time before I can go to Kilcullan again, if ever. Soon enough I will not only need to adjust to being a married woman but to living in another part of Ireland. The actual marriage will probably take place next year, depending on what my father negotiates, so I have time to adjust. My mind has been full of plans just for today's fete and I cannot think ahead to my special day until I get to meet my intended."

To myself I quickly prayed that my stepmother had no say in any of today's plans and especially nothing to do with my wedding plans. What a horrible woman she is and I will be only too happy to leave her out of it all.

Cook stood there with her arms crossed so I continued, "I am so looking forward to this year's festival -- to tonight's party -- to meeting Liam O'Neil for the first time. There, now you know what I was thinking about!" Cook nodded. "My marriage to him will be announced at tonight's dinner." I stopped short, "but of course you know all this. I am excited and scared at the same time – this is an important milestone in my life. Soon enough I will have to live elsewhere – far from familiar places. That's the scary part! The most important thing today is that I have the most perfect dress for the occasion and with my hair all done up I intend to dazzle this handsome fiancé of mine -- this Liam O'Neill."

Just then Niall burst into the kitchen and asked his wife for his gruel, "Make sure porridge is hot wife and has plenty of cream on top -- I am bloody freezing with this dampness and very hungry."

Cackling like he normally does when he sees me, he acknowledged my presence with a formal bow. "And a very good morning to you m'lady. Are you prepared for the trip – do you even want to come what with this cold foggy weather?"

"Of course I still want to come Niall, if you are still willing to take me. Besides you know that today is a special trip for me." Niall was just trying to provoke me, I am quite familiar with his ways. He knows that I love to go to the monastery, so I played along.

Cook cut in to our conversation saying that "Princess Mæl has been in dream land the whole time she has been here. The cold fresh air will wake her up and chase all her fears out of that pretty head of hers. It will do you good too husband of mine, to get away -- out of my hair! I have many preparations to oversee for tonight's dinner."

"Hmmmmm!" said Niall, as he sat down across from me. Whatever was that supposed to mean – men!

Chapter 2 - Kilcullen Monastery

Niall looked across at me after he had finished and asked me to tell him what I knew about the monastery.

"You are testing me right?"

'Hmmmm,' was his only answer. I knew he was killing time till more of the fog lifted.

"Well Old Kilcullen Monastery has a lot of history attached to it as you well know. St. Patrick himself had established the monastery in the 5th century and it was and still is full of religious treasures. So there -- I am very aware of all the history attached to this place. The monastery sits on a hill and boasts a high round tower which houses the scriptorium and has many crosses surrounding it. One of which is very special, a beautifully decorated cross that sits close to the front entrance, the one I especially want to see. The locals simply call it the High Cross and I want to study the designs on it so I can incorporate the less complicated ones into my embroidery. The other smaller crosses are plainer, but just as beautiful in their own way. Old Kilcullen is situated close to the River Liffey so we can get to Dublin quickly via this river, although, being so close to the river also makes us more vulnerable from attacks. There are several main roads that enter into the township but the high walls protect the main village within. It started off as just a monastery but in the last few centuries it has developed into a sizeable town which has expanded to even more houses hugging the outside wall. Inside the walls in the central court there is an active market place and today is a special market day because the whole county will be celebrating the spring fest. There -- is that enough information for you?"

"Tell me what happens in case of an invasion," Niall asked.

Melkorka

"Well, if a likely invasion was sighted from the monastery itself, the bells within would be rung vigorously giving everyone ample time to escape inside and close both gates, front and back. My father had the foresight to set up several early warning stations along the Liffey just last year after expelling all the Norsemen from Dublin. The sentry stations are not far away, they can get to the monastery quickly by horse, in time to warn everyone and as they arrive closer they will blow a horn. It will warn everyone and we can all get inside. Then the horseman will ride off to find help."

Suddenly a man poked his head through the door telling Niall that they were ready.

"Good" he said, "let's go m'lady, the horse and cart are just outside the door."

We said our goodbyes to Cook as she handed me a cloak from one of the kitchen slaves as well as a head scarf in exchange for my fancier cloak which would remain on the peg until my return. This was meant to be a disguise, to hide the fact that I was a princess. Plus the scarf would protect my hair from the cold wind and the mist that hoovered over the land.

"This way m'lady," Niall said as he walked ahead to the cart.

There was some light fog still hanging over the land, how quickly the warm sun had eliminated the mist while I was inside eating and talking. Shivering in the thin cloak but grateful for the scarf, I quickly wrapped it around my hair. Niall waited patiently then helped me up onto the cart, then handed me a wool blanket to put over my knees. He went around to his side and groaned as he got up onto the bench. As an old man he must have many pains but he quickly settled himself then picked up the reigns, slapped them against the hind quarters of the two old hags pulling the cart and we set off on our little adventure. The two guards fell in behind us.

Melkorka

Thinking back to my conversation with Niall I realized how secure my father had made me feel by evicting all those Northmen. But even with all this new security, I don't think he will be very happy with me if he ever finds out about today's trip. Shrugging off any doubts I reminded myself that he always forgives me and besides, since he has sent those fierce Vikings fleeing from Dublin to Northumbria there have been no more problems. So why am I worried about what father thinks.

Bored just sitting and staring at the disappearing mist, I decided to continue our conversation about Kilcullen's history. Being quiet was just too difficult for me and we had a long ride together. It was better than talking about the weather, although it was encouraging to watch the mist dissolving in front of our very eyes.

"As for the monastery itself, it used to be the main part with just a small little village within the high walls. The monastery itself has not expanded and is still located within the walls near the main gate but the village is spilling over to the outside walls. Right next door to the monastery is the brewery. Our destination."

"You already mentioned that part about the village growing m'lady."

"Did I? Yes – so I did. My apologies Niall, my mind seems to be elsewhere these days. Well, the monks maintain extensive gardens inside the walls where they grow mainly vegetables along with herbs for flavouring their food and for medicinal purposes. Outside the walls is another much larger plot of land where they plant the hops needed to brew their beer. Their beer is very tasty, don't you agree?"

I didn't give him time to answer. "I love it too. Haven't they become the most famous brew masters within our local county? Father has even brought it in to our castle at Mullaghat. These beer profits provide a very decent income for the monastery giving them the means to sustain a functional scriptorium as well as the means to add to and maintain all the treasures they possess. Most of which are donated by wealthy landowners, in memory of loved ones. The monastery is a treasure trove of gold religious ornaments as well as many gold and silver vessels which are used by the monks every day. Is that enough history for you? It is certainly enough for me."

All Niall said was his usual "hummmm!"

Suddenly out of the blue, fear gripped my heart. Where did that come from? Why was I thinking like this? I realized that defying father today of all days would probably make him quite angry with me if he knew.

'This will be the last time father, I promise', I silently vowed to myself. Then I made the sign of the cross and prayed he would never find out. *'Stop all this senseless worrying,'* I silently admonished myself.

I looked over at Niall shyly wondering if I had talked out loud. He was shaking his head probably wondering what was going on in my head but I was sure I had not talked out loud. Today is going to be such a perfect day so once again I reassured myself—silently -- that I could always talk my way back into father's good graces.

Before I knew it we had left the forest behind. The high walls of Old Kilcullen came into our view, far in the distance, shimmering in the light mist that was still hovering over their stately walls. Most of it had dissipated, except for a heavier mist lingering over the river itself. Niall must have read my mind. He pointed to the mist over the river,

"Look ahead m'lady, the sun is doing a good job and soon the heat from it should dissolve the remaining mists that still hovers over our Liffey. It looks like it will be a beautiful day."

Niall was referring to the River Liffey which ran along the front of the monastery, past the hill of crosses. The locals just refer to it as 'our Liffey'.

"Yes, I agree. It is turning out to be a lovely spring day and hopefully it will warm up even more. It's almost like the mists have washed the air and left in its' place a clean fresh scent, don't you think?"

Melkorka

"Hmmmm," Niall had fallen back to his normal comment to everything.

The horses clipped slowly along the path. The monastery was just ahead but somehow it never got any closer. I was beginning to feel like we would never get there.

"Is this the fastest the horses can go Niall?"

"Patience m'lady, it's not like the monastery will disappear on you."

I kept my eyes focused and stared at the monastery that loomed through the dissipating mist ahead of us and I thought of St. Patrick, our patron saint and the founder of the monastery. In my head I started a silent conversation with him, I even asked him to bless my marriage and my family. Before I knew it we entered the monastery through the back gate while our two guards carried on towards the front gate to wait for the troop to escort us back to the castle. Once we were safely inside the old horses slowed down even more, they almost stopped moving as they maneuvered through all the people inside. Niall was greeting everyone it seemed.

'Now he decides to talk!' I was quite frustrated with him.

We were moving even slower, if that was even possible! The poor horses could barely continue for people who were not watching where they were going. Nevertheless, we s-l-o-w-l-y made our way towards the front gate where the brewery was located.

I couldn't seem to stop myself – I grew even more impatient, *'darn it'*, I thought to myself, *'I could walk faster, maybe I should get off and do just that, walk! Niall should have gone around to the front gate like the guards did instead of trying to go through all these people. STOP IT!'* I reminded myself, this is one of the character flaws that I had inherited from my father. I must learn to be more patient so I decided to say a few more prayers to get my mind of my restlessness. Praying was a form of mediation for me, it usually calmed me down. The prayers worked – the next thing I knew we had arrived at our destination. Niall jumped down and tied the horses to a post near the door of the brewery.

Over to our left was the main gate which overlooked the Liffey and the hill of crosses that straddled the path from the river. I could see some of them from where I was still sitting on the cart. Sparkling behind them was the thinning mist that still hovered over the river. '*Funny how fog lingers longer over water than land*.' Staring out at the mist over the Liffey, I planned my route in my head as I waited for Niall to help me down. '*Soon the last of the fog will be gone so I shall go see the crosses last I decided*.'

Intoxicated with the freedom of escape and the freedom of discovery I focused my mind on my Book of Psalms which would be in the tower where the scriptorium was located. The book was the main reason for this outing with Nial – a trip without father's blessings. This exorbitant wedding present, a gift which only church bishops or royalty could afford, was not meant to impress me, only my future in-laws but I had an insane need to preview this part of my dowry. It would be the only part of the dowry that would become part of my life. Now to find the abbot.

Niall came around and I regretfully laid aside my warm blanket on the bench seat as he helped me down from the cart. "I shan't be too long m'lady, maybe two bells at most. Where should I pick you up?"

Since I had already decided where my last stop would be I answered with confidence. "Pick me up near the front gate close to where the crosses are located."

Niall answered, "Good choice, the guards will easily see you so you will be safe there."

I found the abbot quicker than I thought I would and he asked me to meet him in the church when they rang the next bell. By then he would have the key for the door to the scriptorium but in the meantime I could tour the monastery on my own or go to the market.

Melkorka

I chose the market and as I wandered off towards it, I thought about my prayer to St. Patrick to bless my marriage to Liam O'Neill. We Irish pray a lot and especially for me prayers had a calming effect on my anxious nature. Lately I was having more anxious moments thinking of Liam and my upcoming nuptials, always wondering what he would be like. Would he be kind, a gentle husband or a rough demanding one? My brothers often teased me about him which did not help my constant worrying. They claimed that he was handsome, brave even, but to watch out, he liked the women.

'Bah! What men don't? My brothers and even my father are quite guilty themselves of liking women!' He had gone on the Dublin invasion with them last year ousting those Northmen. He proved to be a mighty warrior and with my active imagination he had become my prince in shining armour. *'We will be so happy together.'*

Although apprehensive, I felt proud of my future husband. He could easily have been an old man, someone I might have found difficult to live with and to care for but thankfully father had chosen a young man, closer to my own age. My role in this family really is an important one and I hope father realizes that I understand this role very clearly. I am only a woman and women from such a formidable family as mine are used as tools in marriage contracts for political power. Even my brothers are subjected to father's choice of women for marriage.

Once again I thanked God that father's choice had not been some decrepit old man whose power may have been more important than the O'Neill dynasty. I realized then just how much I looked forward to a life as a grownup, especially with Liam by my side. It would be an exciting spring fete and I had that very special dress ready to wear.

Looking up I realized I had already arrived at my favorite stall in the market. There were threads from all over the known world, made from silk, wool, cotton and even linen, hand dyed in the most amazing colours. There were gold and silver threads as well but the brilliantly coloured silk and wool threads were my favorite for embroidery with

Melkorka

just a little gold for embellishment. I made my choices then handed them to the stall keeper to wrap up, I did not want to be late for the abbot.

Chapter 3 – Waiting for Father Michael's return

There was no one at the monastery when I returned but the bell in the tower had yet to strike the hour. The abbot would return soon enough, rather than wait outside I wandered in to look at the relics. The abbey contained an amazing collection and many precious items were just sitting safely out in the open. No local would dare touch them. I had been gazing at the statue of Jesus when the bell rang the hour. Shivering from the cold and damp inside the abbey, I wrapped my cloak tighter around my body. That's when I noticed just how tatty the cloak really was. For these outings with Niall, Cook would make me wear an old wool cloak that usually belonged to one of the kitchen maids and the condition of the cloaks varied, depending on the maid she borrowed it from. Today it was shabbier then normal but it was clean and it covered my plain grey day dress. It also hid the beautiful belt that Mor, my nursemaid, had made. Although my everyday dress was plain, it was made of very good quality wool and would have stood out. The sleeves were bell shaped with a little embroidery along the edges and the exquisitely embroidered belt hung loosely around my waist. This belt would have given me away as someone other than a peasant. Attached to it was a tiny purse holding a few coins, mostly pennies that I could use if I found anything I desired at the market – *which I did*! I had removed it to pay the stall merchant and still had the purse in my hand. Normally there would be a pair of scissors hanging on my belt as well as my room keys but this morning there was no need for them.

Ireland did not have any coins of their own, we used the English coins for bartering in our markets. The Vikings brought them to our land and introduced us to them. Not too long ago I had overheard father talking about minting our own one day soon. He had said if the English and even the Vikings can mint coins than we can too. Smiling I looked at the compact purse in my hand, it looked like a simple medallion, unnoticeable as a coin purse. I kept stroking the outline of the embroidery on the purse, thinking about Mor, *'she is such a genius with the needle.'*

I shivered with the cold and wrapped my cloak tightly around my body. Thankfully no one would take any notice of me in this old cloak and especially with my hair covered like a peasant's, thanks to Cook's crafty disguise. She was always looking out for me and the important thing about the cloak was that it did make me feel safe. The monks, of course, knew me. They knew that I was the princess of Mullaghat castle where my father's primary base was located within the lands of Leinster. They also knew that the High king was my grandfather.

I sat in one of the pews waiting for the abbot to show up with the keys for the scriptorium. Feeling a bit warmer I loosened my hold on the cloak and felt for the hidden pouch under my petticoat. I should put away the threads I had just bought. Since no one was around I slipped them into the secret pouch through a slit in my dress. I felt my rosary beads there and withdrew them and hung onto them along with my little purse. I would need the remaining coins left for the donation box.

This pouch under my dress was a secret place where I carried some of my treasures, like the gold ring band given to me by my father when I cut my first tooth, a small knife with an ornate bronze handle given to me by my nursemaid which I used mainly to cut threads, an ivory comb -- hand carved -- among other silly little trinkets. As a young girl I had always carried a needle and some cotton thread in case I ripped my clothes playing and needed a quick repair and had to appear before father or grandfather before I had a chance to change. Thinking about all these unnecessary trinkets, I chastised myself for not being able to break this habit. I realized that nowadays most of them were unnecessary.

I am much more careful now that I have grown up, I really need to re-evaluate all these things I carry in this pouch,' I decided. *'Maybe I need to get rid of the secret pouch altogether. I will put away most of the bits and pieces I have always carried around when I get back to the castle. At the very least, the sewing items could be put into my sewing case. I am so careful now and too grownup for these childish accidents.'* Somehow I had mumbled the last out loud and startled myself.

"Blessed father... I really need to stop talking to myself."

Needlework and mending were an important skill for young women of my status, my sewing kit was quite large and well stocked and it travelled with me wherever I went. My nursemaid, Mor, was very accomplished at needlework and she had taught me well. She often told me that I was an adept student but the truth was that it wasn't difficult for me. I loved doing it and it meant that I would have my beloved nursemaid all to myself. Embroidery released my creative spirit and it transformed the mundane into a thing of beauty.

From the day I was born, my father had declared that Mor's duty was to make me into a lady and many days I know she had despaired of this ever happening. She often told me so. Just this morning after she had helped me dress she had stepped back with that admiring look of hers telling me that I had grown into a beautiful pious young lady.

Chuckling out loud, *'I know the pious part is more important to her than the beautiful part. Mor doesn't realize that I just look more pious lately as I have so much on my mind, too much to think about.'*

Sadly, Mor is the only female role I have. My mother died in child birth, giving birth to another girl four years after I was born. My baby sister did not survive either after our mother died. Now I am the only daughter, although I do have many brothers to keep the family line secure and now a new stepmother, Siobhan. I looked up at the statue of Jesus thinking he could read my thoughts.

"Forgive me blessed father, I cannot help my feelings about this woman. I just do not like her."

Melkorka

This dreadful woman came from a small tribe just north of father's holdings. Her father was a minor king and had no sons so he made father an offer. He would make him his heir if he married his daughter. She really is a beautiful woman, there is no doubt about that, but she is so full of herself, such an ambitious busy body. She constantly pushes my father into deals that create misunderstandings with his own people. He is an expert at that on his own, he certainly doesn't need her help. With her behind him, egging him on -- these disagreements occur more often than necessary. I certainly agree with my oldest brother and grandfather on this one. Father can be too rash in his judgements and she was his worst decision.

Feeling guilty I looked up to the statue again.

"You must understand Lord Jesus why I dislike her so, but for your sake I will try to find some good in her -- when I get back to grandfather's castle. I promise"

Now Flann, my mother, had been a very different person from my stepmother -- according to my nursemaid. My mother had been born into royalty, not like Siobhan who doesn't have anything royal about her, just a lot of ambition fueled by an enterprising father who through force made himself king of his small holding. My mother was the daughter of the High King Donnchad, my grandfather, the king of Tara. She had the most beautiful red hair, almost the colour of bronze, according to Mor, with incredible green eyes. My black curly hair and blue eyes I got from my father, my temperament I inherited from my mother, well mostly from my mother. My impatience, a definite character flaw, I inherited from my father. I barely remember my mother, all I can recall are her loving hugs plus her smell. I remember vividly, to this day, the feel of her arms and the smell of her lavender water. I like to think that my parents had come to love each other, even though they two, like myself, had been pawns in a marriage contract.

Mor had been my mother's nursemaid, then after mother had children she became our nursemaid. She told us many stories about our mother not just as a young child, but as a young woman. She claimed that my father loved her very much and her death had torn him apart. When we are alone Mor calls me Mæl 'a stor'' which is a Gaelic term of endearment 'my heart'. As children I would sit in Mor's lap with the youngest brothers sitting on the floor. They outgrew her stories quickly but I never did. As I got older I would snuggle beside her, both of us embroidering something together and she would tell me tales of my mother as well as many of our ancient Irish stories. I will never tire of them and hopefully she will be around to tell the same ones to my children. I love her like a mother and I feel blessed by her love and adoration. She will definitely come to live with me wherever I go.

"Praying are we?"

The abbot had crept in so quietly that I nearly jumped out of my skin.

"In the name of God you frightened the daylights out of me, father Michael. Yes -- I was. I was thinking about my nursemaid and giving thanks to God for her training and constant love and affection. She has been my mother role all these years, I feel very blessed and I have much to be thankful for."

"You do indeed young lady, now let us go as I have the keys. It was difficult to find the master of the keys, he was busy with an important landowner so I apologize for my tardiness."

'Yes', I thought to myself, *busy making a list of all that the landowner has and asking when and what would come to the monastery, I bet.'* There goes my suspicious mind again. Maybe I am more like my father than I want to believe.

"I beg your forgiveness Father Michael, my mind is not my own today."

Fumbling with my rosary beads I slipped them into a crudely made pocket inside my cloak and followed the abbot. I kept my purse handy as I would need the remaining coins for the donation box.

Chapter 4 - Tour of the Scriptorium

The scriptorium was an enigma, it was the first time ever I had access to such a mysterious place and today I had a mission. Once we entered the tower we had to climb a steep staircase full of dark shadows but once at the top we arrived at a very brightly lit space from the many openings in the wall. These windows had stretched animal bladders inserted for protection from the elements. As we walked around we discussed the different books the monks were working on. I relished in their beauty, they were works of art which only the rich could afford. Unfair I suppose, that they were so beautiful and so very expensive but then only the rich could read.

'Peasants can't read so why would they want or need a book of such value.'

When we viewed the books the monks were working on he pointed out the special orders and explained who they were for. All were rich landowners who had just made enormous contributions to the monastery, my father was one of them and that was why he was so eager to give me a tour. Father had commissioned a book of psalms for me as a wedding gift which I knew about and desperately wanted to see. My curiosity was the driving force behind my journey today. This precious gift, this leather bound book of Psalms, was going to be beautiful when completed. The front book clasp was ornate with a large amber stone embedded in it, the whole front cover looked like a piece of jewelry. The back cover clasp, although it had no jewel, was just as ornately carved. Two braided calf skin ties were attached to each side of the book which I could tie into a bow to keep the book securely closed. Inside, the cover page was illuminated with some colourful drawings, the iconography was outstanding, as for the text itself, it was in the Irish language hand printed in the classic Gaelic type. *A rare treasure indeed*! The book, according to the scribe working on it, would be ready within the next few months, in plenty of time for the wedding ceremony. The tour completed, I gave my thanks to Father Michael for being such an enlightening guide, then added the few coins I had left to a donation box placed conveniently on the way out.

Before approaching the stairs, I slipped my now empty coin purse into that crudely made pocket inside my cloak along with my rosary beads. As I walked down the stairs behind the abbot I could feel them bouncing around together so when I reached the bottom I took out the rosary beads and kept them wrapped around my hand. It would be easier to attach the purse to my belt later when I got back to the castle. Once we were outside in the sunshine, I bowed to his grace and thanked him again for the tour. He put his hand on my head and said a quick blessing. "May the good Lord bless you and keep you safe. May your journey into marriage be fruitful with many children who will honour and respect their mother and father. In God's name we pray, Amen." We both did the sign of the cross in unison. "Now I must leave you here Princess Mæl. I have to return to the scriptorium and go over the accounts with the monks. I just hope my old bones can handle the climb twice in a row."

We once again made the sign of the cross together, then departed company. Walking backwards for a few steps I said my goodbyes then turned sharply and headed towards the path by the front gate. I heard the loud clunk as the key once again locked the stout door to the tower. Niall was loading the last of the barrels on the cart when I walked by. He assured me that I would be safe with the guards nearby and that he would be there shortly to pick me up.

"Once the troop has arrived we will come for you. They appear to be late for whatever reason and it had better be a good one. They should be arriving soon so do not fret."

Although relieved they were running late, I nodded my assent, turned to continue my way to the crosses, but first I acknowledged the guards with a nod and pointed to the big cross. I was sure they had heard Niall say he would pick me up there. They stood at attention, acknowledging my presence as they should. I walked a short distance then stopped to take a deep breath of the fresh air. As I slowly exhaled I noticed that the thinning mists still hung over the Liffey. It was going to be a beautiful day indeed, I thought to myself. I am looking forward to a wonderful evening with Liam, my husband-to-be, at my side. Life felt secure and I was content with it all.

Chapter 5 – The Viking raid

Fondling my rosary beads, I stood in front of one of the smaller crosses to study the intricate designs. As the sun warmed my back, I felt my whole body slowly relax, my normal, jittery impatience fled from the contentment that flowed throughout me. It was so peaceful here –Niall and the troop can take their time -- I was in no hurry to leave. The heat of the sun continued to caress my skin as I slowly walked towards the 'Big Cross'. Story has it that St. Patrick himself designed the shape of these giants by adding the round circle to represent the sun, one of the most important ancient Celtic pagan symbols of life. This cross towered over me creating a shadow so I used my fingers to trace the designs I could reach, willing them into my memory. A familiar one to me was the trinity symbol or shamrock as we Irish called it but the one I came to see were the shape of birds entwined into some geometric patterns. The atmosphere here was very tranquil, I stood there satisfied with all that was happening in my life, running my finger over a shape of a fat bird that represented the simple wren, the king of all birds. According to our Irish pagan legends it could fly further than the eagle and was the messenger to the gods. A simple wren that lived amongst us, how appropriate that it would be the messenger, of course the wren would be there to witness all of our cares and woes.

Time seemed to stand still, 'there really is no need to rush, and besides, I will see the troop arrive, I will know when it is time to leave.' Sniffing the freshness in the air I could smell the promise of summer and with the comfort of my rosary beads wrapped around my hand, my mind focused once again on the intricate carvings on the High Cross. Rooted to my spot and totally engrossed in these entangled designs, I tried to imagine how I would incorporate them into clothing or other items when a strange rustling noise crept into my trance like state of concentration. I turned to see what it could be, thinking, could Niall be here already?

Melkorka

So startled was I by what I saw, this invasion into my daydreams, I remained frozen to my spot. A giant of a man with long flowing blond hair under his helmet oddly mesmerized me. It must be a mirage I thought, but no, he was coming towards me. Only seconds had gone by and still I stood there frozen to my spot wondering, 'how was this possible, where did he come from?' These questions were tumbling around in my brain when I suddenly noticed that there were many giants coming towards me, with wild looking hair streaming from under their helmets. They were running fast behind the lead giant and they had their swords raised. Panic raced through my body, which finally motivated me to flee. Clutching my beads tightly, I picked up my skirt and turned to run.

Alas, it was too late. I did not get far, the giant was much faster and had a long reach. He clenched my arm in a vice like grip taking me literally of my feet. My beads dropped to the ground as I pummeled the giant with my fists. Laughing uproariously at me, he picked up my rosary and quickly hid them somewhere in his jerkin. He held me tight then turned back towards the High Cross. Taking a rope from his sack he expertly tied me up to it, then left me on my own.

Crying out loud to nobody in particular,

"What the devil just happened? How did these men get passed the river guards? How did the guards not see their ships glide up the Liffey? Why was no alarm given?"

My tears of fear choked me into a horrified silence as I struggled against the rope – but any hope I had was soon dashed. They were tied tight. 'Viking raiders? The early morning fog, was that how they got by the guards?'

Questions flew through my mind with a fearful frenzy as I continued to wrestle with the tightly tied ropes. In the meantime I had no choice but to witness the blood bath in front of me. All I could do was pray for the timely arrival of the troop sent to guard our beer wagon.

The gate sentries were totally thrown off their guard failing to get the stout doors closed in time. The invaders easily pushed their way through the main gate killing the guards, then they immediately split into three groups. One gang of men ran towards the monastery after the religious treasures I expect. They slaughtered the few monks and townspeople who were in their way. Another group of men ran after the terrified locals as they tried to make their way to the back gate, trying to escape the wrath of these Northmen. The guards there had initially tried to close the stout gates but quickly changed their minds leaving them half open, they ran for their own lives along with the rest of the fleeing peasants. Most of them managed to escape through the back gates before the invaders got there, the few that did not, did not survive. Then this group of invaders closed the back gates tight against any Irish coming in that way. The third group guarded the front gate, to keep their escape route secure.

I could hear the group in the monastery as they hurriedly flung whatever treasures they could into the sacks they were carrying. The clatter of them clinking against each other prickled at my ears.

'These beautiful relics will be all dented, they are destroying their beauty and they do not care. Savages!'

The market crowd had disappeared from my sight so, I could see clear to the back gate, now locked tight. The locals that were not killed were probably running towards the forest, hoping to find a safe place to hide. The invaders did not bother to follow them -- they did not even seem to care if they got away.

I prayed that Niall was still alive and hiding somewhere safe. 'Where is that troop of soldiers?'

A couple of the renegades must have spotted the tower door just inside the monastery. I could hear them chopping as they tried to break it down with their axes. I had just left through that door and knew it was very thick and covered in metal strappings.

'Would they succeed? It is a very secure area so I hope they fail.

Then it hit me... "Dear God I should have stayed just a little longer in the scriptorium, I would be safe now within that room, safe with the scribes. Damnation.... why was Father Michael in such a hurry to get rid of me? Or was it me who was in a hurry? Oh blessed father -- what are their plans for me? Save me from these vial monsters...   P-L-E-A-S-E H-E-L-P   M-E!"

Nobody was listening to me so I turned my attention to my bindings. Convinced that I was making progress motivated me to continue, to keep trying to escape. They appeared to be a little looser or was my mind playing tricks with me? Alas, the ropes remained tight, I had had little success with them but I continued to struggle nonetheless, there was no other alternative. Soon my wrists and fingers were red raw, almost bleeding from the exertion of trying to escape, plus my nose was running and I was choking on the tears that flowed nonstop. I tried to wipe my nose on my shoulder but could not reach it.

The giants guarding the front gate started yelling -- the next thing I knew the raiders were back, running out of the main gate, their sacks filled with booty, heading back towards the river. One man came out with a cart full of barrels, Nial's cart!

"Oh dear God, did they kill Niall too?"

I moaned out loud, but no one was around to hear me cry out or to even give me an answer. There would be no beer for the fete tonight. "What a disaster!"

It was not to be my day, the big blond giant who had tied me up came out at last, stopped in front of me and looked hard and long, obviously making his decision what to do with me. Tears were streaming from my eyes, my nose was running and my voice had fled from fear. I silently prayed that he would leave me here but he obviously decided against that idea. He untied me and easily picked me up like a small child. He flung me over his shoulder like a sack of grain as I watched my little coin purse fall to the ground. The crazy giant did not notice it. He continued to run towards the river, then carried me on board their long ship which was hiding behind a grove of trees along the shore line. The last two raiders had given up trying to chop down the door to the scriptorium and ran behind us.

'God help me! They're actually taking me with them, I have been kidnapped! Where are the soldiers?'

I sobbed quietly to myself. I was so traumatised by this attack not a word or a cry of terror escaped from my lips, even though my tears and nose continued to flow. I was stunned into a strangled silence and I vowed then and there that I would remain silent, they would not hear it from my lips that I was a princess. As the hatred flowed through my body I found an inner strength and sunk deep into myself willing my mouth to remain sealed against all those nasty words forming on my tongue.

Chapter 6 – The Journey to hell

On board the ship I found myself locked up in a small square 'crate-like' cage located on the top deck already filled with other women. The space was cramped, we were unable to stand up, but they made a space for me when I was pushed through the small opening, small even for me. Somehow I shuffled into a corner, into the space they had made for me. Later with my cloak I cleaned my running nose and by now my anger had quenched my tears but my fear had seized up my chest with silent sobs – I could hardly breathe. The other women had gathered their arms around their knees, squeezed their bodies closed, and laid their heads on their knees. Although they gave me my little bit of room, they had created a sullen barrier between us all so I remained silent and said nothing.

'Where did they find these women, they cannot be from Kilcullen? They all look traumatized – as traumatized as I must look to them. Were they picked up recently? Somewhere nearby, I would think? God -- I need to breathe – I need air!'

My heart was racing like crazy as I continued to weep internally.

The ship was on the move, I laid my head against the slats and hung onto them tightly and watched the sailors as they rowed. They sat on a box like bench and rowed constantly, without stopping. They all had very muscular arms, they were all very strong looking but to me they looked very frightening, they looked like the devil himself. Not that I had ever seen the devil, but I had decided that would be how the devil would look. Their helmets covered most of their face so they all looked alike – to me they embodied the devil as one -- the devil incarnate. How I hated them.

Melkorka

I opened my hands wishing my rosary beads were there. What I wouldn't give to have them for the comfort I knew they would have brought me but my captor had picked them up. The rosary was made from amber beads and I knew they were valuable and obviously these fierce pagans knew their value too. Instead, I simply wrung my hands in desperation and hung my head praying to God to let me die. My life was over before it had even started. The boat started to bounce more and my heart jumped into my throat as I thought of father.

'HOLY MARY -- MOTHER OF GOD -- FATHER!!! What will he say when he discovers I have disappeared??? He will be so angry with me for going to Kilcullen and even more furious with those who knew I went. Oh my god -- Cook will be in terrible trouble once he finds out who I went with. Liam – now I will never get to know you!! WHAT HAVE I DONE?? Please forgive me father -- I am so frightened. Please forgive me!'

The leader started to yell loudly as he pointed to something behind us, this distracted my suffering for a moment and raised my hope of rescue. He seemed to be giving orders to keep rowing while a couple of men raised the sail.

'It must be our troop of soldiers! Finally! They are probably afraid of an attack from them. I sincerely hope they are right behind us.'

Hope surged through me as I tried to see if anything was following us but I could see nothing. The ship easily sliced through the water with the power of these gigantic men and I knew before long we would be on the open sea. Then there would be no chance of being saved. My slim window of hope was shattered so I bunched my legs up close to my body and hung my head on my knees – just like the others had done. Effectively I shut it all out -- we shut each other out -- we each entered our own silent world of trauma and desperation.

We remained that way, tightly wrapped up in our own little hell until we hit the open water. Once there the huge sail filled with the wind and gave us more momentum allowing the rowers to stop. Meanwhile the big rolling waves made the ship rock like mad – it had gone berserk and shook us all out of our secure coils. We hit the gaps between the waves with a mighty force, so furious, I thought for sure my heart would stop pumping. I had never been on the open sea before and this unstable movement terrified me so greatly I thought my heart would seize up with such fear, but then slowly realized that it was still beating, albeit wildly. The frantic beats of my heart proved I was alive not dead, but the gushing wetness between my legs exposed my aversion of being on the open sea, I had literally wet myself from fear. I remained panic stricken, my arms floundered as I tried to hang onto to something secure. I had grasped onto one of the thin slats of the crate but knew this may not keep me secure. I thought for sure this ship would break in two and that our little prison would fly off into the big black void each wave seemed to create. Before long my stomach started to turn upside down and the next thing I knew I was vomiting up my porridge and buttered bread. My body had totally failed me now -- any shame I could muster had left me – I did not care. The other women moved into a tight bunch trying to keep as far away from me as they could.

Once the ship settled into a rolling pattern, one of the women called out to the invaders in Gaelic, "hey you over there. We have a sick woman in here. We need a bucket of water and a cloth to clean it up."

One of the men came over and must have seen all the vomit, whether he understood her or not he could see what was needed and shoved in a wooden bucket. The woman with the bright red hair crouched over the mess I had made and cleaned it up. Then she set the pail in front me, threw the wet dirty cloth at me and hissed, in Gaelic, "puke into that pail wench and stay away from us. From now on you clean up your own mess."

Much later, my stomach was purged of all it had held, with the evidence of all I ate that morning stinking in the bucket, but my stomach continued to heave. My whole body ached from such violent retching's, I had never felt so ill in all my life. Curled into a tight bundle and quietly heaving I thought back to my childhood days of sickness, which were not many. Whenever I had been ill my beloved nursemaid had been there for me, she would pamper me wiping my face with a damp cloth dipped in ice cold water that had been scented with fresh mint, and would whisper words of encouragement calling me Mæl 'a stor' – dear heart.

'Mor – poor dear Mor -- she will be devastated when she hears I have disappeared. Just like that – in a moment -- she is gone from my life. My future husband – gone! My father, my grandfather, my brothers and even my hateful stepmother – all gone! But mostly I will miss my dear nursemaid – gone – never to be seen again. What will they all say when they realize that I am lost to them, never to be seen again – ever! It will break Mor's heart but my father will be so enraged with me for going to the monastery. I won't get to meet Liam, my intended. What a sad, sad situation I have put myself in, I should have never left the castle. My last grasp at freedom had seemed so important this morning, all because of a book I so wanted to see. What a fool I have been! FREEDOM! I will never have any of that ever again. I have no idea what is waiting for me. I pray that I just die! Here and now! Maybe my prayers are been answered as I feel like death has grabbed hold of me already. I can hardly breathe and I feel so ill. God forgive me! Father, please, please, forgive me. The O'Neill clan will be so angry with you now. What a mess I have made of everything!'

Later that night the seas seemed to calm down. A reprieve from my death sentence – I was still breathing, unfortunately just barely, but I could feel death's grip on me. While the other women were asleep I struggled, but quietly managed to take my belt off. It had been my fifteenth birthday present from Mor. I rolled it up and quietly slipped it into my secret pouch through the slit in my dress pocket, hiding it away from prying eyes. Why did I even care I probably won't survive this journey to *'wherever'*? If I die they will find it anyways.

Melkorka

The journey to *'wherever'* continued to be rough with an occasional calm spell. I curled up into a tight ball and laid down in my corner rather than trying to sit up. For some reason lying flat seemed to help me but I had become so weak from lack of food or water. No matter how hard I tried to nibble on the hard bread they gave us or drink a sip of the grimy water, it all just came right back up. The retching would continue with the dry heaves, so I just stopped eating or drinking. By avoiding food or water there was no longer anything to bring up and then I no longer had the need to urinate or to defecate. I need not even move at all so I remained curled up in a ball. The other women whispered to each other but I could hear and understand their peasant Gaelic. They thought for sure I was not going to survive -- I was too sick to even care what they thought.

'God — just let me die.'

We were far out to sea, the invaders seemed to relax and started talking amongst themselves. They were very happy that they had got away. Astonished I suddenly realized that I understood most of what was said. Then I remembered that many northern people from many places visited my father's court and we were all able to understand each other, except when we spoke Gaelic. Nobody seemed to know that language other than the Irish.

'Did that make us smarter than most people? No, probably not.'

I had been told many times by outsiders that Gaelic was a very difficult language. Years before my father had raised his mighty army to chase out the Vikings, he had been friends with them. He had even been their ally in wars against our own people. I remembered then that father had had a close friend called Magnus who was married to an Irish princess, whose name I cannot recall. He would come often to our castle for celebrations or to hunt or fish. Sometimes he would bring his two children, they were twins. The father would introduce them as Magnus son of Magnus and Solveig dottir of Magnus. They spent much time with us as both father and this Norseman loved to do the same things together as well as discuss strategies for invasions. These two children were close to my age. Then I was only about five years old and we used to play together all the time for several years. Since there were two of them and only one of me, they spoke mostly in their language so they taught me many Norse words and I had understood a lot back then. Now those Norse words were returning to me as I listened to the chatter amongst our captors. I didn't understand every word but enough to make sense of their conversations.

From the sailors dialogue I discovered that their whole cargo was female slaves, at first I thought we were it, but from their chatter realized there were many more of us. They discussed their invasion tactics and seemed to be quite proud of themselves. They had planned to sneak in and out of areas all over Ireland quickly, just to pick up the young girls or women and to leave as quickly as they could. They all claimed not to be afraid of a fight but it made more sense to kidnap women who were not near large villages. They had planned to escape Ireland during the night but the heavy fog forced them to stay put and when the mist started to lift and they saw a monastery right there in front of them, they thought that their Gods had guided them there. They gave thanks to someone called Freya, a female goddess, who apparently controlled their destiny, so they could not pass up the opportunity to take the monastery by surprise. It had all worked out so beautifully for them they were fated to be there and find more treasure. Even that troop of soldiers who had arrived after their takeoff could not keep pace with their ship, Freya was with them all the way. Those hateful men were so proud of themselves, they never stopped bragging about their good fortune. Now my fate had become wrapped up with theirs -- how I hated them!

Later I realized from the men's constant chatter where the rest of the women were -- in the hull of the ship – probably the bulk of their cargo was hidden down there. If I was down there I would have died for sure – the thought of death was soothing while the thought of sailing into the unknown was terrifying. We must have been last minute captures then and thrown into this crate like structure. Staring through the slats all I could see was the vast sea, nothing but water all around us with waves rising and falling. I tried not to look at all the movement of water, instead I would focus on the horizon, but mostly I just kept my eyes shut. Alas, the movement of the boat churned my stomach into a constant frenzy regardless of what I did.

A few days into this horrible journey the weather changed abruptly. The men became frantic -- there was a big black cloud looming on the horizon. This cloud was a gigantic black wall -- a storm was coming straight for us. Everyone rushed around trying to tie everything down, the sails were rolled and tied securely to the mast. They tied a big tarp over our crate, I suppose to try and keep us dry and just in time – that black wall hit us hard -- it was a violent storm. Inside our covered crate we could not see a thing - I thought for sure we would all drown. Even our captors were afraid and prayed out loud to their heathen gods promising sacrifices if they all survived.

Many of the other women were now vomiting into my bucket, I did not need it as there was nothing left for me to vomit up, although my body continued to retch but all I could manage were dry heaves. We all clung desperately to the wooden slats of our cage so we would not be flung up to the crate's ceiling. Our jail creaked so loudly I thought for sure it would break into pieces. Everyone was moaning and crying but the violent storm masked all their noise. I could have screamed out loud too and nobody would have noticed me. Strange how even during this fearful storm no sound escaped my lips -- I had become too good at being silent. I was beginning to think that God had taken away my tongue as punishment. Because I laid my head on the floor to still my retching stomach I could see what the crew were doing. They were frantically bailing out the water with their wooden buckets but the waves kept washing over our ship and filling it up with more water. Their ship just went where the waves took them.

Melkorka

'Where is their goddess Freya now? Would we become lost on this angry sea – would they ever find their way to back to wherever they had planned to sail to?'

Finally the black wall carrying this ferocious storm passed over us, leaving us a calm sea but the sky drenched us with a heavy rain. Finally they had raised the tarp a little so we could breathe, all the rain was a blessing in disguise as it washed away all the sickness and stench of urine from the other women. Many had wet themselves in fear so the soaking rain was cleansing to us all. After watching the others go through what I had in the beginning I no longer felt like I was the only weakling but I knew I was totally alone in this foreign world. These women were ordinary people and chances are they would not warm up to the idea of a princess in their midst so I curled up into my corner, sick hearted and freezing, and feeling very sorry for myself. We were all wet through and all shaking from the freezing cold under our water logged covers. If fear does not kill us this freezing cold will. Once the rain stopped they took away our tarp covering and our wet blankets, then they replaced them with some dry warm skins but we continued to shiver in our damp clothes. They laid all the wet blankets over wherever they could to dry out.

Chapter 7 - Hordaland, Norway

Still reeling from the violent storm we saw land approach and the raiders roared with happiness. It wasn't long before they turned into a very large bay, apparently they were not lost after all. I had no idea where we were and really did not care at this stage. As sick as I was I couldn't help but admire these amazing sailors, they had brought us safely here, *'wherever here'* was? As we sailed into the bay I saw that the coasts were covered in trees right down to the shoreline. Lots of green but a green so different from the greenness of my Ireland. The sun was shining brightly and the water sparkled like gems unlike the emerald lands of my home that were constantly soaked by the rain clouds that clung to it. The bright rocky ruggedness and green forests of triangular trees that framed this bay of glittery waters created a different kind of view unlike anything I had seen before, this strange country was astonishingly beautiful, even to me.

The sailors were vigilant, there was dangers even here in this huge bay of shimmering water, craggy outcrops were everywhere. The captain was always on the outlook. The men called this inlet a fjord, I could sense their excitement about something when we stopped and dropped anchor. The sails were rolled up, then two of the men went down into the hull. One came out dragging a woman, she was screaming and crying, begging to be saved. The sailor just laughed at her as he flung her at the feet of their leader, who was called Hrafn Hviti (Hrafn the White). All these sailors had such odd names but this name I remembered as I had heard it so many times. Plus he was the very one who had kidnapped me. I would never forget him or his name. HOW I HATED HIM!

 The other sailor came out with a live sheep, its legs were trussed together. Hrafn declared that the woman and the ewe were to be sacrifices to the gods and goddess for watching over them all during that raging storm. The poor woman was terrified, she was visibly shaking and begging for her life. The leader ignored her and continued to thank the gods, then nodded at his men. The same two men that went into the hold for them came forward. One grabbed her legs and the other her arms. The poor woman wet herself with fright as they flung her overboard.

'Her screams will haunt me forever! '

The "baaing" ewe was crying as well. There was no sympathy shown from the sailors for the poor little animal, it was thrown in right behind her. They all cheered and called out to Odin in thanks and cursed the woman for peeing on their deck.

The red head in our crate cursed them under her breathe, "May you blasted heathens burn in hell!"

'Dear God, I pray that the poor woman is an excellent swimmer and will foil their sacrifice. Sadly, this fjord looks much too big and cold – neither will probably survive.'

The men went to their chests. They sat down, then picked up their oars and rowed towards the harbour where a large town built entirely of wood slowly came into view. Smoke streamed from openings in the roofs, it was a town unlike anything I had ever seen before.

We had arrived in a place called Hordaland in Norway. I overheard the crew talking about it, they were saying that it was a famous trading center where they planned to sell us women, for a lot of silver. They were also saying that just a year ago they would have made a much shorter journey, a much safer one too, just to Dublin to sell us slaves. Then that Dublin was controlled by the Vikings and they had made it a famous centre for the slave trade. I heard them curse the O'Neill clan along with a king called Mykjartan. That sounds like father's name, Muirchertech. They were saying that this Irish force led by this man had chased the Vikings out, just last year. *'That IS my father they are talking about!'* This Irish alliance had foiled their lucrative slave trade and now they were forced to go all the way north to Norway instead of using Dublin.

When the raiders said my father's name out loud they spit on the ground condemning him to hell. I had reacted to the sound of his name and quickly raised my head ready to tell them that this valiant king was my father but one of the other women snorted so loudly my brave words stuck in my throat. The one with the bright red hair, the mouthy one, snarled,

"A lot of good that bloody Irish king has done for us! He should rot in hell – at least we would still have been in our own country if he had not sent the Vikings running. God willing - if we had managed to escape – at least we would have had a better chance of finding our way home or for our menfolk to find us. Here, in Norway, there is no chance to get home so nobody will even try to escape. We are too damn far away from any help whatsoever. Muirchertech! Damn him to hell."

I hung my head, silence continues to be my only security.

According to these Viking raiders Hordaland was only their temporary slave centre. At least until Dublin could be re-taken or the slave trade re-established elsewhere closer to Ireland. According to them the Irish women were beautiful and worth the risks. Kidnapping was obviously a lucrative trade for them to take such risks. They talked about other trading centers like Northumbria in northern England. It was ruled by some other Vikings that they all knew well. According to them York was one of the greatest trading centres known -- except slaves could not be traded there. Those *"weak Viking leaders"*, as they called them had made a treaty with an English King, called Athelstan, who was a strong Christian, not to use the land granted to them for the slave trade. Our captors all agreed saying that it was a stupid treaty and that this king Athelstan was not to be trusted. The captain of the ship declared loudly,

Melkorka

"We Vikings may be pagans but we have more honour than that so called Christian king. Our people in Northumbria are honourable and will hold true to this ill-considered treaty but I do not trust that English king. Our people are now too immersed into the English way of life, they have become nothing but farmers and merchants and are at the mercy of this king who will eventually stab them in the back. He is just waiting for the right opportunity. How can they not see that? Do they not remember what an English king did to Ragnar Lothbrok and to his people he left there in their care? Christians are not to be trusted!"

I watched these men all the time. I had nothing better to do than lay in my jail, all curled up staring through the wooden slats. Earlier, during the first part of the voyage I had watched silently as they shared their booty amongst themselves. They had quickly stashed their share into their own uniquely carved chests which they now sat on while rowing. These chests were set into neat rows along each side of the ship making them part of it and when they had to, they used them as their rowing seats. *'Very clever,'* I thought in spite of my anger and hatred of these men. The sail appeared to be only used when on the open sea or in the large fjords. I had even witnessed a couple of men sew patches onto the sail after the awful storm we had. It now made complete sense to me that sailors should know how to sew. It looked like the sails were made from a tightly woven wool which I knew was a very expensive commodity. We Irish were master weavers and I knew quality when I saw it. After this journey to Norway I now realized that their highway, this northern seaway, could be a cruel and vicious adversary so maintaining their sail was crucial. These men were now busy docking their ship, securing it with thick ropes to the harbour. My growing respect for these Viking invaders was beginning to break through my hatred. I laid my head into my hands sobbing quietly. But then I sat straight up and glared ahead of me and gave myself a good tongue lashing.

'Stop this Mæl *Curcaig. You have to stop this admiration of the very men that kidnapped you. You must keep your hatred burning in order to*

survive. HATE them always. HATE ALL MEN if you must. Silence is and will be your only chance of survival. Let them think you are a mute. To talk now could very well drive you over the edge.'

Feeling this hatred creep over my body, I wrapped my thin cloak around me and laid down on the wooden deck curled up tight in my corner of the crate to await my fate.

They came for us the morning after docking in Hordaland bragging to each other that the Big Rus' will be happy to see so many females, especially the young virgin females. They unloaded the hull first and I saw all the others for the first time many were just children but all looked to be female. Two men herded them towards the plank that would take them to the harbour. Terrified they stumbled down the steep bridge as they covered their eyes from the bright sun. Once on the dock two other men tied their hands together and sorted them into two groups. These slaves were struggling with the brightness of the sun so they hung their heads to protect their eyes. I counted nineteen in all. There would have been an even number except they needed a sacrifice to their gods. I shivered with rage!

'Yes – I do hate them still. This hatred will keep me sane.'

Then they came for us and herded us down the steep plank that bounced with our weight. I was last down the plank as it took me longer to uncurl my aching body from what felt like my permanent position. They ripped my hair covering off and laughed at me as my hair fell over my face. It felt straggly and dirty. One of them said that they would not get much for this sick little peasant girl.

"She stinks of vomit."

He threw my head cloth back at me yelling at me as well as using his crude version of sign language, insinuating what he would like to do to me.

"Cover up that ugly, messy hair, you stupid thrall."

Melkorka

I understood his crude sign language but raping me was obviously not an option he could afford. We were a commodity that was too valuable to them all. Now 'thrall' was a new word for me but I ignored him and wrapped the piece of cloth around my shoulders in defiance. Keeping my head down with my dirty hair hiding my face I silently screamed at them.

'You can go to hell – in my world you would be nothing. My father would have hung you by the neck until you were dead if he had seen your rude gesture to me!'

Neither the rude one nor the others seemed to care about my little act of defiance, they were too busy trying to organize us into rows on the dock. Our hands were tied and we stumbled over each other, this just added to their organizational confusion. They struggled to form a decent line and I think we all realized this and reveled in confusing them by tripping over each other.

"Stupid thralls" they kept calling us.

'Thrall must just mean woman? Or does it mean slave? After all that is what we are to these horrible men!'

Thankfully my hair hung over my eyes as it gave me some protection from their glaring sun so I managed to get a better look at the other women while they organized us. There were a number of red heads but most were fair haired, blonds or light brown hair. I was tied to one of the red heads from our crate, the one with the bright red hair. She was very brusque, she seemed very angry and kept tugging at my part of the rope making me stumble as I walked. She was the one who cleaned up my first mess and let me know it too. This one I will avoid if possible. All were of varying heights and then there was me, black haired and by far the shortest of all the women.

There were three small buckets of soapy water sitting on the dock, one for each group. We were told to use one of the cloths to wipe our face, hands and as much of our bare skin as we possibly could. Each group gathered around their bucket, undoing the lines that they had just organized.

'Stupid thralls? I think it is more like STUPID MEN! YOU DUMB NORTHMEN!'

I tried to grab one of the cloths because a quick wash would make me feel better, but one of the fair-haired women grabbed the rag from my weak hold on it. They pushed and shoved, fortunately I was the last on the rope line or I would have been trampled to death.

'What an aggressive bunch of women!'

I recoiled away from them all as best as I could. Being attached to them they dragged me hither and thither but I finally managed to get near the bucket and cloth. There was not much water left. The cloth was filthy but I washed myself anyways. After much difficulty, they lined us up once again and then we were led to a warehouse nearby.

'They obviously have a trader they were familiar with. Ahhh – I remember now. They did say there was a trader -- a Russian trader?

Chapter 8 – Sold into slavery

I had thought that all these raiders were fair haired giants until I came face to face with the dealer they had chosen. *'Gilli the Big Rus'* was huge, with hair spilling out over the edges of his clothes. He must have thick hair covering his whole body, like an animal, like a bear, hair so blond it was white. He must have been in many fights too -- his face and arms were full of scars – evidence of battles won -- or lost? Along with all the scars he was covered in green coloured tattoos. His face was an ugly contortion of normal facial features with cruel looking eyes, hard steel blue eyes, that pierced through you and his hands were the size of small shovels. Terrified, I kept my head down, hiding behind my straggly hair hoping to hide from those hard, piercing eyes.

The raiders negotiated for each woman and when one group of slaves, still tied together, were finished, they would shake the trader's hand. Then one of his men would lead the group to the back of the warehouse. Our group was last and I was the very last to be brought forward, I kept my head down with my hair partially hiding my face. The Viking leader, my captor, Hrafn, laughed saying,

"We do not care what you do with this shrimp of a woman we just want her off our hands."

My body stiffened with silent rage, *'I hate you, my God hates you --- if you did not want me why did you not leave me tied to that cross. I HATE you!'*

Hrafn, my giant ugly captor, kept talking, his voice slid through my fury.

"We ask for only one piece of silver for her. She was very sick from the sea voyage, we thought for sure she would not survive. Apparently, she is stronger than she looks but needs to be cleaned up properly. Also, I must be truthful about her, it appears that she cannot speak. Although I do think she can hear and can understand a little of what you say. I don't think she is stupid, but she may be. We took all this into consideration when setting her price. She is quite plain and hopefully will soon fill out like a woman. We should have left her where she was but once she is cleaned up and fattened up you will get more than one piece of silver for her – of that I am quite sure—she is surely a virgin."

'You are right Hrafn Hviti – you ugly excuse for a man – you devil incarnate! You should have left me where I was -- unfortunately you did not!"

Rage rippled through my body but I forced myself not to blurt out that I was a princess and how dare they describe me so negatively. Tasting blood I had literally bit my tongue when the Big Russian agreed to take me. What would be worse, to stay with these Viking raiders or to be sold to this beast or thrown into the street not to be sold at all. With a determination I did not realize I possessed I forced myself not to look up, silently berating my evil captors. This anger saved me from crying out loud. Then the ugly Russian giant ordered his man to take us away. This man led us, half dragging us to a locked room which was part of the warehouse in the back area. As we were untied, he handed each of us a ratty blanket. Then we were pushed and shoved into a huge room where the other women from our ship were taken. Apparently there were other women already there sold previously by other kidnappers so there were a lot of us in this huge holding cell.

In the end the Viking kidnappers got what they came for, even though they got nothing much for me, *'the sickly mute peasant girl',* as they had called me. Once I was in the lock up I walked away from everyone. I settled into a corner of the room with my head against the wall. I tried to isolate myself from all the women so I pretended to sleep. My fellow captures were busy scrutinizing each other and I did not care to be part of this charade.

Suddenly I heard a familiar voice against the wall, it was Hrafn's. It was as if he were right beside me, in the same room. Startled by the sound of his voice I sat straight up but kept my ear to the wall. They were very noisy but appeared to be happy and I could hear what they were saying. Hrafn, his voice I knew well, claimed triumphantly to them all.

"Stop here men where it is private, let's count our silver coins again and divide it up between us. It will be safer that way and once back on the ship we will give everyone their fair share. The Russian, always drives a hard bargain but we ended up with more silver than we expected, even with throwing in that sick peasant girl - almost for free. Let's sell the kegs of beer next except for the one we set aside to celebrate with. Men we have perfected our raiding techniques, our plan to quickly sail in, undetected if possible, and then leave as fast as possible, has been a brilliant idea. Now we must celebrate since we had no loss of life or injured limbs and the raid on the monastery was an unexpected bonus for us. We were destined to be there thanks to Freya!"

Much laughter, then there was silence. In my isolated corner I sat, hugged my knees into my body, wondering what was to become of me? *'A bonus – indeed!'*

Later that day the Russian came to look over his newest purchases. Talking about his cargo to his right hand man, he pointed to me declaring,

"Find me a customer as soon as possible for this one. We will sell her cheap, we need to rid ourselves of this excess baggage, as she might put a stain on the cargo as a whole if we keep her, even if she is a virgin as they claim. She is not up to my usual standard plus she has black hair. There are plenty of black-haired women where we are going. We do not need her and cannot take the chance of her dying on the way."

I now knew that I was not long for this place.

'Not again! I have barely arrived.'

Profit is king to this big ugly man, he figured that he had got a great deal for all of us, even me. He continued to talk loudly as I heard him say that he would get something for me but the downside was that I could not speak or sing or tell stories to entertain men. He called me a mute and that I would be a handicap to him. Good God he even thought that I was stupid.

Well, I will remain mute, just so you do not profit much for me, you ugly man,' I promised myself.

Does he never stop talking? He continued to rant at his man, "my future customer might try to dictate the price so I have decided to keep my reputation intact and to sell her cheaply, but for a price I will dictate, anything to get rid of her. Anything more than one piece of silver will still be a profit to me. Get this done quickly man!"

Chapter 9 – Life with Gilli the slave trader

The next day, I was feeling somewhat better, but I still smelled awful and did not like that. Ignoring my body odour I stood up and wrapped the piece of cloth around my head, tucked in any stray hairs and looked around, taking in my surroundings. Our dungeon of doom was a huge box-like structure with wooden slats, similar to the crate on the kidnapper's ship, only much larger. We were all able to stand up, move about and even find our own space if needed, it was that large. One side overlooked the sea, it had a partial stone wall with wooden slats in the upper part. There were thin spaces between them which allowed in fresh air. Two of the sides looked into the warehouse itself with larger spaces between the slats so our jailers could watch us. The fourth side faced the street, it had a solid stone wall a bit higher than the sea side wall with wooden slats higher up for more fresh air. There was no escaping from here.

'Where would we go if we managed to escape? I must have been sitting against the street side because how else would I have overheard Hrafn and his men when they left here yesterday.

I looked over to the sea side.

'At least there would be some light and fresh air coming through these thin openings by the sea or off the street, but obviously the bad weather like the rain and snow could slip through as well. After the crate on the ship this new jail feels like luxury. Plus we are heading into summer so for now there will be a lot of light coming through. In the bad weather we will probably shift over against the other walls, that is, if we are around long enough to experience any changes of weather and by the sounds of things I was not to be here for long. I am so thankful just to be on solid ground—with no movement – although my stomach is still not settled - it feels like I am still on the dreaded ship!'

Melkorka

The women had their own small groups, likely they stuck together with the ones they came with. Even us, the women that were on the ship drifted off together. Then I saw Deidre, the other red head, beckoning me over to her. I walked slowly towards her as she padded the floor asking me to sit near her. She said to me in Gaelic,

"One thing I cannot fathom is why everyone seems to understand one another. For us Irish I can understand that we know some Norse because we were so used to having the Vikings around and trading with them. That is up until a year ago before they were chased out. I even worked for a short time many summers ago for a Viking called Magnus, who was married to an Irish woman."

Surprised by this name I once knew I nodded in agreement as I curled my arms around my knees.

"This is very confusing to me," Deidre went on, "clearly there is a language out there that we all know."

She became silent, she was obviously pondering over her own question. I sat there beside her with my own thoughts and questions cramming my brain.

'Magnus! I wonder if he was the same man I once knew, my father's old friend, with the twins, a girl and a boy called Solveig and Magnus? If so, what a small world.'

I looked around the room, we were all females, there must be over seventy of us. I tried to count them all but everyone continued to move about, making it difficult to come up with a final number. We ranged from very young women, some still children to older women. We were all shapes and sizes. Some were almost as short as myself, but most were fair haired. Many looked very Nordic.

'They must raid Ireland for the red heads and pick up women of fair hair wherever they can? What did they want with me then, I have black hair? Why didn't they just leave me tied up?' I looked around again and

realized, *'These Vikings must also kidnap their own, the filthy pagans, anything for a profit. Or was it a revenge kidnapping from other Norsemen that they had fallen out of favour with. Now that makes sense to me.*

Fresh air seemed like a good idea to clear my head, so I headed back towards the sea wall, but I could not stop my mind racing, I could not let this theory rest as I argued with myself. Clearly, I was desperate to understand why I was here.

'But I do know men, I was surrounded by them and do know that they don't always get along with each other. They were all guilty of conniving against each other and there is no honour in that. There's father, he was always struggling with uprisings, mostly through his own rash dealings. Then there is grandfather and my brothers, they did not always get along with others either. Several times hiding in the great room at Dun Ailinne castle, I often overheard my oldest brother talk about our father with grandfather. They often discussed just how rash father could be. I already knew that grandfather did not like father very much. Why -- I do not know? Is it possible he blamed father for mother's death? The loss of his beloved daughter makes sense. He was always looking for reasons to point a finger at him. One day last winter I had even overheard grandfather promise my oldest brother that he would be the one to succeed him, not father. If only father knew that,' I chuckled to myself, *"there would be hell to pay.'*

I even had the nerve to advise my brother not to trust our grandfather, but he had simply laughed in my face telling me to stay out of men's business – that I was only a woman and under their protection.

'Where were you when I needed you? I have now decided that there is no honour among any man – period! I hate you all and will forever remain silent! Now why would you do that?' I argued. *'I don't know why – it just seems like a good idea. Maybe I hate the men in my family too because they did not save me. God – I just feel so alone and abandoned.'*

Melkorka

I bowed my head against the slats and silently prayed.

'Help me Blessed father – save me from these awful men! More importantly – save me from my own self-loathing. That disastrous trip to Kilcullen should never have come about. But alas I did go and now here I am in some foreign country – sold as a slave no less!"

Turning away from the sea wall and my self-loathing, I looked at all the others, all beautiful. The Russian will become even richer with all these women to sell. That was obvious - even to me. Again I asked myself.

'Just how do I fit in here? Why couldn't they have just left me tied up to that cross? I will probably ask myself this same question over and over for the rest of my life or whatever is left of it. There was no need to take me.'

Deidre's waving hand disturbed my train of thought. She wanted me to come over to her again so I wandered back to her.

'It will be good to have a friend – maybe if I get to trust her I will tell her my story and maybe even ask about Magnus?'

The next day came and went with still no water to wash myself with, they must have forgotten me. I sniffed my cloak, *'I really do stink.'* I decided to do something, so I used my hands in my own form of sign language with my new friend, Deidre, and I managed to express my need for some water to wash with, sniffing my clothes and pulling faces as part of my actions to illustrate my need for cleaning myself. She laughed and smelled herself, then went over to the locked door where the guards were. She demanded verbally and with using the same sign language as I did demanded that they bring some clean water for all of the new arrivals. Finally they understood her and soon after a large pail of hot water was brought in. They told us that we newcomers had to share. All the woman pushed and shoved leaving me on the sidelines once again. The water came in hot and soapy, but was soon reduced to a grey sludge when it came to my turn. There was only the one rag which soon smelled as bad as we did but what little was left did help me feel better. I washed my hands and face and tried to scrub the front of my grey dress with the slimy rag. The water was too dirty to wash my hair but I did feel somewhat better. I walked back to the sea side and stood by the slats overlooking the sea using the fresh air coming through to dry the front of my dress. The fresh air not only dried my dress but it also helped to air me out, dispelling some more of the odour but the now fainter smell of vomit and urine still clung to parts of my clothes.

'I will never learn to live like a peasant. How on earth do they manage to live with themselves without washing every day? Disgusting!'

My hair was a tangled mess and I would have tried to remedy that but I did not want to bring out my ivory comb. Afraid that the women would steal it from me I kept it hidden and used my fingers instead and raked through my tangles, trying to calm down the curls.

The other women talked about me openly, saying that I was just a child and deaf and dumb to boot. Most were kind enough, only a few were mean-spirited and were cruel to me. They poked fun of me whenever I came near them, pretending to be stupid. I quickly learned to keep my distance from them and to keep my head down, averting their eyes. Deidre was my only saviour. As for the others that were not teasing me they generally just ignored me. Then there were the jailers to avoid at all costs. These disgusting men fawned over all the women, touching their breasts and sometimes licking their faces to their disgust. Mostly, they left me alone probably because I still smelled of vomit but sometimes they would sneak up on me from behind and cup my tiny breasts, squeezing hard. This would always startle me, my eyes must have showed my shock and horror and just how much they frightened me. The men would laugh so heartily, it was all a great joke to them. Then one or two of my defenders would step in and slap them away from me, telling them to "leave the poor mute child alone."

Of course that only made them laugh harder. What horrible men they were. How I managed to maintain my silence with these antics the jailors played on me was very surprising.

'Maybe I really have lost my voice?'

Some of the women finally complained to the Russian about the men squeezing our breasts and when nothing came of their complaints, it became apparent to us that he already knew what they were doing. He would probably kill the jailors if they tried to do more than a quick squeeze. We were the Russian's property and the jailers knew this, but they had their fun in their own twisted ways. A quick squeeze or a lick here and there, kept us all in line, was probably the Russian's perverted way of thinking. His men got a little thrill, no harm done – their bonus.

'Men – detestable hateful men!'

When I wasn't sitting with Deidre and her gang, I would stay by the sea wall away from our guards and curl up into a ball for warmth. To protect my mind from these distorted awful men I would think about my life back in Ireland but mostly I thought about my nursemaid.

'Mor 'a stor' I miss you so much. My life is over and it is all my own fault.'

Thankfully, I had many memories -- wonderful memories -- that kept me sane. The best one was how we would sit side by side and work on our needlework while she told me stories. The memories of the stories she had shared with me saved me from dissolving into emptiness time and time again. When I wasn't thinking about Mor's stories I would try to recall anything else about my life in Ireland. Raised in a castle with a king for a father I would never have been exposed to men like these.

'Blessed Father, how my life has changed.'

As a royal princess, I had been encouraged to learn fine embroidery, even to learn how to mend. Good quality cloth was a luxury and even a princess needed to extend the life of her every day clothes as well as the beautiful formal dresses. If there were any embellishments on these dresses I had probably embroidered them myself. I could also knit well. There were many slaves, mostly peasants, working in my father's castle but most did not have the skills that my nursemaid had. She had come from a middle class family, her mother was a skilled seamstress who had taught her all she knew and in turn had taught me. Mor's father had died unexpectedly when she was a young girl. He had been an excellent craftsman who had made many swords for the army of the High King. Fortunately his family were cared for after his death, they were taken in as servants in my grandfather's household. Mor his daughter, became my mother's nursemaid and Mor's mother, Cait, became the High Queen's maid. Mor had one brother, Eoin, he learned to craft swords like his father before him and was somewhere in my grandfather's army. My mother's name was Flann but I never knew my grandmother, Emer, the High Queen. Mor was but a child herself when she entered service but she soon became a loving and efficient nursemaid to my mother and then later to me and my brothers. Through her stories I got to know both my mother and grandmother much better. Mor loved us both, my mother and I, like a real mother. She never married or had her own children, she always claimed that we were enough for her.

A few days after arriving at the Russian's warehouse I sat staring at my ratty blanket and thought for something to do I would try to mend the little holes in it by embroidering some Celtic design over each one. This little activity would surely relieve my mind from my dilemma. During the night I managed to move some of my collection from the secret pouch into my pocket so nobody would know about my secret hiding place. It did not take the other women long to walk by and inspect my work. Deidre, my friend, asked if I would fix the holes in her blanket as well as mend a tear in her dress. I nodded and before long I was very busy. The holes in their clothing were soon expertly mended, most of the time they could not tell where the hole or the rip was except for the design I had incorporated on some of the bigger holes. Even the bully women became nicer to me, now that they wanted something from me, and realized that I was not so stupid after all. The women even begged the big Russian when he came around for inspections, to provide them with more cotton to repair their clothes and when they received these gifts of colourful threads they gladly gave them all to me. The Russian, once he discovered what I did for them, later sent over some of his personal clothing for me to mend. I was earning my keep, his man informed me.

The two red heads from my group took special care of me knowing that I had come from the same place in Ireland, from a place obviously very close to their homes. They were peasants and a bit brash, so it felt safer to keep my silence even from them.

'I am a princess after all and they are just peasants, not in my class.'

Their brashness did not frighten me but at times it offended me. I suppose I was just so used to peasants being subservient, not bossing me about and they were definitely overbearing, pushy women. The two red heads were very shapely and had the most beautiful hair. Since they were older they were probably not virgins.

'Deidre, I wonder if she is a mother used to dealing with frightened children. Is that why she is so kind to me?'

Most of the other Irish captives were quite young and very likely virgins. They would be worth a small fortune. One of the two older red heads had smoky grey eyes with flecks of hazel in them and flaming red hair, the brazen one. Her name was Brigit, she was the one who originally cleaned up my vomit. My friend Deidre had hazel eyes with a greenish hue to the rims and darker red hair, more of an auburn colour. I did wonder if they were sisters. I liked Deidre more, she was my friend and she was softer spoken then Brigit, although just as bossy but more diplomatic, you could tell she was used to dealing with younger children. She was the one who said she had previously worked for the Viking named Magnus. If we stay together long enough for me to trust her I will ask if this man had a son called Magnus and a daughter called Solveig. Deidre had told me that Viking raiders had caught her and Brigit together, while they were fishing by the river and that now, they were destined for some Arab's harem. She noticed my puzzled reaction and explained what a harem was and what these men expected of them. That was my first lesson on the male/female relationship, she would give me several more explicit ones. Mor had kept me in the dark about all this but expect before I married she would have explained it all to me.

The Russian would get good money for them even if they were not virgins, they were beautiful, shapely and seductive women. He would never get as much for me, I was a skinny kid not yet a full blown woman. Although I was a virgin, which is worth a lot to a slave trader, I was beginning to understand more clearly what the Russian wanted in his women captives, thanks to Deidre's educational talks.

Whenever it was too cold to walk about the room the two red heads would call us over in Gaelic. Anyone who understood Gaelic came over to them right away, they knew it would be story time. We would cuddle together for warmth with our shabby cloaks and blankets wrapped around us in a corner of the room away from the side facing the sea. Unfortunately we would be nearer to the guards but I felt safe huddled within this group. Deidre and Brigit would give the guards such hateful looks that told them to stay away from us. Then they would tell stories in our Irish language, it was a time of escape for us all -- Deidre and Brigit were master story tellers. Every time they had finished telling us stories I would wonder if they had children waiting for them to tell them the very same stories they had told us?

One story they told us was about an Irish chieftain and his son who had been kidnapped by Viking raiders. These raiders, knowing who they had, later negotiated a ransom with the chieftain's village for silver. Brigit was the one telling the story and she claimed that Vikings have a code of honour and once they were paid they would always fulfill their promise and let them go.

Melkorka

After that story I realized what I had done wrong. I should have told my captors right away that I was a princess, that I was not a peasant girl -- before they sailed away from Old Kilcullen. They may have ransomed me for silver and my father would have gladly paid them to get me back.

'Look at me! The way I am dressed, tatty cloak and all, they would not have believed me. Besides, those kidnappers were in too much of a hurry to get away from Kilcullen -- it is too late now – and I am too far away from home! I belong to the big Russian and even if I was to confide in him, he would not even consider this daft venture. He would have to find someone to sail back to Ireland and negotiate with my father and Norway was just too far from there and Ireland would be too dangerous for him. It would be easier to sell me here to whomever would pay rather than support such a risky journey based on my word. He would laugh in my face at this stupid idea! Besides, I no longer look the part of a wealthy princess thanks to cook's disguise -- my tatty cloak. Plus I have lost so much weight, I must look like a starving peasant.'

After that story was finished, I laid my head on the floor and wrapped myself up tighter into my smelly cloak sinking farther into my silent world of despondency. Heartbroken and disappointed with myself for not thinking wisely, for not thinking like the grownup I had thought myself to be, I tried to fall asleep. Why did I listen so eagerly to these stories – after this latest story I just wanted to be alone, I wanted to die.

Melkorka

Chapter 10 – Thrall for sale - cheap!

One warm day days later, the atmosphere suddenly changed. The big Rus had come by and some of the women had become quite agitated with him, crying and creating such a turmoil. He had to scream for silence, even threatening violence. Not knowing what was happening I ran and hid behind the two Irish women fearing he was serious about his threat. One of the women finally spoke up. She claimed that they had heard rumours from their jailors that he would be sailing soon to a far off country where it was extremely hot. Where people had dark skin, dark hair and dark eyes.

He laughed at them confirming the rumour saying,

"Of course, you STUPID IGNORANT women, that is why you are here. These dark haired, dark skinned men will pay a high price for you women of fair skin and they will pay me even a higher premium for the ones with blond hair and blue eyes, as well as the red heads and especially for my virgins. We set sail in about ten days. You had better accept the inevitable ladies, you are here for sale only and I will finally get the profit I deserve and be rid of you. All of you!"

Laughing at them the big Russian collared the first man he turned to, pointed at me cowering behind one of the red heads, and growled into his ear,

"I asked you days ago man, to clean up that skinny peasant girl."

The guard claimed that he had given them all some water to wash with, although he seemed to hang his head with guilt.

"You lazy lout, send in a big pail and make sure it is a pail of hot water with some soap and even a change of clean clothes -- just for her! Although she was useful for a short time mending our clothes - she is the one for sale right now! Do I have to think for you too, you ignorant peasant. Get it done – now -- today! What do you think I pay you for? I don't pay you to squeeze their boobs, I pay you to look out for them so go find an easy mark willing to buy the scrawny one. You have done nothing... now get a move on. Put out the word that she is for sale. Tell whoever you talk to that she will be sold for a decent price. I do not want her to be part of our cargo to Arabia! Do you hear me!!! Find some empty headed person for this deal and hurry! We leave soon and I do not want her loaded onto my boat."

All the time he was shouting at him he was pounding his right fist into his left hand. The frightened jailor sprinted out of the warehouse to get the water and the clean clothes that he was ordered to get. I knew that the Russian was mean enough to use that fist on him. The guard must have thought the same thing as he fled to fulfill the big Russian's demands.

So finally I was to have some clean water and to myself. Meanwhile, I crawled into my corner shivering with fear and dreading what the next few days would bring. Thinking that if I was not sold soon I would be left on the street, on my own. It just gets worse and worse. Despair overcame me and I cried myself to sleep. Sleep and my muteness remained my strong hold onto sanity.

The next thing I knew someone was shaking me awake. Deidre, the Irish peasant, the one with the auburn hair, spoke quietly into my ear.

"Wake up lass, you need to be cleaned up and there are some clean clothes for you."

I sat up and saw the clothes made from some rough looking cloth sitting beside a big pail of steaming hot water. There was even a big rough towel folded beside the pail and a wooden comb. Deidre handed me a bar of soap saying,

"Here is some soap, clean yourself lass, wash your hair and dress into these clean clothes. I think it is made from lavender and it smells lovely. Lucky you! Brigid and I will make use of your leftover water and soap.

Melkorka

Right now, we will hold our blankets up around you to give you some privacy. Go by the sea wall, I know it is cooler there but at least the jailors cannot see you from the sea side. I will hang your blanket on that wall to protect you from the wind and cold. Now hurry... you are to be ready to show off to a prospective buyer if that idiot jailor of ours finds someone."

Struggling, Deidre, Brigid and I carried the big bucket to the sea wall. Shivering with fear and the cool air, I stepped into the hot soapy water right after stripping. Being so small I was able to kneel right into it and it felt marvellous to be able to scrub myself clean and to wash my ratty hair. After I dried myself with the rough towel my skin tingled and looked a healthy pink for the first time in what felt like forever. I got dressed in the clean clothes, rough as there were, they too felt wonderful. I managed to tie my secret pouch around my waist before pulling the clean petticoat over my head. I knew Deidre saw my secret pouch as I dressed but she had turned away. *"She probably thinks it is all thread.'* Afterwards she bundled up my old clothes into the shabby cloak. She must have felt the softness of the grey dress when she shook it out.

Speaking quietly in Gaelic she asked me, "Who are you? This dress and petticoat are made of quality fabric. I know my cloth, I was a wash woman for a very rich family. Tis a pity you cannot speak, you must have quite the story to tell young lady."

She quickly finished wrapping everything into the old cloak so my grey dress was not visible and tied it into a tight parcel with my old head scarf.

Melkorka

Hoskuld

Melkorka

Chapter 11 - Laxardalur, Iceland – Late Spring 937AD

The pelting rain was furiously digging holes in the existing snow banks, even the ravens were trying to hide from Freyr's anger. I was huddled under the door frame of the long house watching the rain fall. Yesterday there was another winter storm with fierce winds, blowing the unexpected snow into huge banks against the buildings, despite spring nearing its end. Winter this year in Iceland has been relentless and today, the rain, although a nuisance was at the same time a blessing, it will help rid the land of this unwanted snow and wash everything clean. I offered up a quick prayer to Freyr asking for some decent weather, I needed to sail for Norway as soon as possible for a trading expedition.

My name is Hoskuld Dala-Kollson. I own a large farm in the Laxardal region and I am a chieftain, a goði in Icelandic. My father, Dala-Koll, had a fjord named after him when he settled here, many summers ago. Dala means bay and that became my father Koll's nickname. My mother was a daughter of Thorstein the Red, which makes me a great grandson of Aud the Deep-Minded, and Olaf The White. Olaf had being the King of Dublin for a short time, but when he was killed, Aud fled with her young son, Thorstein, to the safety of her father in the Hebrides. Years later Thorstein became the king of Northern Scotland sharing the land with his half brother Donald III. He survived as such for many years but was later ambushed and killed. Freya's destiny for both father and son was to be murdered by the very people they ruled over. When Thorstein was murdered, Aud had to flee once again and eventually came to Iceland, she was one of the original settlers. Not all of the sagas tell us that it was Ivar *the Hated* that scared Aud into fleeing first from Dublin, then from Scotland, but I know this to be true because Aud was my langamma. We Icelanders have a deep respect for genealogy and my knowledge of this important lineage has contributed greatly to my power as a chieftain.

Melkorka

This journey to Norway means many riches for me and I am anxious to leave so I made my way back inside the longhouse for the natmal, then bed. I woke up early the next day hoping that winter had come to an end and went outside to see that better weather had indeed arrived. The sun was shining brightly and most of the snow was gone, Freyr, thankfully had listened to my desperate prayers and sacrifices.

It took most of the morning and I thanked Freyr continually as the ship was loaded with the last of the trade goods. My cargo included dried fish, bolts of wool, dairy products, such as butter and skyr, some rope, even some walrus ivory that I had purchased from a merchant who had recently arrived from Greenland, as well as some skins and many furs. The knarr was also loaded with enough food for the crew to survive the trip. Last thing to load was my own chest which stored my stash of silver. There were twenty men going on this journey with me and I would need all of their help to handle our rough northern sea.

As I got ready to board my knarr, what the Icelanders call their cargo ships, Jorunn, my wife, called out a blessing to me.

„May Odin give you knowledge, may Thor give you strength, Freyr – good weather and together may they keep you safe on your path my husband. May Freya, the goddess of love and destiny keep your journey to Norway and back home as part of her plan for you. Also, may Loki give you laughter to enjoy your time in Norway away from your loved ones."

I returned the blessing with,

„The Lady Freya's light shines through you my wife. May her blessings be with you and keep you healthy and eagerly anticipating my return. I will miss you wife."

Jorunn stood alone for a long while as we sailed off to the south, I continued to watch her until she faded into the shrinking landscape. I wished that she could have come with me but she was much too important to the running of our farm. I could not do it without her whether I went to Norway or not.

Waving a final goodbye, knowing full well that she could no longer see me either, I turned my back on her and proceeded to the bow of the knarr to have a word with Thor and Freyr. Their protection was crucial to us all. Our cold northern sea could turn on us with great anger and without warning, so we would need them on our side throughout the journey.

Chapter 12 - Norway

The weather remained balmy, we had an uneventful journey, but with our unpredictable waters it was never an easy voyage and we were always on guard. The sea could change instantly, with storms lingering around the corner, just waiting to accost sailors and hurl them overboard. It is a brave man's world sailing these ships on such a harsh seaway but with the god's help we did arrive safely in Hordaland, Norway. I gave thanks, to them all, Odin, and Thor, for watching over my ship and crew and to Freyr for the good weather. Freya was included in my thanks as she controlled our destiny and had looked favourly over us all.

After we arrived in Norway I made several appearances to the court of King Haakon and was well received even though the king was away in South Möre settling disputes with the Jarls and chieftains in that region. They had called a Thing, an assembly of the leaders of that area, and it was necessary that King Haakon attend. From there I was told he planned to go to the Island of Frædi in South Möre for a rest where he had a country estate. There he would meet up with some of his household and a group of friends who planned to meet him there very soon. They encouraged me to join them but instead I asked his family to pass on my best regards to the king when they would see him and asked that they also pass on my deepest regrets and to explain that I had too many things to accomplish here in Hordaland at this time.

The importance of such assemblies was something I fully understood, we too have a similar event in Iceland called the Althing. Although in Iceland it was held only once a year, while here in Norway they held many Things at all times of the year to manage their many disputes. The population here was so much larger than in Iceland and that necessitated many assemblies to settle disputes and to change laws. As

Melkorka

a goði I went to the Althing (Alþlng) each year, sometimes to settle any discord within my own region and sometimes to speak for people from other regions.

Disappointment flooded my soul that King Haakon was not here, he was a good man and a good friend, I had looked forward to greeting him personally. Although, I was invited back to several feasts at the king's royal long house by the king's family and entourage that ran his large estate in Hordaland, it was not the same without him. The royal family were infatuated with Icelanders, with their sagas and their poetry and they pestered me to recite any that I knew. For some reason all the best skalds come from Iceland and being the showman I am I did enjoy that part, very much.

Iceland has many stories or sagas as we call them. Most of the original settlers that came to Iceland were indeed famous, many were ancestors of chieftains and kings of Norway. A king called Harald Fairhair had began a campaign to unite all of Norway under one crown, his crown. Many battles occurred and as he got stronger, the Norwegians who opposed his drive for a single crown were either killed or they fled for their lives, taking their families and friends with them. They had all become outlaws to Norway, but later they became heros in the Icelandic sagas. Some of these outlaws had eventually settled in Iceland and created a country with no need for kings and queens or any other royal title, thus making our Althing more democratic in nature to Norways. Incredible as it may seem many of the original settlers were my ancestors so I had many stories to tell the king's court with a personal link that I could make into the focus of my story. The sagas were well received since all these outlaws were eventually forgiven, many were even idolized as heros by the Norwegians.

Iceland is also famous for their poetry and poetry is a passion of mine and I know many verses by heart. The court loved to hear them as well as our sagas so I was able to entertain them most evenings I was invited.

Melkorka

They never appeared to be bored -- they always asked me back to perform -- I was in my realm.

The trade goods my crew and I brought to Norway received a high price, especially the walrus ivory and Jorunn's bolts of fine cloth as well as the bolts of shaggy cloth. They were both made from sheep's wool and each one looked so different. The grey shaggy cloth that looked like fur was becoming very popular in Norway. Mostly, it would be made into cloaks because the oils in the undyed cloth naturally repelled the rain. The wearer of these cloaks remained warm and dry beneath them, making them quite a valuable commodity. Since Iceland's settlement, the country's main export was wool and they were becoming well known for their excellent quality. The other products we traded were dairy products and hard fish. The walrus ivory was especially valuable and difficult to find. We now bought it from the Greenlanders as the Icelanders had depleted their own stock by killing off all the walrus living in the northern parts. I got a great price for the ivory. All these products made me wealthy, even more wealthy than before.

A few Icelandic carvers were becoming well known for their skill at carving the ivory into game pieces, for a game called hnefatafl. These outstanding carvings were treasures only royalty could afford. Hnefatafl was a popular game with the Scandinavians, a game for two people where a white army and a red army challenged each other. Slowly they were becoming known for carving beautiful chess pieces as well, which was introduced in Norway and now Iceland, from other European countries. This new game was overtaking the old Scandinavia game of hnefatafl. When I return home I must find our own artist and it was not too long ago that I had heard of one, a woman no less, who lived not too far from my farm. If she was as good as they claim I could make a great fortune selling ornaments and game pieces to the priests of this new religion which was slowly invading Scandanavia, as well as to the Norwegian royal families. They were clearly the only ones who could afford such luxury items.

Melkorka

One night I stood on board my knarr looking up at the heavens. As I thanked my gods for all this fortune I had acquired through this trading venture, I started to plan what I could buy to treat my family and maybe even treat myself to. A good night out was in order for myself and the crew I decided. First things first.

Buoyant by such good prices I went to a drinking house near the harbour with half of the men to celebrate. A few men always stayed on board to guard the items we had so far purchased for the trip home. The ones that stayed had drawn the short sticks, but they would get their turn to celebrate another night.

I had had quite a lot to drink that night and while enjoying my good fortune I met a Norwegian man claiming that he worked for a Russian merchant who had a pretty young slave girl for sale. This man said that the Rus would be leaving soon for the far east and would sell her for a good price. The reason he gave was that she had dark hair and his boss was only interested in dealing with fair haired or red haired women. I was indeed interested, it sounded like a great idea for a gift that I could buy for my wife and I did not want to spend a lot of money. The fact she had dark hair was unimportant to me, she was only a thrall afterall. The thought that she would be suitable for my short term use slipped unheeded into my head at this point, but I quickly shook that thought out of there, telling myself that this was a gift for my wife only. I told the Norwegian to lead the way and I followed the man to the Russian's warehouse which was close by.

The Russian shook my hand, introduced himself as Gilli, the Russian, telling me that he would take only five pieces of silver for her. He explained that she was inexpensive because she was a mute but had great sewing skills. He did not want her in his cargo because she had black hair. He only dealt with fair-haired women or red heads as his market was in the Middle East and they had all the black haired woman they wanted there. Then as he called for the peasant girl to be brought out, his man raised his hand to him and asked to speak to him first but the Rus insisted,

„bring her out now, as ordered man. We have a potential customer and we should not keep him waiting."

He disappeared but returned quickly with a slave girl who trailed behind him with her head down. Gilli explained to me as she approached us that she had arrived wrapped in an ugly dirty cloak and that her head had been wrapped in a dull cloth. He claimed that they had cleaned her up, fed her well and dressed her in much cleaner clothes that were a brighter colour which would better suit her dark hair. Her overdress was a deep red colour with a white linen petticoat, but I could see that the quality was very poor. The guard walked her towards us but she kept her head down and only looked up when she stopped in front of us. Seeing her face for the first time I was stunned. She was not what I had expected, she was actually very beautiful.

‚A bright colour does wonders for her, even for wool as coarse as this,' I thought.

She had the most enchanting blue eyes I had ever seen and her black curly hair tumbled over her shoulders and hung half way down her back. I was mesmerized by those deep blue eyes, they were the colour of the ocean on a clear sunny day with the same dancing sparkles that reflected the sun's rays. Difficult as it was to describe the actual colour I wanted only to drown into them. I had to shake these thoughts from my head.

‚What is wrong with me? I have had much too much to drink.'

I heard the Russian mumbling about something, then I heard that he may want more for her. I shook his hand and told him that we had already agreed on a price and that I expected him to be an honourable man. I quickly handed over the silver. Those sapphire blue eyes had already enslaved me, I bought this mute girl without any more consideration, convincing myself that she would make a good house slave or thrall as they were called in Iceland.

‚The price for her was very reasonable,' my mead induced brain concluded.

Although stunning she looked so vunerable, scared even, all I wanted to do was to take her away from here and protect her from this brazen Russian. The trader could not seem to stop talking, he confirmed that he would shortly set sail for the far east and started bragging about the high profits he would make from his load of slave women. I did not care to listen to his boasting, I only wanted to leave as quickly as possible with my purchase and get back to my ship. She appeared to have only what she wore so I said my goodbyes and left with the thrall in tow.

Once on board I settled her into a small storage room below deck telling her that this would be her private space. I moved a few of the things out then laid out a sleeping pallet for her. Her clothes were not of good quality so I went to my chest and pulled out a fine looking garment and handed it to her exclaiming,

„this will be too big for you but I am sure you can make it fit well. The Russian obviously did not care to spend much or care what his women wore but the garments you are wearing will serve you well for your day to day chores which I will expain later. This new dress will be for special occasions. I will purchase some extra linen for you to make all the necessary under clothes and aprons you women need."

She smiled at me, bowing her head in thanks, as she brushed her fingers over the luxury of the fine wool. The colour was a magnificent lavender blue colour with fine embroidery along the cuffs of the sleeves and around the neckline. I also gave her a plain but beautiful sash to wrap around her waist to pin any items she would need, like scissors and a spindel. The quailty of the dress was so much better than the one Gilli had given her. She could make the dress fit if she sewed as well as I was led to believe.

Melkorka

This alluring thrall was quite inexpensive and at first I had convinced myself that it was a profitable purchase only for my wife. Most nights, previous to her arrival and especially after a few drinks, I had dreams of Joruun only and would wake up sweating, filled with desire. My wife and I still had a very healthy love life together and I missed it desperately. Now my dreams were haunted by images of this raven haired, blue-eyed goddess.

My cargo of timber was not ready and I still had other items to purchase. Looming ahead of me were weeks away from Jorunn to survive through. I promised myself that on our return home that I would hand the thrall over to my wife as her own slave, to use in whatever capacity she would see fit. In the meantime she would be here to satisfy my needs, my desires -- it seemed like a great plan to me. Afterall it is acceptable for men to have mistresses or concubines as well as a wife, even though not all wives liked these arrangements.

‚My wife will not accept her as my concubine but what she does not know will not hurt her. Afterall this mute slave will not tell.'

The first few days I simply talked to her, I told her about Hoskuldstaðir and my family. I found her to be good company and I rather liked that she never talked or questioned my stories. I kept telling her that I realized that she did not understand but that I had this need to talk to her.

"My stories must have a soothing effect on you", I said to her not long after, "you don't seem as nervous or as afraid as before."

Days later she appeared in her new dress that she had adjusted to fit perfectly. Amazingly, she looked more like a lady than a child slave. How she had managed to bundle up all that hair into an intricate braided design was a mystery to me, but I liked that it made her look older, more like a grownup and more acceptable as my companion. My sexual desire soon took over and I could not get those enchanting blue eyes out of my head. I was so lonely for a woman's touch and thinking she was ready I decided to take the thrall to bed that very night. Seeing that she was rather nervous and knowing that it was obviously her first time, I talked to her quietly, explaining her roll.

„ I promise you that I will not hurt you, it may be a little uncomfortable at first but I promise to keep you safe. You will soon enjoy the coupling as most women do. You go into your bunkhouse and get ready for sleep and I will come in later. I am sure you will want privacy to undress."

I felt silly having to explain to her knowing she did not fully understand what I intended but it made me feel better to verbalize this need I had for her. Somehow my message must have got through because she looked over her shoulder as she walked off to her alloted space.

Melkorka

Melkorka

Melkorka

Chapter 13 – Sold again

My jailors lead me out, I kept my head down to stem the tears that threatened to spill. All the women in our cell had lined up to say farewell, many wished me good luck with my new life. Fearing what was in store for me, I walked slowly towards the two men waiting, the Big Rus and another man. When I looked up at them, Gilli, the Big Rus audibley gasped, which startled me. I noticed immediately that the other man was very handsome, quite a bit older than me though. He had beautiful strawberry blond hair that was neatly braided into one thick braid.

"Damn it", the Rus exclaimed to his buyer, "maybe I was a little too rash, I should have listened to my slave keeper and talked to him first before declaring my price. She has cleaned up v-e-r-y nicely. I may need to charge more for her."

The buyer did not seem to notice the Russian's audible gasp or care what he had to say as he was too busy just staring at me, which really unsettled me -- I did not know where to look. The Russian continued talking to this stranger,

"She is very beautiful as you can see, but unfortunately she cannot speak, she is a mute but can understand a little -- it seems. Five pieces of silver for her is too cheap don't you think? Just think my good man, she cannot talk back to you which is a good thing for a woman. Also, I had forgotten about her skill, she is an expert with a needle and cotton, mending is her thing. I may have to charge more for her, you are getting away with valuble cargo!"

The buyer responded quickly shaking his hand, "but you asked for five pieces of silver and five pieces of silver it is. A deal is a deal!"

"Did I? Alright – alright!! You are right -- a deal is a deal."

Melkorka

After the silver was given over to the Russian's man who checked each piece out. He verified that they were indeed real silver, even bit them to make sure, then counted them a second time and put them into a box . Gilli shook his hand again and finally appeared to be happy to be rid of me but he kept on talking. I could see that this Northman was not listening to his boastings and he finally put his hand up to stop Gilli's chatter saying, „I must get back to my ship" and he motioned to me to follow him.

We walked along the harbour and once on board he showed me where I would sleep. It was a small, little room below the deck of the ship he called a cargo hold but now it would be mine. This would be my own private space he told me. I could come and go as I pleased but I was not to leave the ship. I wanted to say to him – *'why would I? Where would I go?'*

Then we went back up to the deck. He went to a carved chest and pulled out a beautiful dress which he handed to me. If I understood him right, it was mine but I would have to make it fit me as it was too big. My collection of silk thread could now be used to embellish it and I would use my own embroidery designs once I made it fit me properly. The fabric felt luxurious as I swung around hugging it in my arms, I almost laughed out loud with joy. I will have to be careful with this man, I do not want him to know that I can talk until I can fully trust him.

'Remember Mæl *Curcaig, men are not to be trusted! Nobody is to be trusted!'*

He told me that his name was Hoskuld Kollasson and that he was from Iceland and had a large farm there which he called Hoskuldstaðir. He went on to explain that he was the local chieftain and that he had many people to look after. He had come to Norway to trade his goods for things that they could not get in Iceland and one of the main items was timber. He had explained that the need for timber was great in Iceland as they did not have trees for their buildings. The original settlers had devastated any forests that were there to make charcoal for cooking fires, to heat their buildings and for building fences. That was all the trees in Iceland were good for, they were not tall enough or strong enough for buildings. They had to conserve what trees were left now to make the much needed charcoal for heating their long houses. They struggled with any new seedlings that tried to grow as they were eaten by the sheep and goats while they grazed freely over the summer. Charcoal was fast becoming extinct. As for the long houses it was always necessary to come all the way to Norway to buy the necessary timber for the structures. Drift wood sometimes worked but there was never enough or of good enough quality for his needs. Timber was essential and his order would not be ready for approximately two more full moons, then we would sail to Iceland. So he was planning to take me home with him from the sounds of things --wherever this Iceland was?

Thank goodness I did not have to cook, he had a good cook which was very fortunate. My lack of cooking skills would have exposed me and I may have felt the need to explain my situation. He explained that we would eat two meals a day. The first one in the morning, the day meal or as Hoskuld called it, the dagmall, a few hours after rising from our sleep. According to him they all tended to their immediate chores before eating the ‚dagmall‘. My job would be to tidy up his temporary bunkhouse on deck and to do any laundry and mending that he and the crew had. It did not sound too difficult. The second meal called the night meal or ‚nattmal‘ was eaten in the early evening after everyone‘s chores were completed. At this meal we would all enjoy some beer or wine. Each crew member had their own vessel to drink from, mostly drinking horns, many of them were beautifully engraved. Hoskuld had a fancy silver vessel, similar to a wine vessel that I would drink from if I were home in Ireland, but mostly he drank from a fancy carved horn, just like his men. Mine turned out to be a wooden cup, acceptable I suppose for a slave, which I was in their eyes. I must always remember that this is how they see me but this Norse man appeared to be more civilized than the few I had encountered so far. My life as a slave looked more promising than I had anticipated.

Melkorka

I did not find this system of dining strange at all. It was very similar to what I had grown up with in Ireland except there I would have a snack mid day, usually a chunk of cheese with a piece of bread washed down by a small vessel of mead or water. Here, like back home the food was cooked for me, although it was different, or at least it tasted different. Here they ate a lot of fish, fresh mostly. The man that did all the cooking would buy it from fish mongers on the dock sometimes already grilled or if he cooked it would be boiled with herbs. Sometimes we would eat fish that was dried, salted or pickeled in whey. They had barrels of fish preserved like that, obviously that would be what they lived on while on a sea journey, but mostly it was fresh while docked at the harbour. Sometimes stew was on the menu as it was an easy meal to cook in one pot and Hoskuld 's cook liked to present this meal to us. He seemd to be very proud of his one pot meals and his soups, so I would smile and nod my head as a thank you to him. Stew was a very common meal back home in Ireland as well but it tasted different here. I could not always identify what meat it was unless fish was used or what herbs they used but it was very edible. The stew was always full of vegetables, delicious really. The fancy meals of grouse or wild boar were the ones I missed most and even cook's sausages that she always made. My brothers loved the sausage that she made from blood and oatmeal, which I had normally found too rich, but now I missed even those.

Deidre had talked to me about the roles we would have to play as a slave. She had explained that most men would force themselves on us women and had explained what was expected of us. I was partially prepared and thought I knew what to expect, thanks to her. She also said that there were a few good men out there who could be kind and gentle. At first I was terrified of Hoskuld but every night he would just tell stories – wonderful stories. Maybe St. Patrick heard my prayers and found me a kind master? I started to relax and even began to enjoy my new found surroundings. Although, I would need to constantly remind myself that if life was really fair I would be safe and sound back in Ireland, getting ready to marry my knight in shining armour. But life

Melkorka

obviously was not fair. I must remember this always and be on my guard around everyone. I must not trust anyone -- ever! Especially men!

The first night I wore the dress that Hoskuld had given me was the turning point in our relationship. I had taken special care that evening to put my hair up. I had made a long braid leaving the hair soft around my face, then twisted it into a knot. Hidden in my secret pouch was a bronze hair pin and a hair net which I used to keep the knot together. When I walked out of the bunk house that evening Hoskuld just stared at me. I thought that he too had lost his voice but he finally spoke.

"You look like a lady now, not like a child. You really are quite beautiful!"

That comment brought tears to my eyes and he immediately apologized. I shook my head at him and smiled.

"Aaah," he said, „you are not offended and you obviously understand more than I thought. That is good. Sit and share our meal, here is some wine."

He handed me my wooden cup filled with wine. That night he told me a story about the goddess Freya. She was not only the Norse goddess of love, fertility and beauty but was also a warrior goddess and he said that I reminded him of her.

"Your eyes are deep and steady, I can see that you are a brave woman, you are a survivor, "he said to me. „I can see your inner strength even though you cannot speak for yourself."

My chest was tight with emotions but that night I felt alive. There was a flicker of hope for the first time since I was caught unaware in front of the High Cross at Kilcullan Monastery.

After his story he took my hand and explained what my new role was to be while on this ship, besides the laundry and mending. For some reason this did not frighten me, strangely I felt safe with him. He asked me to go and get ready for bed and that he would join me in a few moments. I climbed down slowly to my bunk house, got undressed but left only my petticoat on and crawled under the covers. I waited not fully understanding what I was to do but that night was to change me forever.

Our life on board the ship slipped into a cohesive routine for the two of us. Hoskuld treated me well and did not push me into anything out of the ordinary. Diedre had described some of the abnormal acts men expected so I was very relieved when he did not expect anything as strange as she had described. The chores I was given kept me out of everyone's way during the day. Hoskuld gave me some more linen so I worked on making another petticoat as well as two aprons. He also gave me another piece of nice wool to make another overdress for day use and a warm cloak. These few chores kept me occupied but my mind was free to dwell on my situation. Content so far with life onboard I decided to keep my voice silent until I could trust him completely.

As I sewed or embroidered I often thought about what could have been. I was extremely thankful that I had escaped the journey with the big Russian to some foreign land, of being sold as a sex slave to some dark foreign man. I shudder to think what life there would be like. The situation here was not right either. Here I was still a slave, but it was not as bad as I thought it would be. My daily life on the ship, or the knarr as Hoskuld called it, was tranquil, even his men showed me respect and what Hoskuld wanted from me was not all that unpleasant. Maybe in the future I will be able to confide in him. First I will have to tell him that I can speak – but some inner voice told me to stay silent. For now I was content with this man -- I am alive and I must admit that I loved his stories so I always looked forward to my time with him. Mor would tell me that it was nothing but childess optimism but my new plan of survival, besides my silence, was to treat this as an adventure.

Although, my days were calm and peaceful, some days my loss would overtake my mind as all I could think about was ,what if?' Obviously I did pine for the life I had or would have had in Ireland. I often wondered if they missed me at all. Did they even search for me? Sometimes I pondered over what my life would have been like as a wife to Liam O'Neil and especially now that I knew what would have been expected of me as a wife. Would Liam O'Neil have been as gentle and kind as Hoskuld is?

'I will never know now will I?'

On some of the days when I was alone in the bunkhouse, I would get on my knees and pray for forgiveness. I blamed myself for what had happened, if only I had not gone to Old Kilcullen with Niall, my life would have been so different. That dreadful curiosity of mine had led me into this danger.

'Poor Niall, was he dead or alive? At least here I am -- still alive and now I even want to live. There is hope that my life will be worthwhile after all.'

Chapter 14 – At the king's command

One bright warm day Hoskuld was summoned to the king's court for a feast. As a slave, he could never take me with him but he promised to bring back some treats. He returned late that night with an apple, a plum and some blue coloured berries that he called bilberries. He was very excited, he told me that the king wanted to see him. He was talking so rapidly that I simply tilted my head sideways and shrugged my shoulders to let him know that I had not understood a word.

"Never mind", he said as he handed me the treats.

"Tomorrow we leave for South Möre, to the king's island estate and then you will understand. King Haakon has summoned me there for a feast with his family and friends to greet me personally before I leave for home. I cannot refuse a king's command now can I? Although my timber is not here I can spare the time now that I know when it is to arrive. Years ago when I was a young man I was part of his regiment. It will be wonderful to see him for he is getting older and may not be around the next time I sail to Norway."

We set sail first thing in the morning. Once the harbour horn blew the crew rowed away from the dock before raising the sail. There were many outcrops of rugged rocks so it was important that Hoskuld direct his men to avoid hitting them. When we hit the open water in the wide part of the fjord they hoisted the sail with men lined up on the side to lookout for any jagged outcrop, ready with their oars to push away if necessary. Once we hit the mouth of the fjord Hoskuld and his crew set the ship in the right direction. They turned and headed northward but sailed close to the coastline, always keeping the beauty of Norway in sight. The ship glided smoothly over the water which was a surprise for me. If only the sea was always this calm, maybe then I would enjoy being on a ship that actually moved. There was always some movement even when we were docked but that did not bother me as much as sailing in the open waters. This time my stomach was only a little queasy, not as bad as the first time, but I decided to avoid eating until we docked in South Möre. I did not trust my stomach. It was, after all, a short trip so I shook my head no to Arnor, the cook, when he handed me my bowl. He nodded as if he understood my delimma and I was very thankful not to have to explain.

Hoskuld was sitting on a big crate covered by furs eating his dagmall. He asked me to sit by him.

"My crew are in control now and I want to tell you my story about King Haakon."

I made myself comfortable and he continued.

"The king's family and some close friends have already set sail to South Möre to join him. They left yesterday and since they will be there before us the king will know that I am on my way. Now I must tell you all about King Haakon... although he is an old man now he was the youngest son of King Harald Fairhair? Incredibly his father is the very same man that chased most of Icelands original settlers out of Norway or from whatever other country they were in. Iceland may be a very young country but we Icelanders have long memories and a passion for reciting our family trees. Haakon is unlike his father or his brother, he is very wise and very kind. The one thing against him is that he converted, he is a christian believer. His foster father was King Athelstan of England who was a christian and raised him to be one."

I knew that name, Athelstan, from my captors. They did not like or trust him, if I remember correctly. Hoskuld 's voice brought me back to his story.

"His father, King Harald had sent him to England to keep him safe and look what happened, he went against the Norse Gods and changed to believing in this new god. He can even read and write. Of what use is that?"

Melkorka

I wanted desperately to tell him that I too could read and even write a little but I did not want to disrupt his story. Now was not the time. Hoskuld continued, „when Harald Fairhair died his oldest son Eric Bloodaxe took over, he ruled for years but later had to flee for his life when his own people turned against him."

Hoskuld cleared his throat and took a long drink from his mead horn. I recognized these pauses as his way to organize his story in his head.

"Eric, unlike his brother Haakon, held onto our Norse beliefs but he was a cruel and selfish king. Quite different from his young brother and not nearly as wise. This young brother, Haakon, later convinced the people of Norway to turn against his older brother Eric. He managed this as a very young man who lived a great distance away, in England. I must clarify that he could not have accomplished this change of leadership without some strong backing within Norway itself. Haakon had powerful men, like Sigurd the Jarl, on his side. I am looking forward to seeing him too... he will be a guest as well at the king's feast. Sorry – sorry! Back to my story. Haakon promised that he would not tax the land owners when their heirs inherited their father's land, this was the most convincing argument to rid them of Erik. Erik took whatever he could and more from the people and they were fed up with his greed. Sigurd the Jarl called a ‚*Thing*' in Trondheim and invited Haakon to leave England with the promise of safe passage if he would come to his Thing and speak to the people. At this assemby with King Haakon by his side Sigurd conveyed the king's message to the people of Norway. He promised that Haakon would respect their pagan beliefs even though he had converted to the new religion as well as promising the people not to enforce a death tax. Sigurd even claimed that he, himself, would never convert and that King Haakon respected his decision. Haakon spoke to the people after Sigurd, confirming all that the Jarl had said. After the king had spoken the people all agreed to take him as their king."

Hoskuld took another break here. He had some hard fiskur with another drink of his mead. This time he offered me a drink and some of the dried fish. I shook my head no to the fish, but let him pour a small amount from his horn into my cup, just to wet my lips. I was still getting used to how they ate their hard fish, lathered in butter, then they peeled it off the skin with their fingers. Even though it tasted just fine it was the smell and the greasiness that lingered on my fingers that bothered me. In Ireland the servants would have had a bowl of rose water close by so we could rinse our hands at every meal along with a linen towel to wipe them dry. Now the smell simply revolted me as I was sea sick again even though only slightly. It was not as bad as the first time so I blamed the smell of the fish for it this time. I was determined to overcome this malaise. Hoskuld continued with his story.

"Later with Sigurd the Jarl's help, Haakon organized a very large army and together they chased his brother Eric Bloodaxe and his family out of the country. They fled to Denmark where the King there took them under his wing. Fortunately for them there was animosity between the two countries, Norway and Denmark. Soon the people of Norway started to call their new king, Haakon The Good, because he was and still is a good man. True to his word."

He smiled to himself as he leaned back against the mast, "he is truly a great man and I will soon get to see him. The Norwegians did not like Eric's wife, Gunnhild, either. Many claimed that she was a witch, this also eased Haakon's takeover of the crown of Norway. Amazing how two brothers, Eric and Haakon, can be so different in the way they think and rule. Although I think Gunnhild had way too much influence over her husband, Eric Bloodax. She was too ambitious for her own good and did not think of the people either, she was not a good advisor and was as greedy as her husband and sons."

South Möre, according to Hoskuld, was not far from Hordaland but they had to sail out of the fjord and then head north around the large cape to get to the Island of Frædi near South Möre where the king would be waiting for him. Hoskuld had much time on his hands for his storytelling. His crew were experienced sailors but kept their ears open to his stories as well. They all listened attentively while going about their duties sailing the knarr northwards. Later that evening Hoskuld took over the steering of the ship for a short while, the coastal view faded as he directed the ship further out to sea to avoid the shallow waters he knew about in this particular area. Darkness had descended upon us when he gave back control to one of his men as we moved to sit on another crate. This time the crate was covered by a thick skin of fur for more comfort and we covered ourselves with warm wool blankets because further from the coast we had more wind. Hoskuld continued his reminiscing telling me about Haakon's father, King Harald Fairhair.

"As I explained earlier King Harald Fairhair, Haakon's father, was one of the main reasons people settled in Iceland. He was very busy uniting all the lesser kingdoms of Norway under one crown, his crown, and fighting battles against the chieftains or lesser kings. The ones that lost or decided not to fight fled and became Vikings, many settling and conquering areas in England, Ireland, the Hebrides, the Orkneys, and other places. Some took their families and others had none to take but eventually married into local prominent families. Later when Fairhair had control of Norway he went after these Vikings or sent armies after them. He killed some but many got away from him once again. He forced them to flee from his might and wrath. Some fled to Iceland and named the country Iceland in the hopes that Harold would avoid such a cold desolate place as the name infers. They settled the land bringing their women and families with them and became farmers. By the way, not all the women were Norwegian but that is another story. The important thing about the ‚Settlement of Iceland' is that they all gave up any idea of becoming kings or jarls or anything connected to a royal name. Most settlers were descendents of such men either from Norway or whatever country they had fled from even though a few settlers were slaves or descended from slaves. They all wanted the same thing -- to be equal. They had seen what those titles accomplished and by this time the settlers had had enough. Although we still maintain slaves, they do have some rights. As for the name – Iceland -- we chose well. Harald

Melkorka

Fairhair never ventured that far north. Once the settlers established their farms they made Iceland into their own country without the need of a king as a leader, instead we have an elected chieftain or a goði for many sections of the country. I am one myself. Although the chieftains are elected for life, they are there to look after the people, to argue for their rights and to help make laws to defend these rights, even the rights of slaves. We maintain that type of governing to this day."

He had many other stories to tell, some of when he was a young man and about the many battles he fought for King Haakon The Good and even some stories as the chieftain of a large area in Iceland. He chuckled, mostly to himself I think.

"Reminscing for me is a good thing but to you it probably means nothing since you can't possibly understand all of what I am saying even though I am beginning to think you understand more than I think you do. Ahhh, there were such good times and being Haakon's man meant much wealth for me. My brother Hrut was also there for a short time with Haakon and even earlier with Eric Bloodaxe, his brother. Sadly my brother has passed on a few summers ago. I hope he is enjoying the feasting and love making in Odin's palace in Valhalla."

He raised his horn to his brother's memory and took a long drink. He wiped his mouth on his arm then stared off into the heavens. Probably remembering something about this brother he loved so well.

'Little do you realize that I understandstand most of your stories.'

He had so many to tell, and I especially liked the ones about himself growing up in Iceland. With these stories he was describing this mysterious country for me, this country which in all likelyhood would become my new home. The time passed by quickly. The weather too, was especially nice and the lull of his voice calmed me. The sea's movement made me feel ill once again but this time only slightly - my stomach did behave as I prayed it would – no actual vomiting. Maybe I was gradually defeating this weakness of mine, this sickness that

99

Melkorka

plagued me with the motions of the sea and had almost destroyed me when I sailed here on that awful slave ship? We continued our journey north and that night we slept soundly as we slowly skirted the land northwards. We arrived at our destination early the next morning.

Chapter 15 – Battle at Rastarkalf

Hoskuld went to find the king and returned later that day excitedly telling me all about it.

"It was wonderful to see King Haakon. To be expected, he has aged much. There has been a change of plans. Our arrival was well timed as he has need of my assistance. Apparently the sons of Eric Bloodaxe will soon arrive with an army of Danish soldiers. They have forced Haakon into battle. He wants me to lead a group of men with them to Rastarkalf where the battle will take place. King Haakon does not have many men here with him and he said that he trusts my judgment and needs all the support possible."

Taking my arm he led me to his bunk room. I thought that I knew what he wanted, except Hoskuld kept talking about King Haakon telling me about his mission. Not touching me, he continued to explain his mission, apparently not caring if I understood him or not.

"The sons of his older brother, Eric Bloodaxe, are south of here at the Stad with a great army they have raised in Denmark. Thinking about it, we were very fortunate that we did not run into them on our journey here. We were probably saved from their sight as we sailed by that area during the few hours of darkness we had and we were further out to sea, away from the coastline. These sons of Eric continue to threaten his rule here in Norway and this time King Haakon has been caught sitting with a smaller army than normal. His wise men, Egil and Sigurd the Jarl, advised him not to sail back to Thronheim to raise a larger one. That would put him at a disadvantage, they would see just how small his army really was and give him chase and if they caught him they would surely win this time. King Haakon has sent word to them that he will fight on land at Rastarkalf. Egil has asked for eight brave men and extra standards in the hope that it will fool the Danes into thinking the army is greater than it really is. I am to follow the king with one standard along with my few men and a small group of young men from this area. He needs all the men he can get. Sigurd and the king will each lead a full battalion with a standard bearer. Then Egil will disturbute the rest of the standards amongst the few men remaining."

He found a large sack and threw in what weapons and armour he had for himself, talking all the while as he did this.

"I will be taking my men with me but I will leave you in the care of my cook, Arnor. He used to be a great warrior, sadly he is too crippled to fight now, but he is a very reliable man. I leave him to guard you and my ship – there is a fortune here and I trust him like a brother. If we lose the battle someone will get word to him and he will know what to do. You are safely hidden in this fjord so do not worry your pretty little head."

My heart sank fearing for us all. He turned to leave without ever touching me, without really acknowledging my existance. I knew then that if he did not return he had already advised Arnor to sell me or do with me as he liked. I was only a tradeable commodity after all.

'Silly woman, did you really think you were anything special.'

Armed with this new knowledge I became very angry with him but it did not dispell the terror that gripped my heart. The thought of losing the only person in this country who cared anything for me and the fact that death could be lurking nearby for everyone, including me was frightening. Before Hoskuld I may have welcomed death, now I fear it. He has given me the desire to live - how did this happen?

Hoskaulð, however, did return safely to tell his story. I heard him arrive before I even saw him. The horse's hooves kicked up the stones on the path alerting us to their arrival. Next thing I heard was his voice as it rang through the air. He was jubilant telling Arnor that they had sent Eric's sons running back to Denmark. Relief for my life and for his, washed over me. Fickle girl, that I am, I quickly forgave him for his cold goodbye. Hope was revived once more. My heart raced as I lifted my skirts to get on deck as fast as possible. Hoskuld looked up at me waiting near the gangplank. He sprinted up the ramp, grabbed my arm and pulled me against his muscled body and held me tight. I laid my head against his chest and my heart soared as he cradled my head softly with a bloody hand. He rocked my body in tune with the motion of the knarr, which was bumping softly against the dock from the waves he himself had created as he ran up the gangplank.

'Oh my God, is this love? It can't be possible that I love this man... a married man... a man who buys slaves?'

Breathless, my mind was racing with too many questions. I wrapped my arms around his body, not wanting to ever leave his embrace. He gently put his hands on my shoulders and pushed me lightly away from him, still holding my hands in his.

He looked into my teary eyes and exclaimed softly, "I am not afraid of death but I was terrified I may lose you. Now that I am back and you are safe and sound I just want to drown into those amazing sapphire eyes." Laughing out loud, "looking into your incredible eyes I just realized that your tears are on the verge of spilling over and they look like sparkling ocean waves. How you do that?"

'As if I do that on purpose – what a crazy thought!'

Then he looked passed me towards Arnor. I could tell he was still very excited from the battle, I had listened to his heart pumping wildly as he held me. I was learning what made this man who he was and hoping against hope that it was not just my so called *'sapphire eyes'* alone that moved him. One thing for sure, my previous doubts have not stopped my heart from longing for him. I not only discovered hope and a desire for life, now I realized I wanted it to include this man. This brave, wise, kind man.

Melkorka

"The ruse worked Arnor. I cannot believe it -- but it worked. I will tell you all about it but first," he looked at me. "Get some hot water thrall and wash all this blood off me."

Thrall -- that name did not even sway me to anger as I moved my hands lovingly along his arms and gave him a soft squeeze. After all he has no way of saying my actual name now does he? I smiled at him through the tears that had finally overflowed and nodded. If there was a time to admit to him that I could talk, now would have been that time but I was too overcome with emotions. Relief that he was safe, relief that we were all safe, and the shocking realization that I might actually be in love with this man, virtually rendered me unable to speak. My emotions once again were choking me into this continued silence so I swiftly wiped them dry on my sleeve and went to get the towel and hot water he had demanded.

As I carefully washed the blood off him he described the battle scene to us.

"The ruse worked.... King Haakon's battalion and my battalion each carried one of the standards as well as Sigurd the Jarl, who led another battalion with another standard bearer. We were all in hand to hand combat with Eric's sons and the Danish army when they saw all the other seven standards approaching, they thought that the army was huge so the Danish army turned and fled leaving Eric's sons on their own. They had no choice but to flee as well. Amazingly we won with a very small army. Once the Danes hear this story Eric's sons will hang their heads in shame and hopefully give up their quest for the Norwegian crown".

Hoskuld loved to tell this story of the battle over and over again. I soon knew it by heart, I was becoming quite fluent in Norse with all his story telling. If I needed to talk I would surely be capable of making myself understood.

'One day soon!'

Melkorka

There was a large drunken celebration at King Haakon's summer home. I even got to go this time but as a thrall helping the others to serve the feasting army. His long house was very large with an enormous central fire. There were beautiful tapestries hanging everywhere depicting other famous battles. Hoskuld would most likely know all the stories they depicted. They entralled me but I had no time to check them out.

King Haakon sat in his high seat surrounded by his entourage, along with his wife and daughter. The next level had his close friends and his advisors which included Hoskuld. It was my duty to see that they were never without a drink. The rest of the men were spread over occupying all the rest of the space available. I couldn't believe how civilized these heathens could be but then later changed my mind about them. As the evening wore on the regular soldiers got so drunk and rowdy, puking and corousing openly with the other thralls. No one touched me though as they knew I belonged to Hoskuld. He was respected and feared and thankfully he respected me enough not to try anything in front of all the guests. Amazingly, the king, his wife and daughter as well as his special guests all ignored what was going on. That baffled me, the king being a christian should think this all a disgrace. It didn't take Hoskuld long though to notice all the goings on so he sent me back to the ship with Arnor. He asked Arnor to send the few men left behind on guard duty back to the party.

"It is their turn to have fun." Then to me he said „I can tell from your face that all this carousing is too much for you but I must remain as long as the king remains. He would consider it bad manners to leave but I am sure he and his family will not last too much longer. The king does not approve of all this merrymaking but he is so excited over his win I don't think he has noticed what is going on yet."

I was only too happy to leave and go back to the safety of my pallet and wool blanket. Hoskuld would be back soon enough and Arnor was a safe guardian to have. The others were too drunk to care.

Chapter 16 – Jounrney to Iceland

Many days later we returned to Hordaland. We had had a glorious time together in South More. The king had invited Hoskuld to stay with him and gave him his own bedstofa where I too was allowed to sleep on a mat while Arnor and the rest of his men remained on board the ship to guard his precious cargo. Hoskuld was wined and dined every day while I played my role as the diligent servant but I am sure the Royal family knew what their guest got up to during the night as they all slept. During the day all those beautiful tapestries were mine to enjoy during my free time and if Hoskuld happened to be nearby and alone he gave me his undivided attention and unlocked each story they had to tell. Between those few precious moments alone during the day and our time together during the night I was falling in love with a man I knew would never be mine alone.

Not long after we returned we felt the change in the weather, there was a chill in the air telling us that autumn would soon be here. Hoskuld was getting anxious, time was fast approaching to set sail north before winter arrived. In this northern country, he explained to me, winter could very well come early. The last while in Hordaland Hoskuld would come and go, he was busy preparing for his return voyage to Iceland. When his timber appeared it was quickly loaded from the ship it had arrived in onto Hoskuld 's. The two ships were anchored together with a wide plank as a gangway between the two. The men walked back and forth over this precarious gangway carrying their loads of timber over their shoulders from the ship that had delivered the load. It was fascinating to watch these agile men navigate such loads over this narrow passage, all the time rocking the ships so much I feared my stomach would fail me again. The timber could not be loaded fast enough for me.

The knarr was ladened down with many items, most important was the grain for consumption and some for trade stored safely along with his prized timber. We were almost ready to leave when another slightly smaller knarr sailed in beside us. This mysterious ship was flying the king's standard and loaded with just timber. The captain of this knarr came over to ours and told Hoskuld that this now belonged to him, explaining that it was a gift from King Haakon in thanks for his services. Astounded by the king's generosity, it was a totally unexpected bonus.

He now needed more men for his second crew. He rushed off, frantic to find them, they would need to be decent sailors as well. Later that night he returned.

"It was not so difficult after all to find men," he claimed, "good men at that. There are plenty here who are looking for their own piece of land and thought that Iceland still had some for the taking."

Hoskuld later told me that he did not want to discourage that dream even though he suspected that there was not much land left. He assigned one of his top men to become the new captain giving him half the original crew and split the new crew members between them. It had all worked out and now we were ready to head northwards to Iceland. That night he dressed in his finest and went to the castle to thank the king personally.

Two days later we were to leave, the king himself came to see us off. He presented Hoskuld with a beautifully decorated sword. While Hoskuld thanked him the king took off a gold ring from his arm and gave that to him as well telling him,

"I am an old man and I may not even be alive when you return. You are an exceptional man Hoskuld, you have always been faithful and I thank you for your continued support. Fare thee well my good friend, may you have a safe journey home. I know that you are not a christian but you think like one. I pray that my god will keep you all safe, I also pray for the protection from your gods. May Odin, Thor, Freyr and Freya look

out for you and your crew." He was indeed a ‚*wise king*,' as Hoskuld
claimed.

The king hugged him tightly, then Hoskuld came aboard. Both crews
were at the ready, sitting on their chests with their oars in the water.
They could start to row as soon as the harbour guards blew their horn
giving both knarrs the right to leave. Hoskuld had paid all the harbour
taxes they had demanded for his ship and the kings gift was exempt so
it was safe to go – finally the horn blew and we were off. King Haakon
remained on the wharf for a short time while both our ships rowed
away. I watched as Hordaland, the town made entirely of wood,
disappeared from my sight, wondering what surprises Iceland held for
me. I could see that Hoskuld 's heart was heavy as he directed his crew,
in all likelyhood because he would never see King Haakon again.

Onboard, our ship was tight for space as the timber took up a lot of the
room, plus he had another ship loaded with timber following us. The
wood was a very valuable part of his cargo, he would use it for the
support structures of the turf buildings that were so common in Iceland
and for the walls inside the buildings. He was happy because he could
build so many now and could even cover many of the turf walls inside
the turf long houses. These inside walls made from his precious timber,
he said, would all be hand carved, they would be beautiful and would
show off his power and wealth.

Other items onboard included luxury goods to sell back home. Items
such as honey, walnuts, a few jewels, and candles, many candles. When
candles were not available, Hoskuld explained, they used fish liver oil,
shark or whale oil with a wick made from wild cottonweed that grew all
over the country. This oil and wick would float in a well carved in the
middle of a stone.

All the luxury goods did not require a lot of space but they were what
the wealthy chieftains in the surrounding regions would gladly haggle
over. He said that they would pay him in silver for such exotic goods and
he needed to rebuild his stash of silver for future trading voyages.

Melkorka

Although It would be quite a few years before he would need to return to Norway for more of the much needed and prized Norwegian timber to build more of his long houses, he explained. Now that he had an even larger stock of timber he had expanded plans for his future developments. After all he was a wealthy chieftain, a goði with many responsibilities. Many people worked for him and depended on his wealth and power which in turn provided them with a roof over their heads along with their food and clothing. Selling off some of his cargo, he should more than recuperate any costs for this trip. Plus there was sacks of grain and salt as well as other items you could not get in Iceland. Lastly, he made room for some gifts for his family and friends, which included me, of course, a slave for his wife.

'What would she be like? Where will I fit in?'

This new concern troubled me daily and haunted my dreams.

Sailing northwards, most of the time I sat on a crate which was secured to the mast. I clung to the mast for safety with one hand and with the other I clung to my bucket, not surprisingly the rocky sea made me sick again. This malaise of mine was set to destroy me. This northern sea was very rough, rougher even then the Irish Sea, if that was possible. I was obviously not meant to be on a ship -- I was a poor sailor indeed. Hoskuld did not assign me any duties, he could see I was not well. When I was not vomiting all I did was dwell on what to expect on arrival. Hoskuld had no time for me and by shutting me out, the fear of the unkown was invading me body and soul.

At the beginning of our journey Arnor gave me a herb he called ginger root, it looked like some sort of tuberous root. He said that he noticed on the trip to South More that I was not a good sailor. He claimed that this spicy herb came from some exotic country and was difficult to find but he searched for it in Hordaland before we left. All I needed was a small piece each day. He explained that it was best to peel and slice it into smaller pieces then boil it in a little water. Mostly the rocking ship made it difficult to do even this small chore so I would just bite off a

Melkorka

small bit, peel it with my teeth then nibble on it. It did seem to help settle my stomach. I valued this precious gift, hoping the piece I had would last for the whole journey. It was quite hot and spicy at first but I persevered as it cleansed my mouth so well of the taste of vomit. Laying on deck in the cold fresh air calmed my stomach slightly, but it was often too cold and too wet for me to remain there for long. I could not face food and could not understand how Hoskuld and his men could devour so much and actually enjoy it. Most days my ginger was all that I consumed.

Mostly I stayed out of the way on my pallet down below trying to sleep the time away occasionally nibbling on my ration of ginger before forcing myself to eat a small amount of the dry hard bread that Arnor, our ship's cook, gave me daily. Although Hoskuld was too busy to bother with me he sent the cook to check on me periodically. When Arnor could he also made me a tea from the flower he called the meadow flower (anemone), it helped slow the vomiting which was basically dry heaving as there was nothing much in my stomach.

Curled up on my sleeping pallet in my little bunkhouse or on the crate attached to the mast I thought about all of the stories Hoskuld told me about his homeland and about his dreams for the future. Even though I was scared to death of the unknown life waiting for me in Iceland I prayed constantly to be off this ship sooner than later. Just to be on solid land and to be well again and Hoskuld had painted such an impressive image of Hoskuldstaðir, his domain. Not knowing what to expect or where I would fit in I simply hoped and prayed that I would be a part of his life - somewhere – a small part of his life.

Part II

Iceland

"Olaf was a peerless child, and Hoskuld loved him dearly."

Laxardal Saga

Melkorka

Melkorka

Jorunn

Melkorka

Melkorka

Chapter 17 – The unwanted gift

"The landing onto our shores will be rough today son, the winds are very strong and your father's knarr is loaded, so Odin and Thor must continue to watch over him as he manovers his way into the Laxa River. Freyr must be testing your father's skills with this strong wind he has sent us today."

What I thought to myself though was ,*I wonder what your father has been up to to deserve this horrible wind?'*

Smiling down at my beautiful son, I shook that untrustworthy thought from my head.

"Your father will then bring the cargo ship into the Bay of Breiðafjord then steer the ship onto the shore at the mouth of the Laxa River. There our men will greet him and help unload and transport his prize timber up river to our farm. Fortunately our farm is very close by. Then they will move his ship further in land and erect a shed to protect it until he will need it for another trading expedition. Bjorn just told me that there is a second ship sailing in with him. This is exciting elskamin -- it will be fun to find out why this ship is with them, don't you think?"

"Does pabbi only bring home timber mama?"

"No son, he is bringing home many things. These other items will be loaded onto smaller boats to haul the few miles to the waiting storage areas which I have already made ready. Also, I am quite sure that your father will have some gifts for you and me. Are you happy that he is home."

"Yes mother, but where will pabbi put all the timber?"

"The timber will just sit in the farm yard until they can build protective sheds for it all. He will assign some men to guard it in the meantime. This wood is very valuable. Come along inside Thorleifur, your pabbi will be here soon enough. Go play with your toy animals while I check on everyone."

Once inside I sent my son over to play with one of the thrall's sons with his toy animals that Bjorn had carved from horns from some of our animals. With him out of the way I could monitor the activities in the longhouse. Everyone was full of excitement, people were running around preparing a huge feast for Hoskuld and all his men. Now with the second ship there would be more than expected. It looked like mayhem but everyone actually knew what they were doing.

'However, this organized chaos would soon fall apart if I was not here watching, ready to direct someone to their proper chore.'

Time flew by and before I knew it Hoskuld had arrived. I could hear all the commotion in the yard, all the dogs were barking with excitement, so I grabbed Thorleifur's hand and ran out.

"Quick, Thor elskamin, pabbi is here."

I was so happy to see Hoskuld, I gave him a big hug in front of everyone. To show so much emotion in front of my workers and the thralls is quite unusual for me but I did not care. Normally I have a tighter control over my feelings but I couldn't stop touching him. Thorleifur, our only child, hugged his father's leg and wouldn't let go. I was happy to see that this expression of love from his son had a profound effect on Hoskuld 's emotions. He continued to hug us both tightly. Oh Freya -- it feels so good to be in his arms once again. I have missed him too much and I pray that tonight will be a special night. Hopefully I will finally conceive another child soon.

Hoskuld shouted out to Bjorn, „control those darn dogs Bjorn. Why were they even allowed to be loose?"

Melkorka

„The men have all just returned from bringing in the sheep for the winter and were busy caroling them into pens. They will be taken care of right away."

He whistled loudly to the dogs and silence descended on us all as Bjorn led the dogs out. Something caught my eye, I noticed a frail looking woman trailing behind him but I held my tongue. Hoskuld would explain her presence eventually. She looked wet, cold, actually she did not look well at all. He must have noticed that I was staring at her so he turned towards her and presented this frail looking woman to me as one of my gifts. He explained that she had been quite seasick, but claimed in a couple of days she would be back to normal.

He appeares to be a little uncomfortable around this child like woman, my new thrall? I wondered if there was more to her than this sickly looking appearance gave out. Hoskuld stressed that she was a skilled thrall and that he was sure I could find a place for her in this household. He listed her skills, which were few, but he stressed that she was a wizard with the needle, obviously hoping to make her more acceptable.

'Hmmm? 'I thought, 'I will get to the bottom of this -- later. No sense upsetting things right away.'

I looked her over with a hard look and asked, „what is her name?"

"Believe it or not I do not know", replied Hoskuld. "She cannot speak but she can hear and understands most of what you say."

"Hellavitas, it gets worse, a sickly thrall and a mute no less."

I waved my hand to Thora and asked her to take her away from here. For some reason I just wanted her out of my sight as fast as possible. There was an ominous shadow hanging over her -- I sensed trouble. Thora is my head house maid and will know what to do with her. She took her away and offered her some skyr which the thrall refused by shaking her head in a negative manner. Thora was very kind, too kind, I thought, she tried hard to comfort this thrall.

Melkorka

"I understand how you feel, food will not be something you desire just yet. Drink lots of water and you will soon feel better. Nibble on some flat bread with a thin coating of butter if you can. It will settle your stomach. We make the best butter and skyr in the whole region here."

"Thora, "I called out, "stop rattling on and just take her to the thralls quarters." For some reason I just needed her out of my sight.

Hoskuld quickly turned his head away when she looked over her shoulder at him but I could not miss the look of relief on his face. He was with his family now and I could see that he forced himself not to look her way. I wonder, he must be avoiding her look for a reason. Maybe Freyr brought this wind to forewarn me of trouble? I knew that I was brooding over something and maybe for good reason. I could see that he was trying to make it clear to her that he was with his family and she was not to be part of it? Well I will make sure that this thrall gets no special treatment from anyone. The die was cast and my gut told me to be on my guard.

'This thrall is trouble.'

After she had left the room Hoskuld gave out all the other gifts. The gifts to me included some new vessels, two new iron cooking pots and some utensils, a new cloak pin and a beaded necklace. Such luxuries and I was thrilled with them all -- except for her! I was not enthused with the gift of this mute thrall. I decided not to wait and told him upfront that I was not happy with having to take the time to teach a mute, a handicapped girl, how to do the chores that I would have to assign to her.

"It will take extra time, time that I do not have. Hoskuld, you must realize the difficulties of running a large farm, this dumb girl will just take up too much of my precious time".

Hoskuld responded holding tightly to my hand,

Melkorka

"Jorunn, I really do understand but please make the effort. She mended my clothes and appears to have a great talent with the needle. That must be of some value to you, no? Back in Norway I thought that I had found the perfect gift for you. I regret that you do not like this gift but now we are stuck with her. We will have to make it work somehow."

I agreed -- begrudgingly. Just then something clicked in my head. I understood it all now – she had that look. She had not only been sea sick – she was with child. Hoskuld may not realize her predicament just yet and from the way the thrall focused her eyes, beautiful blue eyes at that, at Hoskuld as she left the room, I suspect that he is the father. This has spoiled the whole home coming for me now. I am well experienced with pregancies, my own for one and most of the women living on the farm. I have acted as the midwife at many births. I rejoiced with them all, at the births of all their children, but there will be no rejoicing when this one came along.

'I promise!'

I hung my head and told myself, *there is nothing you can do about it right now. You have to accept that he is the master and can basically do as he pleases. Although, by law in Iceland, I could divorce him if I was unhappy with our marriage and could probably get a very decent settlement but that will never happen! He is mine, she will not destroy my life. I like my life, I am very happy with my marriage and don't want things to change. There will be some adjustments for us with the arrival of a new baby but I will make sure that I take control of these impending changes -- now. This upstart thrall will soon know just who is the real boss around here.'*

Feeling quite confident that I now knew what to do, I joined my husband on the high seat and waited to be served the natmall reassuring myself.

'I am queen here she is only a slave!'

Melkorka

I ate my meal and toasted to Hoskuld 's return. While he talked to everyone else I thought about our life together. Our farm was the largest in the area. I had many chores to oversee, like the making of the fine cloth that rated such a high price in Norway, plus the new shaggy cloth that was fast becoming a popular item, as well as the food products for both trade and for consumption. Besides the trade goods, I needed to make sure that there was enough of everything, to feed and clothe everyone, as well as organizing it all for storage. The thrall, I suppose, could help with the mending, there was always plenty of that to do. Later, I will figure what else she could do but I will never acknowledge her full value to my husband.

'Extra hands are always needed here and If there is any value to find in her, I will use it, but never will I admit it to him.'

The men on the farm generally looked after the catching and drying of the fish as well as any other meat they consumed, but my job was to organize and store it all. I know that I am a brilliant manager, the storage of such vast amounts of food and trade goods was a big job and even Hoskuld recognized and acknowledged my skills. My life was not easy even though I am a very efficient and a very organized person. Without me the farm would not run as smoothly and this so called efficiency did not always make me well liked by the farm hands or the house maids. I understand their dislike and do not care as long as they respect me. That is all I want, their respect, whether it is out of fear or not is of no concern to me. That mute thrall will more than likely fall into the category of dislike for me too.

'Do I care? Not at all – but I do care if Hoskuld *tries to make her a part of this household besides just the mending. I must be aware of his actions around this woman at all times and especially when I tell him she is with child.'*

In the days following Hoskuld 's return, I found running the farm even more demanding, with all the new items to store plus it was more work than was necessary to get this mute girl to understand my orders. It was an exhausting time in my life.

'Was she just ignoring my commands plus this thrall has an air about her and walks with a pride that drives me crazy. Who is she? Is she just being arrogant and putting on airs because she has slept with my husband and is rubbing it in?'

Slowly I managed to get throught to her and make her move more quickly at my command. She understands my feelings of dislike because I can read the fear in those blue eyes whenever she dares to hold her head up and look at me.

'Finally! That look of fear confirmed the power I now have over her. I am rather enjoying this, she may be useful after all, besides her mending skills are really excellent and there is never a shortage of that here.'

One day I was concentrating on my drop spindle spinning wool, deep in thought about the situation with this thrall. I must have mutter to myself, not realizing I had said it outloud.

"Damn you, you stupid thrall. You have wrecked my ideal life here and I cannot trust my husband ever again. You must be some sort of a witch and forced Loki, the trouble maker, to mess with our lives. I will get you somehow, you stupid arse of a woman. You dull-witted thrall."

When I realized I had spoke some of my thoughts outloud I looked over towards Thora and realized that she must have overheard me. I can tell from the sideways looks she is sending my way.

'So what!' I told myself, careful not to speak outloud, *'She won't go running off to tell Hoskuld. Her husband's job is too important.'*

I ignored her strange looks and continued my spinning, thinking how I was to deal with this issue.

Melkorka

Chapter 18 - Hoskuld's confession

After that incident of muttering out loud I realized that I had to do something to get this thrall out of my mind. Muttering my thoughts outloud would not do. When we were alone in our bedstofa and before we even got into bed I told Hoskuld that I suspected that the new thrall was with child. He immediately hung his head with guilt.

"Jorunn, I am so sorry but I missed you too much. I made a big, big, mistake and cannot tell you how much I regret it. The drink was in control of my brain when I bought her as a gift for you. When I arrived home and saw you and Thor I made a promise to Odin that it will never ever happen again -- I will always be true to you. Can you forgive me, even though I must acknowledge this child and look after it. It has always being you who I love, my dreams of you and the mead took over my common sense while I was away from you. Forgive me?"

Relief passed over me. Of course I forgave him, I love this man. He took me in his arms and carried me to bed and make such passionate love to me that I am convinced I conceived that very night.

Months later after the thrall gave birth, I found the strength to bury my hurt and humilation over this new arrival, all the time secretly despising this young innocent girl -- even more than before. I cannot understand why I let this stupid woman get to me.

'She is only a thrall and Hoskuld has been true to his word. He has had eyes only for me and I am indeed carrying his child.'

Thora looked after the birthing and I consoled myself that this woman was indeed a slave. Such a small woman and she had no problems giving birth to such a big baby. Only a slave would give birth with such ease. A big baby boy came out of that small body and he was a beautiful, healthy child with Hoskuld 's red blonde colouring. I must not let him steal into my heart. My other consolation was knowing that I was with child – our love child from that night of passion.

'*I know now that* Hoskuld *will always love me and only me.*'

A few days later, after the birth, Hoskuld had the nerve to claim him as his child in front of everyone and to personally name him after his favorite uncle, Olaf Felain.

'*Of all people. Will I never get control of my feelings and my hatred for this scrawny thrall?*'

In the name of Freya I muttered curses at her under my breath to help relieve my anxieties and anger with it all. Thora sometimes looked shocked and gave me such funny looks so I realized that I had been muttering outloud again. Thora's sideways glances at me were enough to still my tongue, at least for the time being. I must learn to control this hatred before Hoskuld overhears me talking to myself and not just Thora.

'*This thrall is driving me crazy with jealousy. In the name of Freya – why can't I let this go?*'

Melkorka

Melkorka

Melkorka

Chapter 19 – Unwelcomed in Hoskuldstaðir

It was pouring rain as we trudged up the path from the small boat. I saw Hoskuldstaðir for the first time. There were many buildings, buildings unlike anything I had seen before. The roofs were covered in grass and I knew from Hoskuld that the sides of the buildings were all cut from turf. The blocks of turf were laid in some sort of pattern. The walls were black but I could make out a thin line of green turf forming the pattern.

The front of the long house appeared to have wood panels and he did say that his long houses were framed with timber to support the weight of all the turf required to insulate the house. Interesting and so different from the stone houses, monasteries and castles I was used to. The poor people in Ireland lived in small stone houses which had a thatched roof, similar idea except thatch was dead grass and the roofs here had living grass. Even in father's compound there were thatched roofed buildings but they were for the animals or his workers. These people are wealthy and they live in grass roofed turf buildings?

Hoskuld ducked down to enter the carved front door of the long house and I followed closely behind him. No need for me to duck but when Hoskuld straightened up and I peered around him I saw a huge room with many people standing about, near a big central fire. It was warm and even inviting. All the walls were paneled in wood with intricate cravings, quite beautiful really. There were a few wall hangings, they looked to be all embroidered. I will take a closer look later. Wood benches were built in all along the walls and they were covered in furs and wool blankets with cushions everywhere, beautifully embroidered cushions, sheep skin cushions and even knitted ones. Now I understood his need for all the timber.

Melkorka

The dogs were in a frenzy as Hoskuld hurried towards a very tall, beautiful blond woman with a small child at her side. Jorunn -- it had to be her. That woman smiled lovingly at him and he hugged her and the child, kissing them both over and over again, I saw that there was much love between them. The child clung to his leg, he had obviously not forgotten his father.

After he had shouted to a man called Bjorn and got the silence he demanded, he turned to me to present his gift to Jorunn. Her smile faded immediately and I could see the coldness stream from her grey eyes. I understood at once that I would not be welcomed here -- my heart sank.

Quickly Jorunn dismissed me and Thora took my hand and lead me out of the big room. She offered me something white and creamy to eat but I could not face food right now and shook my head to say no. Thora was very understanding and smiled at me. At least someone will be kind to me here. Nothing was working out as I had hoped, Hoskuld appears to have abandoned me and now totally ignores me. Heartbroken by his disregard I gave thanks that I kept my silence a secret. Thora, what a godsend, at least she appears to welcome me. My immediate concern was my need for sleep, a good rest would settle this stomach. Then I will assess these surroundings, I consoled myself as I followed her to my lodgings. I am on ‚terra firma‘ and at this moment that is all that matters.

We climbed up a ladder to a small room that I was to share with some other thralls as well as Thora and her husband Bjorn. They had a private area in the back part of the loft. I later found out that this loft was located above the barn that housed some animals. The body heat from these animals kept our area warm and surprisingly there were no bad smells. The barn must be cleaned very often.

We would all eat in the main room of the longhouse, Thora explained, since all the meals were prepared there and she was the main cook. My small box of clothing was soon brought up to me but I understood immediatley that to wear the dress Hoskuld had given me would be the wrong thing to do. Thankfully I still had the clothes from the Russian and had worn them traveling to Iceland. Tomorrow I will wear the other plain overdress I had made from the cloth he had given me in Norway. I took out a clean dry petticoat and Thora later brought me a brown overdress to wear for the next day, plus an apron so apparently there was no need for my own clothes. It was very like the one she wore and I now understood that this would now be my uniform.

'I am a slave – will always be a slave – never to be a princess ever again. My continued silence will be my refuge here too. '

Thora was kind enough but kept her distance at first, which dissapointed me. Later she did mellow towards me, probably after she saw just how cruel Jorunn could be. Thora loved to talk and told me that she was a second cousin to Hoskuld. She was thankful for her position and that of her husbands at Hoskuldstaðir, but that did not mean she had to like Jorunn she explained. She claimed that she had much respect for her management abilities but that she must keep her real feelings well hidden.

"Safer that way" she confided in me. "You must learn to do the same. There, there, you probably don't understand me so I can tell you anything right?"

I nodded and just smiled at her as I continued my mending.

"You really are brilliant with the needle young lady. Now, if only you could talk you could tell me when your baby was due?"

I looked at her in surprise.

"Aaah – then you do understand," she exclaimed. "I thought you just might understand more than you let on. You do realize that you are pregnant, don't you?"

I nodded slowly to acknowledge that I did know. I had only just realized myself that I must be with child when my queasy stomach remained with me on land plus my bleeding had stopped. There is nothing I can do about it now. I am stuck here in this foreign country and I am pregnant. Do I admit that I can speak? Tears escaped from my eyes so I stuck my needle into my garment I was mending and tried to wipe them away. Thora took my hands into hers and squeezed gently.

"Do not fret dear child, babies are always welcomed in this country whether they are born out of wedlock or not. We are a small population and a birth is always a joyous occasion. We will be here for you, even if Jorunn will not. Hoskuld is obviously the father, right?"

I smiled through my tears and squeezed her hand back nodding my head, acknowledging that she was correct about who the father was. It was my way of saying thank you. A great relief washed over me with those words - I would not be alone with this pregnancy. Thora then handed me a clean linen rag to wipe away my tears.

Chapter 20 – With child

My first days in Iceland had felt strange but I managed to find my place amongst the others working in the long house with Thora's guidance. She set me up with a basket of items to mend and told me to stay out of the way so I sat near a tapestry I could study. The long house was mainly one big room, a very big room, just as the name described it with posts and beams holding it all up. The turf was an ideal insulation against the force of nature and they shut out all outdoor sounds. The carved wood walls inside were a luxury according to Thora. She was very proud of them saying that not many people could afford such walls. There was a big fire pit in the middle where she cooked all the meals and this same fire kept the massive building warm and, surprisingly, smoke free. There were large openings in the ceiling right above the fire where the smoke was sucked straight out. The only times it was too smoky was when Thora was cooking lamb, the fat would spit everywhere creating a smog that burnt my eyes. The room was very bright from all the openings, the big central fire and from the stone bowls hanging from the ceiling. Thora explained that there was fish oil in these bowls with a cotton wick made from a weed which grew wild in Iceland. On special occasions they would use expensive candles placed in huge candle holders hanging throughout the large space.

Inside, the longhouse was cozy. The intense heat from the huge fire pit kept the building quite warm, almost too warm at times. The benches all along the walls were where everyone sat for their meals or when at leisure, which was rare. Then they would turn them into beds at night. Very efficient really. During the day was the only time I sat on them with my mending so it was quite easy to separate myself from everyone. Often it was only Thora and her workers and myself in the long house so I would position myself near a different tapestry each time and study it. Jorunn and Hoskuld had their own room at the other end of the building called a bedstofa which had its' own doorway to the outside. They slept separate from everyone along with their only child Thorleifur. '

'There will probably be more children eventually,' I thought.

Jorunn had her own loom set up in that room so she could weave and have some privacy.

One evening after the nattmall Thora and I were on our own. We had gone for our normal walk outside to get away from everyone and to cool off. The northern lights had just started to appear since arriving in Iceland and Thora promised that the lights from the north would give us a spectacular show tonight as it was cooler than normal and the sky was very clear. I stood in awe with my hand covering my mouth desperately trying not to exclaim out loud over this dance of colours. There were muliple shades of greens, blues, pinks, purples, and yellows, it was an amazing experience for me. I felt as if I could put my hand out and touch them -- instead I rubbed my pregnant belly, thinking that I will have to tell this child growing inside me just how beautiful this show was.

Thora could see that I was excited.

"They are beautiful child, are they not? These lights are created by the Valkyries. Oðin chose this powerful group of women to pick up half of the souls of his bravest and most valiant warriors who had fallen in battle. These women take the dead warriors in their chariots to Valhalla. All these beautiful colours you see are the lights reflecting off their armour and off the golden chariots on their journey to Valhalla. Once there these men are revived, there they fight all day and feast each night until they are needed for Ragnorok, the final battle."

'That was the silliest explanation I had ever heard. Don't they know that God created the world, all the stars, the sun, the moon, even these colourful dancing lights? We even see an occasional dance of green light on a cold clear night in Ireland but nothing can compare to the closeness and the colours produced here. Ahh – but she can think what she likes. I just want to revel in God's work, in all this beauty.'

Melkorka

This dance of the northern lights continued for the whole week lighting up my heart with a joy I had not felt since arriving in this strange land. According to Bjorn and Thora, Iceland's winters could be harsh with a cold darkness that will descend upon us for many moons. I was not looking forward to this long season of darkness and cold but now I had just discovered that there was an incredible beauty that came with it.

'Even though Thora was quite wrong about it's creation. Will I learn to love it like Hoskuld *does?. Will our child? Will I even love my own child?'*

Winter was quickly approaching, the days were getting very short. The sun would rise only to set within a very short time virtually sealing us all in constant darkness. Although the long house was bright, the fire pit gave off light for close work but I had to sit close to it to see properly to do any mending or knitting. Sitting so close any smoke created was enough to make my eyes run and burn. I had to constantly blink to clear my vision and I soon got overheated. Often I would go out for a walk before bed to cool off in order to sleep and since Thora cooked over this fire pit she felt the same as I and would usually walk with me. We both enjoyed the dance of the coloured lights and Thora told me stories as we walked. One night she even confessed to me what she thought about how Jorunn treated me. Thora revealed what Jorunn muttered outloud about me.

"Many times I would overhear her whispered curses to you. I think my look of shock and despair would stop her mutterings, but as a servant myself there is nothing more I can do. I wish I could but it would mean my job and that of Bjorn's. Plus she obviously does not care what I think. If only she would accept you as a servant, as a person, even give you a modicum of kindness, life here would be great for us all."

'Is this the time to tell her I can talk? No, I think not.'

Instead I gave her arm a hug, my silence remains my only strength, it gives me a sense of power over my own life.

Melkorka

"There there child. I know it must be scary for you to be here so far from home. Wherever that may be? It is time for us to get to sleep now as tomorrow will be a very busy day. They will sacrifice several lambs to celebrate the sonargolttr or ‚Yule' as we like to call it."

That morning several men carried in two lambs that had been cleaned and prepared for cooking. They set them up so they hung over the open fire. Jorunn was ordering everyone about but I think these men would have been better off without her there. Then she pointed to me.

"You over there, you dumb lazy slag. I want you to turn the meat so that it cooks evenly."

I came over to do as she bid but being so much shorter than most I could hardly reach the handle, let alone turn it. Unable to accomplish what she wanted me to do she threw her hands in the air.

"I should have known you would be incapable of doing anything right. Why, oh why am I stuck with such an idiot?"

Thora came to my rescue.

"Jorunn, it is my job to watch the meat. I have more experience and I am taller than her so I can reach the handle. Besides, I would prefer to do this so please leave it with me. There are many other things for her to do that need doing for today."

Jorunn went off in a huff to her weaving in her bedstofa, Thora looked over at me and winked. I had to hang my head quickly or I would have burst out laughing, she had got the better of our tyrant and I loved it.

Hours later everything was ready and it was indeed quite a feast. Roasted vegetables lined the centre of the table but before we were able to eat the meal all the people there raised their horns and made a toast to Hoskuld and Jorunn.

"Til ars ok til friðar"

Melkorka

'Arse -- did they say arse? To arse to peace -- it can't mean that? It doesn't make sense. When I finally speak I must find out exactly what that means. This is obviously a pagan ritual to celebrate the winter soltice. Soon each day we will have a little more light, another one of God's wonders. In Ireland everyone will be celebrating the navity, the birth of our saviour, Jesus Christ. I am missing out on such a wonderful time of year but I have only myself to blame for my situation. Holy Mary mother of God-- will I ever forgive myself for this situation I have got myself into?'

Thora pushed in behind me and proceded to tell me what to do. As we all lined up to receive a piece of lamb carved personally by Hoskuld himself, she whispered into my ear.

"We are celebrating the rebirth of the Sun Goddess. The lambs are our sacrifice to them as well as to Freyr, the God of farming and weather. With this sacrifice we thank the Sun Goddess for the return of the sunlight and we ask Freyr for a good harvest next summer. We used to do it later than this but the King of Norway, Haakon the Good, insisted everyone should celebrate Yule time at the same time as the christians celebrate the nativity, the birth of their Jesus. He is a christian and a good friend of Hoskuld 's. So now we start early and celebrate for twelve days instead of one or two days like we did in the past. We needed a reason to celebrate each of the twelve days so over the years we have invented a different ‚Yule lad' for each day. Some are good, some are naughty and a few are down right bad. Anything to celebrate this darkness that envelopes us at this time of year. Hoskuld, a story teller himself, accepts all our little fables, our little celebratations and once a year he humbles himself by serving us. I suppose it is his way of giving thanks for our service. Life is good, no?"

'I know just how much of a friend the king is to Hoskuld *and I got to meet this good wise man. Maybe he will succeed one day and convert all these pagans?'*

Melkorka

The meal was delicious but the drinking went on and on. Thora and I will have much to clean up tomorrow so I went to bed to get some rest. From the looks of all the celebrating it may be just me cleaning up in the morning!

Melkorka

Chapter 21 – Two sons for Hoskuld

There were hints of springs' arrival. About seven full moons had appeared since I had arrived in this country when I gave birth to a healthy baby, a beautiful child with a smattering of red blond hair. I was very afraid when I went into labour, not knowing what to expect. Thora was there with me during it all while Jorunn kept her distance -- thankfully. Thora talked to me all the while, explaining everything that was happening and this gave me great comfort. The pain was excruciating and I audibly gasped at times but fortunately the labour was short and before I knew it, I was holding my baby in my arms. Thora cleaned me up while another thrall washed the baby. It was a boy – a beautiful boy! Thora wrapped him up in a soft linen blanket and handed the bundle to me stating,

"Now that was the easiest birth I have ever seen, you so tiny and all and still a child yourself. Congratulations dear girl – he will be welcomed here by us all. He is so handsome and very strong! Look how tightly he holds your finger already!"

The year was 938 and although it was spring, winter still clung to the land. The day my son was born the sun was trying to break through the heavy clouds, but to no avail. As I looked at my son I saw all the sunshine I needed. I now realized what real love was all about. I cuddled him close to me and whispered in his ear that for him I would break my vow of silence and tell him many stories in Gaelic and even in the Norse language now that I understood so much.

Hoskuld showed up a few days after the birth and named the baby Olaf after his uncle, Olaf Felain, who had long since passed on. After the naming ceremony, I tried to recall some of the stories Hoskuld had told me about this Olaf Felain when we were on our own in Norway, but there was not much to remember. Later, after Olaf was born, the story of this Olaf was expanded by Thora who was also a relative of his. Everyone seemed to have some connection to each other and they were not ashamed to talk about it. This was very strange to me as some were servants. In Ireland this would not be acceptable.

Before, on our evening walks to cool off she would tell me stories about their family and their famous ancestors. After the birth, she elaborated more on the story about my baby's namesake thus filling in several blanks for me. I felt as if I now intimately knew this man, Olaf Felain, and readily accepted this name for my child.

Since the birth was so easy I was soon up and about. Somehow we got into some sort of routine. Jorunn later taught me how to weave and I promptly took to the craft and I could see that my quick learning had astonished even my cruel master. There was a weaving house but according to Jorunn there was no room for me. Instead Hoskuld set me up with my own loom in a small storage hut with the only light coming from a stone hanger with the fish oil and cotton wick or the small fire or from the doorway which was open only on mild days. Jorunn thought she had somehow punished me but little did she know, it was a godsend! I loved it there. We muddled along together and life was surprisingly smooth for the next two years. We managed this truce by ignoring each other as much as possible. Since Jorunn had trained me to become such a proficient weaver she was able to leave me on my own, with my child, in my own work hut. This kept both of us out of her sight and I could tell that this pleased her, if she only knew how much it immensely pleased me. Any mending I had to do could be done there as well, giving Jorunn back even more of her own space. Hoskuld continued to keep his distance from me but never ignored Olaf. This was quite acceptable to me - it appeared that we had all reached a truce of sorts.

Braids were another item I had learned to weave. They required a tiny loom which was very portable. One of Hoskuld 's men set me up with one in my hut. There I created beautiful braids that trimmed their own better quality clothes. The surplus was used for gifts or trading. These braids were not allowed on my clothing but I could adorn anything Olaf wore and took full advantage of this. When the weaving was complete both the new cloth and the braids for embroidery were then sent to the dye hut. Some yarns were dyed first before weaving but it was easier to do it after. The workers there were experts in dyeing anything Jorunn wanted dyeing. The colours were bright with red being a favorite of all. Outside the hut were vats where each moon the men were given a designated vat to urinate in. It was then left to go stale. The smelly stale urine was used to seal the colour in the dyeing process. Once the colours were deemd permanent the cloth or yarns were washed in the nearby river or in a designated hot spring to remove the smell. The river water was very cold and would not shrink the cloth but if they wanted some cloth to shrink they washed it in the hot spring. This cloth would shrink drastically and it was then used to make hats, belts, bags, a few horse blankets and protective vests for the men. This shrunken cloth was dense, heavy but warm and it could last for generations. Mostly they used the beginner weaver's cloth or cloth where mistakes were made, because once it was shrunk and beaten you could not tell how badly woven it was. The weave matted all together and the beating with wooden mallets smoothed the cloth out evenly. Nothing was wasted. The farm, itself, had two hot springs. There was the one that was used for washing our clothing or any new cloth and the other one we bathed in. This natural hot water was rather stinky, it smelled like rotten eggs but I eventually got so used to the smell that I no longer noticed it. Also, the stinky smell of the natural hot water dissapated from the shrunken cloth when it was laid on racks to dry in the fresh air. Later the ells of cloth were carefully folded and put away into storage houses. All the cloth was eventually laid out on wooden racks newly built with some of the precious cedar timber brought back from Norway. This wood protected the valuable cloth from bugs and eventually it took on the fresh clean smell of the cedar wood itself.

Melkorka

After the dyeing process I chose only the finest coloured braids to embroider using my own designs on some and the normal Icelandic designs on others. I kept only a few aside for Olaf's clothing as I did not trust Jorunn's generosity. She could take away as easy as she gave. She must have liked the braids well enough to store them in a chest hidden away in her own bedstofa. These embroidered braids were a valuble bartering tool for her with her neighbours and relatives.

I usually embroidered in the evenings while in the long house, it had more light plus a bigger fire that gave off better light for close work. On warm summer days I would sit outside with the natural sunlight as it was there almost the whole day. My life felt complete now with my son nearby, with work that I actually enjoyed doing. Between them they filled my days and with Jorunn generally out of sight, somehow I had adapted to a life as a slave. My life revolved around my beautiful boy, he filled my heart with a mother's love, finally erasing any thoughts of Hoskuld from my head and from my heart.

During Olaf's first summer a second child was born to Jorunn and Hoskuld, another son. Hoskuld named him Barður after Jorunn's grandfather, a good man apparently, one whom he remembered with great fondness. As they grew older and started to walk Barð and Olaf played together whenever Jorunn would allow them too. Despite her interference they became inseparable. Hoskuld was very happy when he was with the two boys, not choosing one over the other much to Jorunn's chagrin. Strange how happy that made me.

Chapter 22 – A two year truce

Mostly we were left on our own but when it was time to feed him I would whisper to Olaf lovingly, telling him stories in Gaelic or in Icelandic. Rarely did anyone, other than Thora, come to the weaving hut. Often she would take Barð out for fresh air and stop by to tell me any gossip. There was a path to my hut and to warn me of anyone approaching I had stewn pebbles laced with sea shells picked up from my walks near the river. These shells would crackle when anyone stepped on them, warning me to keep my silence. Strangely enough Hoskuld thought I was very clever to do this and had his men do the same on all the paths. Muddy paths would become slippery when wet and the pebbles made it easier to walk on and kept the wet mud out of the huts. They would sink into the mud eventually but Hoskuld made his men replenish the pebbles every spring and I continued to drop any shells I found among the pebbles on the path leading to my work hut.

I think my first real story for Olaf was to introduce him to his ancestry. As he suckled at my breast I whispered into his ear.

„It is time you learned about your family dear child. You have a very important lineage and now I am going to tell you all about some of your more famous ones. You were named after your father's uncle, Olaf Felian. This Olaf was a red head just like you. He was the son of Thorstein the Red, who apparently had flaming red hair. At one time this red head, Thorstein, controlled most of Scotland and he had even declared himself as the King of all Scotland. Thorstein's parents, that is Olaf Felain's grandparents, were Aud The Deep-Minded and Olaf The White. Now this other Olaf, nicknamed the White, was once a king of Dublin. He did not have red hair, he must have had very blonde hair hence the nickname. These northmen made Dublin into an important trading centre which is located in Ireland where I was born. Actually

Melkorka

Dublin was one of the most important trading centres in the world at that time. Aaah my Ireland! I do miss my beautiful country but one day you will sail there and see it for yourself. Olaf the White, Olaf Felain -- these northmen really do love their silly nicknames elskamin, but I understand why they do it. So many of them have the same names and it would get even more confusing than it already is if they didn't have a nickname. Thorstein's father, Olaf the White, was murdered and died in Scotland while fighting to help retain the King of Scotland's control over his throne. Maybe he should have just stayed home in Dublin and history would have been quite different. But dear heart, the point I am trying to make right now is that you come from a long line of kings, on your father's side. On my side there are even more kings. My father, Muirchertach, who is your grandfather or in Icelandic your afi, he too is a king, King of Leinster. Then there is my grandfather, Donnchad, your langafi, he is the High King of Tara. That is highest seat in all of Ireland. I will tell you all about them another time in Gaelic so I can practice telling stories in my own language. So many names to remember dear boy but I will tell you the story many times over in both languages so you will become fluent and remember them all."

I rocked him for a few minutes then continued whispering my story to him.

"When Olaf the White was killed, Aud had no choice but to flee Ireland with Thorstein, so she journeyed to the Hebrides or was it the Orkneys? At any rate, his death left her vunerable and alone in Dublin, no support was forth coming from any of their Irish friends or from other Vikings who only saw her as a threat once her husband was no longer their king. Her father was a famous jarl so it was to him she escaped to. His name was Ketil Flatnose. Now that is quite an interesting nickname, don't you think? His nose must have been quite flat to deserve such a name? One day you will get a nickname I am sure, as there are so many Olafs around. Now back to my story -- Aud fled to the safety of her father, Ketil Flatnose, who at that time controlled the Orkneys, the Hebrides and the Isle of Man. It was a safe haven for them both, for her and for her son Thostein."

I wiped some milk that had slipped from his mouth while he was sucking, gave my precious boy a kiss on his forehead and continued.

"Elskamin -- Ketil adored his grandson, he taught him much about leadership and Thorstein clung to his afi's every word. After his afi died Thorstein was a young man by then, he took control over his holdings and later with some help from the Jarl of the Orkneys, Sigurd Eysteinssson, Thorstein made many other conquests and in due course made himself the king of all Scotland and the Scottish Isles. Thorstein remained in power there for many years, setting his centre of command up in Caithness, with his mother as the Queen Mother. He was married to Thurid, the daughter of Evind the Eastener. His mother, Aud, had organized this marriage as head of their household just like most royal families do. I will tell you about my marriage contract one day so you will understand the royal system of marriage. Aud was quite ambitious and wanted to maintain the royal connections so she made sure he married well. They had one son, Olaf Felain, your namesake, and many daughters. He ruled for many years until he met with his half brother Donald lll to declare peace, they had agreed to share the land, he was to rule the northern part while Donald would rule the southern half. Unfortunately Thorstein *the red* was sabotaged and was killed, leaving his mother, once again, in a very precarious stituation. Rumour has it that Donald's mother had planned it all and without his knowledge. Mother's of kings hold much power don't you think?"

After burping him I moved him to my other breast, he continued to feed seemly content with my story.

"The story is almost done, dear heart. After Thorstein was ambushed and killed Aud was once more alone with no Scottish support. They would have killed her and the rest of Thorstein's family as soon as look at them. She must leave and as soon as possible. Aud was an extraordinary woman, the power she wielded over Scotland was gone but, she still had much power over family, close friends and servants. With her power and wealth about twenty of her people helped her organize this escape in secret. She planned to go to Iceland where both of her brothers had settled. Back then it was still a new country and there was still much land available. With her supporters she managed to have a boat, a knarr, built in secret by promising to take them with her. When her knarr was ready she sailed away from Scotland via the Orkneys and the Faroe islands. She even married off two of her granddaughters enroute to men from prominent families. Finally she landed in Iceland with her grandson Olaf Felain, also with several grandaughters she had yet to marry off along with her daughter-in-law, who was quite frail from the ordeal of losing her husband and the long journey by sea to Iceland. Sadly she did not last long. Later Aud married off her remaining granddaughters to prominent Icelanders. Remember her ambitious nature now, these men had to have the right lineage for her to consider such a match. Even here in her new homeland it was all about power. Aud hoped that one day her family would regain all the power they previously had in other countries. She also hoped to establish a powerful hold here in this new country called Iceland. Little did she know they had no intention of having a king here."

Olaf finished feeding and I held him upright against my shoulder until he burped a second time. Smiling tenderly at him I wiped his mouth and rocked him some more. Olaf burped loudly, seemingly satisfied, I could not help but smile as I cuddled him close to my heart.

"Did you know, dear heart, that when she arrived in Iceland safely she claimed one of the largest tracts of land here, and divided it amongst the twenty or so people that had fled with her, some of whom were slaves just like your mama. To these slaves she gave them their freedom along with land. She had converted to christianity while in Dublin and later became well known as converting many pagans in Iceland. She erected many crosses on her land. Funny though, how both your father and Thora, his cousin, remained pagans. Thora told me that only Olaf remained christian, even his children fell back into the old pagan ways

Melkorka

once married and settled away from him. His sisters, the ones who had married Icelandic men, became pagan believers like their husbands as well. Sadly they all fell back into the pagan ways probably because Aud was no longer around to enstill the christian virtues to all. She was a woman with a powerful belief in God – in my God. Enough talk of pagans, let me get back to your namesake Olaf Felian. A few years after settling in Iceland, Aud arranged Olaf's marriage to Alfdis of Barra, from the Hebrides. He was the youngest and last of her grandchildren to be married. She sent a trusted nephew there to arrange it and to bring Alfdis back to Iceland with him. It was a huge celebration that lasted for three days. Aud claimed that it would be her last feast and people came from all over Iceland to attend, including her brothers. They were both famous in their own right, but that is another story for another day. On the third day Olaf was married and at the marriage feast Aud made the announcement that he would inherit all her holdings when she was gone. After this speech she thanked everyone for attending and promptly went to bed. Olaf watched her walk away and observed how old she suddenly looked. The next morning they found her still sitting up in bed -- dead! She must have died immediately upon going to her bed. What a woman! He quickly organized her funeral because everyone was still there so they had another big celebration. Do you think she had planned it this way? Apparently they buried her in a small ship with many valuables like a queen would have been. Now my beloved child -- wasn't that an incredibe story. I have many more -- so sleep well for now."

I laid my son back down in his ornately carved cradle, a gift from Hoskuld, one of only two gifts. His first was the acknowledgement of fatherhood and the naming of my child. Content, I went back to my weaving and to my life of silence. Only my child heard my voice. My voice was the one thing that I had control over and that gave me a feeling of independence and a deep sense of power over my life here in this strange land.

Melkorka

Hoskuld

Melkorka

Chapter 23 – Hoskaulð's discovery

Haying season was over for another year. Counting each stack as I walked through the field I marvelled at my boys. All three sons were strong and healthy. This last summer had been quite warm, a very good season for the grass, but it was over and my men had just finished stacking all the hay. Now I needed to know if I had any extra stacks for sale. As I walked leisurely through my hay field counting I dwelled on the passing of time. Olaf had had his second summer already and Barð was right behind him. Those two boys were very close and they were constant companions -- despite Jorunn's interference. Somehow it had been a peaceful summer, my wife appeared to have adapted to the thrall, finally! But for some unknown reason I do not trust this truce. Then there was Thorleif, our oldest son, who was growing up too fast, soon I will need to find someone to foster him. This was an old tradition in Scandinavia to have a close friend, or sometimes even an adversary, to foster your sons. It is a creditworthy tradition to carry on here in Iceland.

Thinking proudly about my children as I made a knot in my thin rope to keep track of the stacks when suddenly I heard a soft voice and for a brief moment I thought it could be Hudlafolk. Many Icelanders believe they exist but shaking my head I realized that that was not possible. The language was very strange, I did not know it at all. Then I heard a child's voice.

'That voice -- I know it -- it is Olaf's voice and he sounds so excited. But wait! What language is he speaking?'

Hearing it shocked me to the core! He was talking in a strange language I did not recognize and that soft female voice answered him in the same language. If that was Olaf talking the only other voice it could be was the thrall's voice, his mother's voice. Then I heard his laugh – it is definately my son Olaf! Hearing her voice for the first time and speaking that strange language, but speaking nontheless, stunned me to the very core of my soul -- I could not believe my ears! Anger rose up me like a volcanic eruption and instead of steaming lava, the roar that exploded from my mouth was as loud the thunder that Thor's hammer detonated when he struck a storm cloud.

"Loki are you playing games with me. What is this? THIS MUTE CAN TALK! This thrall has kept this from me... all this time.... for over two years!!!"

By then I was on her side of the hay stack. She was fore-warned of danger by my screaming at Loki, she was trying to stand but her apron was tripping her up. I rushed up to her ready to choke her with my rage.

"My wife is right – you are wicked and deceitful. if you can speak you must have a name thrall?"

Terrified she scrambled to her feet, tearing her apron, but she managed to stand up straight. She squared her shoulders and looked me straight in the eye with those magic tears of hers floating on those amazing blue eyes that made them sparkle like the sun's rays upon the sea. Her voice quivered as she spoke to me for the first time.

"My name is Mæl Curaig."

"Melkorka? What kind of name is that?"

"I did not say Melkorka, I said Mæl Curaig! "

"WHAT? How dare you talk back to me! Whatever your name -- it sounds like Melkorka to me! You have much explaining to do thrall."

Olaf whimpered as he tightened his hold on his mother's leg. He had never experienced anger from me before but his fear of me did not stop me from grabbing her by the shoulders. Something inside me had suddenly snapped -- she had deceived me and I wanted that strange voice gone for good,. I wanted to shake those strange sounds out of her but Olaf's whimpering seeped through and I managed to stop myself. My anger was still bubbling over but because of his fear of me I released her. Slowly my common sense returned, I stepped away from them, my hands up in the air as a sign of resignation. Aggression would not solve this issue so I took a deep breathe and asked as gently as my anger allowed me,

"ALRIGHT -- ALRIGHT! Now that you have a tongue that *APPARENTLY* works -- tell me about yourself. Who are you and where are you from?"

My violent behaviour must have terrifed her back into her muted silence, her eyes showed her fear. She hung her head then she crouched down to cuddle and sooth Olaf. A few moments later she seemd to regain her composure, with her arms around Olaf she began to speak. Slowly at first, then the words tumbled from her mouth.

"I was kidnapped by some Vikings on one of their raids in Ireland. I am from a very... important... family... who control a large county.... the County of Leinster... which is situated close to Dublin. My father is a king, King of Alleach. Muirchertach is his name in Gaelic but I have heard him called Mykjartan in Norse. Obviously all you Northmen have difficulty pronouncing our Irish names. My Irish name is Mæl Curcaig. I.... am.... a.... princess! You have no idea how relieved I am that I can finally speak with you and that you want to hear my story."

"Right! But you have much more to explain. Jorunn is going to be livid... you do realize that, don't you?"

"Yes, of course I do!"

She paused here and took a deep breath and continued her story. I could see that she was trying hard to keep her voice from quivering,

Melkorka

"I have a family... in Ireland, a father, a stepmother.... although... her I do not miss... but I have brothers, cousins, uncles, aunts and.... a nurse maid, Mor... whom I miss very much. She was like a mother to me"

Teary eyed from mentioning her nursemaid, she settled herself down and continued her story.

"I was kidnapped along with some other women and we were taken to Norway. I was so mortified with being kidnapped that I seemed to lose my voice so I remained quiet but I thought it was just for the time being. We sailed to Norway, which for me was a long way from Ireland. I had never been on a big ship or sailed the open seas and I was so sea sick on that journey -- I really was too ill to even talk. I was unable to eat or drink and I thought for sure I would die. I actually prayed for death, at that time it would have been a blessing. Once in Norway I was sold cheaply to a Russian merchant who dealt in slaves... as you know.... you bought me from this man, Gilli. The raiders were only too happy to rid themselves of me because they thought I was a mute. Part of me – I think - wanted to foil their money making scheme by remaining mute, but I became even more unhappy and afraid with this new situation. Somehow my voice remained stifled by my own fear, from my trepidation and horror of all these horrible men and especially from the fear of the unknown. I just could not seem to retrieve it. Both the Viking kidnappers and the Rus' merchant, assumed I could not speak, they all called me the ‚mute peasant.' My shabby cloak and head dress established me as a peasant but it was meant to cloak my real identity. It obviously worked too well, so by this time I just played along, it seemed safer not to talk to anyone, even to the other slaves. My mind was that distressed I am sure that that I would have fallen apart if I spoke. All of us were traumatized by being kidnapped and each one of us learned to deal with it differently. We were not only scared we were angry with our situation and to keep some semblance of sanity some exposed their anger while others became indifferent. For me, silence kept me sane. It was only later that I realized maybe I should have spoken before leaving my land, told the invaders who I was. Why did I not speak? I keep asking myself that but I guess it was for a couple of reasons. One, I was so traumatized by it all and secondly I did not think I would have made myself understood. It was only later while we were on the open sea that I realized that I could understand some of their language. If I had been brave enough to speak at the beginning they may have understood and tried to sell me back to my father for silver. My father would have paid dearly to have me back. The O'Neill family would have paid dearly too. My marriage contract was to be signed that very day I was kidnapped. Just how unlucky is that? I was to marry their son, Liam O'Neill, who is a son of a very powerful family from the north of Ireland. They would have contributed to the ramsom, I am sure. I was simply in the wrong place, at the wrong time, sadly because of my chronic curiousity. I wanted to go to this monastry to view the gift my father was having made for my wedding present. My father must have been extremely angry when he discovered I had defied him and went to the monastry without his permission. He may still be angry with me. He may never forgive me and he may not even want me back – ever! I ruined everything over a book. I will never forgive myself for going to Kilcullen Monastry that morning."

She started to cry after she mentioned her father.

"That is an incredible story. I want to belive you but find it hard to believe that a princess was on her own like that."

She took a deep breathe and continued as she wiped her eyes with her ripped apron.

"Well it is the truth. I had done it several times before, always unbeknown to my father. Cook would always cover me up with one of the maids cloaks so I could escape for a short time with her husband, Niall, as my guardian. Father usually found out but I always manged to talk him into forgiving me. This time though, we even had two guards travel with us to the monastry and there was to be a troop of soldiers to guard us and the beer on the way back to the castle. What happened to them – I do not know. This time I am sure my father will never forgive me. "

"Why then, did you not speak to the other women?"

"Sadly, I was a coward -- too afraid to even tell my one friend Dedrie who I was -- afraid she would ostracize me -- that she would exclude me from her friendship if she knew that I was a princess. The stories she told in our language brought me back to the land of the living, I love stories so I craved her attention. Also she protected me from the nasty jailors and the women who were too angry to care about anyone, although eventually most of the women did protect me from the jailors when I started to mend their clothes and ratty blankets. I became useful but to them all, I was always that *poor mute girl*. I played my role so well I even began to believe it myself -- I began to feel safer not speaking - everyone felt sorry for me and they were kind to me. I liked their kindness, it made me feel more secure. I know – I know! What a silly child I was – what a coward! Not long after we were all sold to the Russian I overheard the other slaves talking and they said that he was going to take everyone to some distant land called Arabia and sell us all as sex slaves. Apparently they would pay much silver for us fair skinned women. That place sounded very far away and I felt like my life was really over -- I felt like death would once again be my only saviour. Then you came along and offered to buy me. You were kind and gentle with me and I began to feel like living wouldn't be so bad after all. You may not realize it but you may have saved my life Hoskuld. Thank you."

Her thanks humbled me into an even more gentler manner. I had to know how buying her as a thrall had saved her life.

"Just by taking me away from the Russian you saved me. He terrified me and the thought of traveling so far away, again by ship, put the fear of God into me – I really just wanted to die. I truly believed that I would not have survived that journey. Your ship became a safe haven for me.

Melkorka

You had so many stories to share and as I told you I love stories. They filled me with such wonder and adventure I began to look forward to living in Iceland. The short time we were together in Norway you were my friend and I really did plan to explain everything to you and the few times I tried my emotions were too powerful, they seemed to strangle my voice. Once we left Norway you became different – distant. Then for the second time, I was very sick on a moving ship. Then nothing seemed important except to reach firm ground, anywhere that did not move. When we arrived in this strange and beautiful country you totally ignored me. At first I could not understand why you were no longer my friend, then I got to know Journn. Your wife can be a cruel, hard master. She is a very jealous woman. Once again I lost all hope and again silence became my only friend. A few months later my son was born and at that moment I realized for the first time in my life what true love really was. Because of you I have this precious child -- now I want to live. Now -- because of your discovery I am relieved that I can finally speak to everyone. Yes I am afraid too – very frightened actually -- to face Jorunn as well as everyone else. I am sure they will all feel betrayed by me but it was simply a matter of survival and quite possibly cowardice. Some will understand and forgive but well, we both know who will not. My muteness has simply been a matter of survival, a sense of power over my own destiny. I hope and pray that you will find it in your heart to forgive me for deceiving you."

"I will try but it is difficult to comprehend all you have told me."

Melkorka hugged Olaf tightly to her and continued her story.

"Our son has brought me unbelievable joy and now I not only want to see him become a man, I am determined to teach him all about my family, my country, my language and the stories my nursemaid told me. Thora and Bjorn are really wonderful people and they like to share the sagas of the Icelanders with me --- the sagas you no longer share with me. They do not know that I can talk so please be kind to them. They too will be shocked to learn I have a voice. I have been telling these stories to our son, explaining his heritage to him as you explained it to me. He is such an amazing child. As you know -- he can talk and he is not yet two years old. He can even speak some words in Gaelic. How amazing is that?"

"Why did Olaf not speak Gaelic in front of everyone if he can speak such a language."

"I am only **just** teaching him stories in this language. He is such a smart young child and I have told him that this language is a secret between him and me only. He understands so much and learns so fast Hoskuld."

"Another question! I am very curious as to why you were able to understand us northmen so quickly?"

"My father had a good friend who was from Norway. That was when the Vikings controlled Dublin and at one point my father was one of their allies. That all changed later but in the meantime this friend, whose name I recall was Magnus, had two children, twins. A boy also called Magnus and a girl called Solveig. They came to our castle many times and I played with them a lot over several years. They taught me many words in your language. When I was a young child I wished I had been born a boy, I loved to run and jump, get dirty, so playing with Magnus was a real treat for me. Solveig, his sister, younger by a couple of minutes, idealized her brother and copied everything he did so we all played games boys would play. Plus there was two of them and only one of me so they talked more in their own language which I quickly picked up. I am a fast learner, I have been told that many times. While on the raider's ship since I did not speak, I listened to what they all had to say and later I did the same in Norway. The guards there were mostly Norwegian so the language was all around me. I absorbed it all while in my silent state. Then there was you. You told me so many wonderful stories and I soon understood everything."

Melkorka

After hearing her story I realized that now Jorunn needed to be told, but thinking she doesn't need to be told the whole story just an abbreviated version, it might prove easier for all concerned. I knew she did not care much for this thrall I had gifted her with and I feared her anger when she found out that she could not only speak but that she was a princess as well. This would not be an easy task.

"Stay here and compose yourself. I will send Thora to get you after I have spoken to Jorunn. I will need the support of all our gods on this endeavour."

I left Melkorka in the field and hoped she would manage to gather her wits, to gain control over her emotions. She would need to be strong to face Jorunn later that evening. Haystacks forgotten, as I hurried back to the long house I went over Melkorka's story and came up with a shorter version. It was really very straight forward and there was no time to waste. Jorunn needed to be told.

Chapter 24 – A wife's fury

"A PRINCESS! A PRINCESS! What an outrageous tale! This can not be true!

After revealing the thrall's ability to speak, my wife went berserk. This extreme reaction was not what I expected. Anger, yes, but she was so astonished she wasn't thinking clearly.

„She is nothing but a slave girl who has lied to us all – and for almost two years! She would most likely tell another lie, say anything to save her skin, knowing that I would be angry with her for pretending not to understand me. She has had all this time to devise such an astounding lie. I cannot and will not believe her."

She pummeled her fists on my chest crying,

"Kidnapped – of course I believe that part – that is what Vikings do -- they kidnapp women to trade for silver. Maybe she could even be a merchant's daughter because she does have a trade, I can accept that story. I just cannot believe that she is a princess. Damn her – she has made complete fools of us. Can't you see this?"

I grabbed her hands, hugged them to me tightly to stop her from hitting my chest anymore. It hurt, she was strong when she was furious.

"Her story that she is a princess -- well that is just too much for me to believe and I will not accept it -- ever! Hoskuld I just cannot accept that she is better than me. Can you not understand how I feel? She was bought as a thrall. She just CAN NOT be a princess."

She ranted at me for quite some time, I wished that Melkorka was truly a mute and that I had never revealed her secret to my wife, Jorunn's response should not have surprisd me so. I let her go on and on, not once trying to argue with her to accept Melkorka's story but Jorunn did not tire of her ranting. So much anger and hate she was venting , it looked like she would never cease, so I had decided then and there I had to find a way to side with her, to let her think she was right. Then it came to me -- this so called Irish princess was not just a thrall – but our thrall. That was the only way I could think to save Melkorka and myself from such venom.

I held her tight to me and tears spilled silently from her eyes. This strong woman never cried.

"Jorunn – Jorunn – elskamin." I whispered into her ear. "I really do understand. Just realize something – nothing is going to change. She will always be a thrall, but at least now we know her name. It is a different one at that -- Melkorka. But how to pronounce it does not concern us. She is in Iceland now and she will have to accept our way of saying her name. Besides, she cannot be a princess here, we do not have such people here, remember? It is not our way, so relax Jorunn. Remember only this -- you are a chieftain's wife which makes you better than her. You are my wife, my choice and I care ony for you."

Jorunn nodded, she finally settled down with that explanation.

"I do not want to see her in this hall tonight. I need to digest this and calm down before I talk to her or I may wring her skinny little neck!"

She left our bedstofa. I followed right behind her and called to Thora.

"Thora, go to the hayfield and find that thrall."

Jorunn cut in, „You have all probably heard the news that she has duped us, all of us, and is not a mute after all. What a false character she is. Make sure she just goes straight to her room and keep her out of my sight Thora."

Melkorka

Jorunn walked haughtily back to our bedstofa. I informed Thora which field Melkorka was waiting at and off she went. Later she made sure Melkorka went straight to her room and told her to stay there until she was called.

The very next day it was obvious that Jorunn was still very angry. She made her do extra work shouting at her,

"you have been very lazy in the past and I have been too kind to you thinking that you did not -- could not -- understand. All this time you were pretending to be deaf and dumb, you were laughing at us behind our backs. You believed your own story so much that you even put on airs to pretend to yourself that you were really a princess. What a role you played! You are nothing but a wicked liar"

I tried to intervene but the look I got from Jorunn kept me silent. With hands up I pulled back and let her go on. I now understood Melkorka's need to keep her silence, now I was able to forgive her for deceiving me . When it came to anything about this thrall I too had become a mute, at least around Jorunn.

Melkorka did try to explain her reasons but her arguments fell on deaf ears and her chores increased dramatically because of Jorunn's twisted version of her life. Now I felt badly for this unfortuate woman that I had brought into our life and sincerely wished I had never laid eyes on her or had at the least sold her before sailing back. One of the new chores forced on her was to help Jorunn undress at night. I discovered this by accident one day as I overheard them in the thrall's weaving hut. She wanted to make it quite clear to her that she was getting ready for bed with me, her husband, and I think Melkorka understood this too. She was letting her know where her place was and probably secretly hoping that this would upset her. It appeared to Jorunn that I was defending this slave, even to the point of believing she could be a princess. How could I make Jorunn understand that this slave of ours only cares about her son, she has no interest in me or anyone else.

Melkorka

"What a load of lies is this? " I head her exclaim out loud. "My Hoskuld believes your princess story but I do not so save your lies for those gullible enough to listen to your false stories. Your fantasy will fall apart and he will see that I am right."

I prayed that this revelation would not undo her sanity, I needed my wife's strength. I knew then that she would break if I gave any attention to this thrall, to this so called princess. Melkorka was right, her jealousy spoke volumes and it broke my heart - I cannot afford to lose this woman – my wife.

Hissing at Melkorka Jorunn spoke with venom in her voice.

"He may have fathered your child but he will never leave me and he will always take my word against yours, you wicked, wicked witch. I don't know how you tricked him into sleeping with you. Loki must be your God and he helped you to trick Hoskuld."

"LOKI! I do not believe in your gods – I am a christian!"

"You are a thrall and my thrall so do not talk back to me! Nevertheless, it is quite clear to me that you are an evil woman and as a christian It is obvious that you are capable of any trickery."

I quickly disappeared before Jorunn left the hut. I did not want her to know that I had overheard this conversation. I must show Jorunn somehow that I support her over this thrall.

The tension in the longhouse was ever present, the short truce had been shattered. Jorunn was always angry with her and made it quite clear that she disliked her enormously. For awhile after her story was revealed Melkorka did try hard to please this woman, I could see that, but nothing she did was good enough. She finally gave up the effort and went about her chores in a stilted robotic mode. She would simply walk away from her rantings which would only increase Jorunn's anger, she

Melkorka

would fume and send daggers at her back as the thrall turned and walked away. The only safe place for Melkorka was her weaving hut and now even that was contantly interrupted by Jorunn's extra demands.

A few months later, on an extra cold evening, she was helping to remove Jorunn's long winter socks, socks that Melkorka had knit for her. She had laid them on the bed as I stood by helpless as usual. Then Melkorka turned to walk out of the bedstofa. Jorunn saw only that stiff proud back and picked up her socks, stood up and whacked Melkorka on the back, snarling at her, *"you wicked witch!"*

It was impossible that these woolen socks could have hurt her, but this was obviously the last straw. Melkorka turned around, her eyes were spitting fire, and punched Jorunn in the nose drawing blood and yelling,

"you are a very.... very evil.... spiteful woman... and I hate you!"

Jorunn covered her bleeding nose with the socks in her hand, crying out,

"you're nothing but a self-centered, arrogant person who deserves nothing better than to be a slave and I despise you."

The fight was on. Thankfully I was close by, I rushed over and managed but with great difficulty to break up the women. Arms were flying around my head and I got whacked several time trying to split them apart. With my arms wrapped around Jorunn, I ordered Melkorka to her room and not to show her face until permission was granted! After this ugly situation, I dared not show any favoritism to anyone but my wife. Melkorka hung her head in defeat , but only momentarily, then she looked up with a defiant look at both of us, she turned, straigthened her back and left our bedstofa.

'What am I to do about this situation? Odin – save me! It cannot go on like this. Freya – have you decided that this is their destinies, this constant hatred and fighting? I beg you to change their paths.'

162

Melkorka

Life was more difficult from then on, for all of us. Jorunn went out of her way to make her life even more burdensome, if that was possible, even when I was around. She promised me that it would never escalate to another fight like the one I had to break up but I did not trust that promise. Fortunately it was winter and I could stick around to monitor Jorunn's activities.

Finally, an idea came to me, I knew then what I had to do but it involved making Melkorka a free woman. She had to leave this farm – there was no other way if we were to have our sanity back.

Jorunn fought me on my plan but I had to be firm with her. I insisted that Melkorka become a free woman and gave her several reasons. One was that I could not handle their squabbling any longer and secondly, the more important reason was that Olaf was getting older and I felt that it was important for him to have a mother who was not a slave. Reason number three was that as a slave she could not live on her own – she had to be free. I tried to convince her that I loved all my children, including Olaf. Jorunn could not argue with that, even she had developed a soft spot for him, despite her denial of his existence. She gave in stating,

"Fine – fine. So long as I don't have to see her ever again!"

"Never again, if that is what you desire elsakamin."

I hugged her tightly, then got on with the move. I had a small abandoned farm that would work not too far from here but far enough away for us all. It was still winter and it would need to be cleaned before I could move them over, so I sent some men there, ordering them to get it done quickly and to get some heat in it. After the men left I went to find the thrall to tell her she was now a free woman. I did not expect this to be an easy task either.

'Odin – my life has become much too difficult. I need your support here.'

Melkorka

But Melkorka surprised me and accepted the move without a word said. She immediately started to pack up her small loom for braids as well as her and Olaf's belongings. By late morning she was ready but in reality had to wait until the next day. Then Bjorn moved her and Olaf over, along with her big loom and some food.

'It was done! Peace at last!'

Melkorka

Melkorka

Chapter 25 – Freedom?

My secret was out in the open, I was not a mute. What a relief it was but soon Jorunn made my life ,*hell on earth.*' This black cloud of depression I had come to know absorbed my waking moments. I only found peace when alone with Olaf and that was not nearly as often as before. Thora seemed to have Olaf more than I did, Jorunn had seen to that. Hoskuld managed to stay invisibe when around his wife. At first, after my ability to speak was revealed and whenever he saw me walking on my own, he would stop to talk to me. He would ask about about my life here in Iceland, at Hoskuldstaðir, curious to hear what I thought of his country. He even claimed how wonderful it was that I had a voice and wished I had spoken to him right away. We would talk about Olaf and what a fine child he was. It had felt so good to talk to him but now after the fight, Jorunn somehow saw to it that he never talked to me alone again.

'What kind of power does she have over him? He is a chieftain, a powerful man, and yet he listens to her like a scared child. I am nothing but a slave, why does she fret so over my talking with him? It's not like I can lure him away from her or even want to.'

He chose to take his wife's side even though in my mind it was Jorunn who had started the fight. Now he totally ignored me and his lack of support left me broken and demoralized. How many times was he going to break my heart? Defiance was the only thing that kept me going, hate was my only saviour. I decided that this time I really did hate Hoskuld Kollason. He was a weak man and did not deserve any respect from me but hate was a very unchristian emotion. It was the devil's grip on me, so I prayed to God constantly to release me from Satan's influence. The Northmen had Loki to blame for messing up their lives and we christians had Satan. We were really not all that different afterall.

Melkorka

Once I had my voice, I lost no time in asking Thora to explain the toast they made at Yuletime to Hoskuld and Jorunn. „Til ars ok til friðar." I explained that it did not make sense to me, something about ‚peace‘ and that one of the words sounded lik an English word ‚arse.‘ She laughed so heartily her belly bounced.

"No no child, it simply means to a good year of harvest and feast. Some men like to think it also means good luck with women in bed. It is an old, very old, expression originally used to swear loyalty to kings. We still use the same ancient words which can longer be translated literally, but now , to us, the words symbolize a prayer for a good harvest."

Thora and her husband became a godsend in the evenings. She was especially happy to find out I could speak and badgered me for stories about Ireland and life as a princess. Bjorn - well Born was Bjorn. He just listened and never really said anything but at least they both believed my story. She wanted to know what we ate, what the castle looked like while, Bjorn wanted to know if we had sheep too and what crops did we grow. So on and so on, constant questions were asked about Ireland. Thankfully, the evenings flew by and I managed to get Jorunn out of my head for a short time each day.

Thora's questions and my new found anger at Hoskuld may have saved my sanity but Jorunn's daily heckling and name calling continued unabated. Everytime she ranted at me I would stiffened my back and hold my head high and walk away. This drove her even crazier but that small motion was my only lifeline, the only act of defiance I dared. By having the strength to walk away I convinced myself that I was worthwhile but she thougth that I was simply been an arrogant ‚slag‘ whatever a slag was. I no longer cared.

"You arrogant slag! Just remember you are nothing but a worthless thrall and will always be a thrall. Keep this up and you will be cleaning the barn."

Melkorka

Hoskuld would simply walk out of the long house and disappear for the day. Her rantings must have become too much for him to live with. Finally today he told me he needed to have a peaceful house so he has decided to move me and Olaf to a small farm a short distance away from the main homestead. At this point I did not care – if it meant that I could escape Jorunn I would go anywheres.

'Why not leave? I will manage somehow.'

Hoskuld 's men had cleaned it up so I could move in quickly. They had built a fire, hung up a stone filled with fish oil with the light we would need inside the small house. They had set up my loom, hauled in wool for me to work with, as well as a big basket of mending. My few belongings as well as Olaf's that I had packed and some blankets were sitting on our bench. There was a small barrel of skyr, another with fish pickled in sour whey, and some milk plus a small sack of grain. I noticed a leg of smoked lamb hanging in a sack outside the door beside a pile of precious charcoal to burn. It would be enough for us to survive for a short time then we would need more supplies, but I did not ask. Before the men left one of them explained that Hoskuld would send over food once a week so my silent question was answered. I need not wonder where our food would come from. That was a relief but in reality, at this point, I still did not care. He also said that a female goat would be brought over in the next few days for milking and installed in the shed attache to the turf house. First the shed needed to be reinforced as it was sagging, then they would clean it out and a new grass roof would be installed in the spring. They would be back tomorrow to fix what they could. That shed would have to do for now, winter was still with us, they claimed.

Although, I did not care what they did or did not do, I nodded at the men as they left. The next thing I realized I was alone in this small space with Olaf pulling at my apron. Suddenly the reality of our situation hit me.

Melkorka

"Holy mother of God. This is ours now – no Jorunn! Ha! Thank you Lord and Saviour -- I will give this place a Norse name – Melkorkastaðir – just to remind me why I am in this country! But it will be my very own home where I can practise my own religion! Thank you Lord, Saviour of the weak and tormented."

These few words revived me from my stupor -- my freedom had finally sunk in -- I will no longer be exposed to Jorunn's bitterness. This black cloud of depression which had dragged me down for days, lifted from my very soul. Relief washed over me. The best part was that I had Olaf all to myself, every day, all day and now this tiny place was our own. I knelt down after my thanks to God to hug my precious son.

"Olaf this is our home now and it will be only you and me. Isn't that wonderful son?

"Yes mama but I will miss Barð."

"Oh I am sure you will see him often, so have no fear, your father will want you to visit and soon. Now join me in a prayer of thanksgiving."

Hoskuld kept his promise of support with the supplies I required. My loom from the weaving hut had been installed in the corner of main room so I had work to keep me occupied. My braid loom I could easily set up myself whenever needed. Also, he arranged to pay a farmer, Thorbjorn "Pock Marked", my closest neighbour, to help me with some of the farming once spring arrived. For now Thorbjorn would milk my goat until I could manage on my own, goat cheese was a staple. Also Hoksuld would supply me with our daily need of cow's milk until the spring when he would send over my very own cow. Milk was crucial for a growing boy and to make skyr and provide us with sour milk and the cream to make butter which left us with delicious butter milk to drink. Dairy products were staples in Iceland along with some lamb meat or fish. Now, I would have to quickly learn not only how to make these items, but how to milk the goat and eventually the cow. That was my

first priority. It was a new beginning – a new chapter in my life. Hoskuld
came by a few days later to check on us and he brought Bjorn with him.
They did not stay long but inspected the shed and grounds before
leaving.

"At the Althing this spring I will make your status offical. Now Bjorn here
will see to your needs and will be the one who will check on you and
Olaf from time to time. Send Olaf over to the farm with Bjorn when he
comes here next time – that will be in two days to pick up any finished
work you have. Then the boys can play together and I can get to see
him. Goodbye Melkorka."

*'Goodbye indeed! You coward! Why did you not stand up for me? In
Norway you bragged about your wonderful laws here and that even
slaves had rights. Liar! Well -- maybe not? You may be a weak man
when it comes to your wife but you did give me my freedom and I do
trust you will make it legal!'*

Inevitably I will have to pay Hoskuld back for this new found freedom by
weaving the wool he would send to me on a regular basis so in a way I
was still his slave. Normally I was allowed to keep back enough cloth
and braid to make clothes for Olaf, now I planned to hold a small piece
aside for me. I did not require much but Olaf was growing fast and
always needed something new. The first thing I did was to rid myself of
the ugly brown overdress, the uniform of a slave and I started to wear
the red one from the Russian. It would have to do until I was able to
make another as for the linen aprons and under dresses I had sufficient
stock in my chest that were never used here.

When he first broke the news to me about leaving Hoskuldstadir he told
me that Jorunn had strongly opposed it. This surprised me, I had a hard
time to understand why she would want to keep me around. I had
become a real thorn in her side but apparently she relented when she
finally understood the positive reasons for me to leave. I had no trouble
accepting his decision, anything to get away from Jorunn.

Melkorka

Surprisingly, after several days of revelling in my new found freedom, it suddenly hit me.

'I am totally alone, with only a young child for company. Nobody is here to protect me from any danger. Can I really cope?

It had finally sunk it -- I was totally on my own. This sudden realization made me feel sad as well as happy, even a little afraid of my own self-determination. I no longer had my muteness to help me control my life so now I must learn to control it with independence. Was I capable of independence? My whole life someone else made the decisions for me, as a child, later as a young woman, then as a slave. Even now as a free woman I am dependent on someone but one day, I pray, I will be totally independent. With that goal in mind I gradually convinced myself that having my own place with my son living with me and having my freedom was the second best thing that could have happened to me since that tragic, fateful day at Kilcullen Monastery. The birth of Olaf being the first. Finally, after constant prayers, I felt I had shook off the devil's yoke.

'Thank you Hoskuld. *You may be a coward around Jorunn but this had to be your bravest act so far. I am no longer a slave!'*

Unfortunately, I was to learn that the people of the Laxardal region still thought of me as a slave. First my nickname was the *mute thrall* - now they called me - with much sarcasm - the *thrall prinsessa*. There was no getting away from it, either way I would always be classified as a slave. Jorunn's opinion of me would always matter more to the locals than the fact that I had been a princess or even now that I was a free woman. Icelanders had this strange need to nickname people or maybe my name was just too difficult for them to say?

Chapter 26 - Melkorkastaðir

Thorbjorn "Pock marked" lived on a farm close by with his mother, Halldora. He came over every day with his faithful dog carrying a small bucket of fresh milk and while here he showed me what small chores needed to be done. Gradually I managed to handle things on my own and I finally learned how to milk the goat properly. That was the one thing I did not like to do but knew it was necessary. He was a very kind neighbour and I looked forward to his daily visits, to some adult company. Olaf looked forward to his visits as well, he especially loved his dog. A few days after I arrived, Thornbjorn's mother came with him to teach me how to make butter and skyr, the two dairy products that were staples for all Icelanders. Then on another day she taught me how to cook the basics, how to grind the grain for pan bread cooked over the open fire. She had to return several times for it all to sink in. I feared I would never learn and that my son would starve. I kept apologizing to Halldora.

"Cooking is something that I have never done my whole life and now it just seems like I will never grasp the concept of it. I am so sorry it is so difficult for you to teach me Halldora."

"We are such close neighbours and I think we will become good friends so please just call me Dora. You will probably end up being the best cook ever, my dear, even better than me."

"In that case please call me Mæl or rather Mel will do too."

Kindness oozed out of this woman but I could see that she was also a very determined person. She was tireless with her efforts and encouraging words spilled out of her mouth. I would have given up on me but for her I did keep trying and eventually did learn some of the

Melkorka

basics. Cooking was never to be one of my strengths but slowly there was some improvement. At the very least we would eat. Olaf was young enough, thank goodness, not to care what he ate.

We had been together so often by now I felt comfortable enough to ask Dora why Thorbjorn was called 'Pock marked'. She laid her hand on her heart and I thought she was about to cry so I immediately apologized.

"Please, Dora, it is none of my business. I am so sorry I asked."

"No, no, it is okay. Really Mel, it is fine. His nickname was aptly given as his face is pock marked from smallpox he had contacted as a child. At first he was called Thorbjorn the "Feeble" because he was so ill. We, as well as all our neighbours, thought he would never survive. Many others who had the same disease did not. He surprised us all, he was stronger than we all thought and survived but was left with many scars. Later our neighbours would refer to him as Thorbjorn "Pock Marked" and that nickname has stayed with him. It never seemed to bother him so we did not allow it to upset us either, even though it really did annoy us at first. When Icelanders decide on a nickname you may be stuck with it for life so what is the point of allowing it to get to you. You do know that our neighbours call you the thrall prinsessa now, don't you?"

"Yes, of course I do. I do not let it bother me either. Jorunn will make sure that some things around here will not change."

"That is good, you are a wise woman. Behind all those pock marks, Thorbjorn is really quite handsome and hopefully he will find the right woman who will look at who he is and not at those scars. He was such an easy going child and now that he is becoming a man, his character has never wavered. It has been two winters since his father passed on. Thorbjorn took over the farm and runs it very well for such a young man. His father was well known for training sheep dogs and now Thorbjorn has surpassed his father as the best dog trainer in all of the Laxardal region. Every day I give thanks to the gods that he survived such a terrible disease. I could not live without him or run the farm without him."

Even though my holding was small there was much to do and gradually I took over the chores as I learned how to handle them. Dora and Thornbjorn were such good mentors, I eventually managed everything about this small farm, although I definitely did not have Jorunn's skill of efficiency. Nor would I ever!

Thorbjorn's mother was the only close friend I had since I no longer had much contact with Thora and virtually none with the other maids. Bjorn, I saw more often as he came with our weekly supplies but he was as quiet as always so I learned nothing much from him. Jorunn had made it abundantly clear that I was not welcomed near Hoskuldstaðir but fortunately for Olaf, he was always welcomed. Bjorn would take him or I would walk him to a big rock near the farm and Olaf would run up to the long house himself to play with Barð for the day. Later in the day I would wait on the rock for him and we would walk home together. He told me whatever little news he had, mostly he just chatted about what he and Barð had done that day, which was fine with me too. I did not need to know about Joruun or Hoskuld. Sometimes Thora would walk out with Olaf so we would get some time together to catch up on her life and the news of Hoskuldstaðir itself, although it seemed as though nothing ever changed there. Olaf was always delighted to see his half-brother, Barð, who had been born the same year as Olaf but later in the year. I recalled how overjoyed Jorunn was, she had given Hoskuld another son, another legal son, which pushed Olaf further down the line. She would gloat over her child reminding me that Olaf was third in line and that she would have more children to push him even further down. Hateful woman! Regardless of what she did to prevent their attachment to each other, Olaf and Barð became very close, closer than Barð was with his older brother. Thorleifur was four years, almost five years older, than his little brother and generally found him to be a nuisance, his annoyance only pushed the two boys together.

Melkorka

As for Dora, she became my strength and dispensed sound advice to me. Thorbjorn, became a good friend too, but it became obvious that he was smitten with me even though I was slightly older than him. He told me over and over again, *'your stories are pure magic.'* His constant compliments built up my confidence. I was content with him in my life but could only ever see him as just a friend which became tricky at times when he exposed his desire for me as a wife. He seemed too young to me and I did not want to hurt his feelings, his friendship meant a lot to me, but I wanted no man in my life at this time.

It wasn't long before two more goats were added to my small holdings as well as a sheep dog to keep my few animals in line. It was Dora who suggested the dog for company in exchange for some sewing, then Thorbjorn came up with the two goats. Olaf and the dog became fast friends and we decided to give him a name, Bassi, Little Bear, because he was as cuddly as a bear. Thornbjorn appeared one day with a kitten which we called kisa which simply means pussy cat. She kept the mice away and both animals became great company for us. The next year I bartered with them for two sheep in exchange for my sewing skills. Dora's eyesight was failing and this arrangement worked out to the benefit of us all.

Dora had her own skills, she was an amazing cook and often treated us to a wonderful meal, meals that were seemingly impossible for me to make. I just could not fathom how the same ingredients I used came together with such amazing flavour when she put them together. Life was looking good for both Olaf and I. I began to feel very comfortable in my newfound freedom even though total independence was impossible at this stage, I still required Hoskuld's support and the work they provided me with. I was at ease with this work, weaving Jorunn's wool into cloth or into braids, even doing their mending was not a big chore for me. Some braids were woven into intricate patterns from dyed yarn and some were woven into a plain weave which were later dyed. Once the plain braids were dyed they were sent back to me to be embroidered, this was the creative part that I loved the most. I worked tirelessly on Olaf's clothing, embroidering every piece where I could. He was the best dressed little boy around and I gloried in this knowledge. Even my clothing changed, I was independent enough to choose my clothing needs. At least I did not have to wear the ugly brown over dress that all the thralls in Hoskuldstadir had to wear so I started to wear colourful clothing over my linen which were now beautifully embroidered. Some days I even felt pretty.

Thorbjorn had promised Hoskuld that he would continue to do the haying for me and to clean my shed attached to the farmhouse where the cow over wintered and now shared with the new born goats and lambs. During the summer they grazed freely on the land. One day an old stray cat suddenly appeared in the shed but soon proved her worth and settled in with our few animals each winter. Every fall a couple of the older goats and sheep would be butchered and smoked, then hung in the rafters in the cold house. This would sustain us over the long winter months. Occasionally Thorbjorn would come over with several fish and I learned to clean and filet them, then how to dry them in the sun. Dora had already taught me how to forage for wild herbs and vegetables. During my first summer I had created a small garden where I transplanted some of these herbs making it easier to access what I needed. Father Michael would be proud of me even though he would most likely not want to eat what I cooked.

In the summer Olaf and I herded our few goats and sheep to the high hills near Thorbjorn's farm so they could graze all summer long guarded by two of his clever sheep dogs who kept his herd plus our few together and safe from falling off cliffs or into crevices. Despite their constant care we would inevitably lose a few who managed to stray. I kept the young ones newly weaned off their mothers near me to milk and from this milk I made the soft cheese that Halldora had taught me to make. Soon our little herd of animals expanded despite the need to butcher some of them. Bjorn built the small smoke house that I used to preserve the meat that sustained us over the long winter besides the dried or pickled fish. These goats and sheep were hardy little animals and prolific breeders, soon my small farm was expanding into a larger concern. Even Hoskuld was quite impressed with me whenever he came to visit with Bjorn. This was not often but now at least he came.

Whenever Thorbjorn was around the farm performing whatever small duties he did for me, or just to visit, I would give him some of my skyr. He never failed to compliment me on how well it tasted, finally I had succeeded at something edible. Skyr was so simple to make, it was a no fail process. When he had time to stop longer he never failed to ask for a story. Stories about Ireland and about my life as a princess were his favorite. Sometimes he would even ask about my kidnapping. I would always tell him that I enjoyed reminiscing about my life in Ireland but that the kidnapping was still too painful for me, I would rather put it all behind me by not talking about it. It took a few years but I was finally able to tell him why it pained me so.

"Although traumatic it was not so much the actual kidnapping - I blame myself for going to the monastery in the first place and I went without my father's permission. All because I wanted to see the Book of Psalms my father had ordered for my wedding gift. For sure father's anger with both me and Niall would have been extreme for he has a terrible temper. This brazen act of mine cost me everything, the loss of my family, my beloved nursemaid, my life as a princess and even my life married to a great man."

As for this part, married to my knight in shining armour, I could not and did not elaborate on as I had no knowledge of what it would have been like. That was another one of my regrets, I never got to know Liam O'Neill but kept this to myself.

"This escapade of mine probably cost the loss of a powerful ally to my father as well, but I feared most for cook. She would have had to face my father's wrath for conspiring with me. Chances are Niall did not escape alive so she would have lost her husband in this daring caper of mine and maybe even lost her role as the chief cook. Who knows? Father would show no mercy and maybe had her sent to the gallows. The possibility of Nial's death haunts me to this day as well as her possible death."

Several times over the ensuing years, he worked up the nerve to ask me to marry him. As flattering as this was I could never see myself with any man and always said no as kindly as I could.

"Thorbjorn, you are the most wonderful man I know, a dear – dear friend, but all I want from you is just that -- friendship. I do hope you understand. You have no idea how I treasure our relationship. I value your belief in me -- that you don't doubt who I say I am. Also, I am still getting used to my freedom and I have to say that I like being on my own with just Olaf to think about."

He never seemed to take offense to my refusals.

"You do know that I will never give up hope. You are the only one I will ever want as my wife," was all he would say.

With Dora's help I started to take small commissions for embroidery. She praised my work so much that some neighbours would bring a piece of clothing that they had made to have me embroider designs on them in exchange for wool, leather or food. Life was improving for me every year but I sensed that my neighbours would never accept the truth that I had been a princess. The few that dropped by came mostly out of curiosity at first but then they returned because of my work. That was my only consolation. In my worst moments I even wondered if Thorbjorn and his mother just humoured me by saying that they believed me, but would soon shake that nonsense from my head. Long dark days and loneliness can suffocate any positive thoughts and although difficult it was very necessary to keep the devil's yoke at bay. They were such trusting people unlike my other neighbours, few as they

Melkorka

were, who relished in gossip. Jorunn had done too good of a job convincing everyone that I was a liar, that there was no way I could be a princess. Icelanders had strange beliefs but Thornbjorn and his mother were the best of them all. I must never doubt their sincerity.

'One day!' I told myself, *'I will prove everyone else wrong and Olaf will be the one to do this for me.'*

Chapter 27 – An Ancient tradition of fostering a child

Time passed, Olaf and I had settled well into our new life alone and before I knew it we were celebrating Olaf's seventh birthday. That day Hoskuld came over with Barð with a gift for Olaf, a beautiful game piece carved from a walrus tusk. It was very beautiful but useless really as it was only one piece. I did not say anything but thanked him for it. Hoskuld then clarified my doubts about the gift saying,

" Eventually I hope to complete a set in ivory for all the boys, but they will be adults before this set will ever be complete. It is a gift fit only for kings or catholic bishops. There is a carver from the Laxardal region, not a man but a woman, who is the talented artist. Several years ago before the King of Norway, my good friend Haakon, passed on he had sent over a catholic priest to try and convert us pagans into christians. I was a little disappointed he did this but I also know that there was a lot of pressure from the catholic church to spread their message. This priest lives in Skalholt and calls himself a bishop and we cannot seem to rid ourselves of him now, some Icelanders seem to be listening and slowly converting. This priest has requisitioned her to complete several chess sets for him to send to Norway and this piece was one of the few rejected. It is still beautiful but cheaper, otherwise it would cost a king's ransome for a set with no flaws. I have two other pieces, one each for Barð and Thor. Ideally I would love to purchase a complete set for each but I do not want to pay such a high price. In the meantime I have comissioned a hnefatafl set for these two boys to be made from wood from another carver I know. Thor already has one and is proficient at the game and it is time these two youngsters learn it too. There is another game called chess but that can be another gift for another time."

Melkorka

Before the boys were allowed to run outside to play Hoskuld announced that he had some very good news for Olaf and I. The first bit of news was that Jorunn had had another child, a girl this time and that they had named her Thorgerður after Jorunn's mother. This was old news to me but I congratulated him as if this was a new revelation. There were no other children between this new baby and Barð and so far no more sons. Jorunn must have difficulty conceiving. Hiding my smugness instead I rejoiced in the news and hugged both Olaf and Barð, telling them how lucky they were to have a baby sister.

The next bit of news was profoundly shocking to me and put the fear of God into my heart. He told me that he had found a foster-father for Olaf, a wealthy chieftain, a goði named Thord, from a different region, not too far from Laxardal. This meant that Olaf would have to leave me and go live on another farm, far away. I quickly gathered my wits about me and shooed the boys outside to play before I exposed the terrible fear and anger that had gripped my whole being. Then I turned to Hoskuld,

"How could you do this to me? You never come to visit and now you come only to bring such bad news. You know Olaf is better off with me." I begged and pleaded with him, "I have many things yet to teach him, he is still too young to be away from his mother. Plus he will miss Barð too much." On and on I came up with excuses why. Even the mention of Barð did not help.

"Soon enough I will find someone to foster Barð too, like Thor his brother. This is our tradition here in Iceland, you must accept the inevitable Melkorka."

Nevertheless, I continued with my objections to this adoption, clinging to my one point that he was too young. I even tried another route saying that this inheritance wasn't good enough for the son of a princess.

Melkorka

"Being a princess has nothing to do with this and you know it. Do not play that game with me Melkorka, you have no idea what a winning situation this is for all, especially for Olaf. You do realize that my two sons come first for inheritance and between them the farm will have to be split up, leaving very little for Olaf. This way he will inherit a farm all of his own as Thord has no children. Olaf can become a wealthy landowner in his own right so we must not pass up this opportunity. Like I said before, it is not uncommon here in Iceland to foster out a son and even without inheriting anything it builds good relationships between landowners, between leaders. In this situation Thord will leave him everything. It is a win win opportunity so I intend to accept this offer – with or without your approval".

Defeated, I knew I had lost this one so I finally relented. I believed that this man would do as he said regardless of my feelings. My heart broke at this news but my head told me that this was indeed a very good offer for Olaf. He would eventually inherit a good farm and Hoskuld promised me that I could see him whenever I wished.

"Whenever he returns home for a visit," Hoskuld promised, "Barð and Olaf can see each other as much as they like, that is until I find a foster father for Barð. When Olaf comes for a visit he can also get to know his new baby sister as well."

Accepting the inevitable, we called in the boys and discussed it with Olaf. He looked shyly at me not knowing whether he should be happy or sad. Poor child, I can see that he wants to stay with me. This is such a silly tradition. Before leaving Hoskuld admitted to me why Olaf was offered this opportunity.

"Thord is involved in a messy divorce with his wife Vigðis Ingalsdottir. It was because of this divorce that he first approached me. He asked for my support against Vigðis and her kinsman and asked that I speak at the next Alþing for him. He made his offer to foster Olaf as his thanks for my support even though Olaf may be a couple of years younger than most sons fostered out."

"So I was right, he is too young."

"Maybe, but we cannot pass up this chance for him to inherit such a great farm. Since he is so young I will make sure Olaf spends the passing of one moon with you and then one with Thord until he is old enough to spend longer time there. Is that a deal?"

"Yes, of course I understand what an opportunity it is for him. Alright, we will work something out."

That night I prayed fervently to my Christian god asking him for his support and guidance, begging him to keep my son safe when he would have to leave my side. Later we would find out that by naming Olaf as his heir, it had complicated the litigation. It would take several other smart law speakers, besides Hoskuld, to untangle all the mess they were in. Thord had purposely named Olaf as his heir so his ex-wife or her kinsmen would not inherit his farm when he passed on but they were fighting it with other smart law speakers. This divorce almost ended in a blood feud.

Chapter 28 – The divorce is final

At the end of the summer Olaf left to spend his first month on his foster father's farm. Heavy hearted, alone without my ray of sunshine and with the darkness of winter drawing near, I set about doing my chores. I must keep busy so I won't dwell on my loss. He will soon be back with me, Hoskuld promised. Somehow I managed over the next winter and adjusted to sharing my son with Thord. He turned out to be a very dear man and you could see that he too had become quite attached to Olaf.

After seeding, Hoskuld and Thord travelled to the Althing hoping to finalize the divorce and in the meantime Olaf was allowed to stay with me. I prayed that they would take their time in returning but alas it was not to last. They returned frustrated with it all. Thord was still married to this awful woman and it appears that they were threatening a blood feud so Olaf could no longer stay with me alone. He would have to stay with his foster father continually until it was settled.

"Come and spend part of the winter with us Melkorka especially over Yule time." Thord kindly offered. "You understand that Olaf will be safer living at Thordstaðir as I have more people around to protect him than you do."

The divorce proceedings, all the haggling over property, all the animosity over Olaf's inheritance, continued unabated over the next year, forcing me to go through another dark and dreary winter and this time with no visits from Olaf to look forward too. Hoskuld managed to find other men from different areas to speak on Thord's behalf. They claimed that now they were really prepared for the next Alþing in the spring, that Vigðis' claim would be null and void this time. I was totally excluded from all the negotiations but I heard enough about it to stress me greatly. Gossip always distorted the actual thing but nevertheless I whittled every day over all the arguing between Olaf's foster father and his wife's kinsmen. Olaf's very existence was in question and I prayed endlessly to my own god, asking him to watch over my son, to keep him safe. The ex-wife and her kinsmen were very angry over this adoption, they thought Thord had tricked them out of what should rightfully belong to Vigdis. I believed them to be capable of terrible treachery and agonized the whole time over his safety. This was a very trying time for me, although I did realize that Olaf was safer at Thord's farm than with me, a lone woman. I had no one to defend Olaf if it came to a physical fight and fortunately Thord did. The dark cold winter did not help and the loneliness, the detachment from my son, nearly finished me mentally. Bessi and kisa were good company during the long dark nights I was alone but they could not replace my son and the only thing that prevented my complete breakdown were the short visits to Thordstaðir. Thorbjorn and Dora took good care of my place whenever I was gone.

Every day that I was alone and while I milked my one and only cow and my few goats, I would pray out loud in a rhythmic chant to the milk hitting the bucket, repeating it over and over again.

"O' God above I'm begging you...
Protect my son from the few...
Feudal lords who tender their swords...
Be my shield against these hordes.
Keep him safe upon this land...
For he must grow and become a man.
He is destined to fulfill my goal?
Keep him safe - guard his soul."

This was the state of my mind during that second winter without Olaf.

Being Irish, of course I was raised as a Christian. Ireland was a Christian country and I had explained this all to Thorbjorn and his mother, telling them that I derived much comfort from my new found freedom and been able to pray to whomever I wanted to. They assured me that they did not care who I prayed to. Still, thanks to Dora, my other neighbours would sometimes drop in with small commissions of work for me so now I needed to be even more vigilant. They would not be as understanding as Dora and Thorbjorn, if I was caught talking out loud or singing to a different god than the ones they were used to. Without Olaf desperation had set in, my mind was slipping and I needed some sort of comfort so this rhythmic chant helped somewhat. Thinking if I also had a rosary this might be even more consoling and I would stop all this craziness so I asked Thorbjorn for his help. I explained what a rosary was, that it was like a necklace except no one wore it as one. He carved some beads out of bones and a small cross from wood and I strung them together with a long leather lace. Leather that I had tanned myself from my goat skins. Every year I made soft leather shoes for summer from this leather, with laces to tie them tight so they stayed on our feet. This time I made an extra-long lace for my rosary. These shoes were soft and supple with insoles made from thick wool cloth I had shrunk in the hot spring but they only ever survived a single summer from constant wear. Our winter boots on the other hand survived more than one season, they were made from cow hide or goat skin and they were lined with the same thick wool shaped like a boot as well. The snow was not as hard on our footwear as the summer was, the rocky passes shred the soles and I was constantly mending them. The rosary beads and cross were completed in record time and I threaded them onto my long leather lace with much anticipation. Although it could never be blessed I found the feel of the beads in my hands soothed me as I prayed. Now calmed by the feel of the rosary around my neck, my rantings ceased, and now I was able to continue my sing-song chant in silence while I milked the animals. Amazing what comfort I got from this small gift, from this ancient catholic tradition. They made me feel closer to my god whenever I prayed. Tradition was everything, it soothed my troubled soul.

Melkorka

During one of the visits with Olaf at Thordstaðir he asked me how I was managing without him living with me.

"What a caring soul you have my son. I have tried to teach you about my religion many times before so you must know that that is what helps me survive without you. I pray to my God just as you pray to Thor. To me my God is the God Almighty and Jesus, his son, is our Saviour. He died to save our souls but before he died he performed many miracles."

After telling him some stories of the miracles Jesus performed in the name of God, Olaf confessed to me his confusion.

"Sounds like you Christians have more than one god to pray to just like us pagans do mam. You know that Oðin is our high god, who sacrificed an eye to become the wisest of all and the rest are lesser gods, each with their own strength. Besides this Jesus, you have the Virgin Mary and all the other saints you talk about as well."

Laughing at his observations I hugged and told him that he would understand one day. Not once did I denounce the pagan values that the Icelanders believed in. I was smart enough to realize that that would be a huge cross for Olaf to bear if I made him choose since he was surrounded by pagan believers. It was too important that he fit in here.

Right from the beginning I had encouraged him to choose his own favorite pagan god but also encouraged him to pray to my god at bedtime telling him never to reveal this to anyone. It would be a secret shared by us only. Then after our prayers to my god he could pray to his chosen pagan god, which was Thor of course, like most Icelanders. Hoksulð, Olaf's father, talked much about the God Freyr when he discussed the weather which was always a concern in Iceland and for serious situations and for travel he prayed to Oðin or to Thor. Praying to Thor, a warrior god, impressed Olaf more than a weather god. Thor was considered the main God by most Icelanders and he was the chosen god of most Viking warriors. Even Loki had a role to play in pagan worship but Olaf had chosen Thor, of course. He was a warrior god. When he left to live on Thord's farm I advised him to stay true to Thor or any other pagan gods he may one day decide to choose, but never to speak about my Christian beliefs.

Spring arrived finally, the assembly at the Althing was fast approaching and I had survived a second awful winter.

'Will there finally be an end to this worry?'

Chapter 29 – Olaf receives a nickname

It took two years and two trips to the Althing to negotiate the divorce, but at last it was all settled. Thord could not have accomplished this outcome without Hoskuld's powerful backing and advice. It was through Hoskuld's influence that Thord managed to acquire the other lawspeakers who eventually untangled all the charges against him and had them all thrown out. Vigðus was an angry woman but smart and wealthy enough to finally realize that if she or her kinsmen hurt Thord or Olaf they would all be outlawed and that her new found wealth could revert back to Thord making him more wealthier than her. She finally succumbed to the divorce but walked away with plenty. That very summer she found another wealthy farmer, married him and erased Thord and Olaf from her life. She was still a very attractive, desirable woman and apparently had several other offers. When we heard this good news we all relaxed and started to enjoy life without looking over our shoulders all the time. The best thing was that now Olaf could safely come to visit me -- that in itself was worth rejoicing over.

Plus Olaf had a bright future, a father figure that doted on him and a guarantee that he would inherit all that he owned. Life was good once again and the future was looking even better. Finally I was able to count my blessings, my poor rosary beads were almost worn out from all my previous concerns and now from my prayers of thanks to my God for looking over my son. The rosary was always with me as I wore them like a necklace hidden under my clothes and only took them off to pray. The most important thing to me was that Olaf could come to visit me, another rosary was not that important. Although one day soon I may ask Thornbjorn for more beads before this one fell apart.

Olaf loved fine things and his foster father gave him what he could and I continued to make him his colorful clothes he loved so much. Dressing

Melkorka

well was a status symbol of wealth and power in Iceland. I had become an expert weaver and combined with my embroidery, Olaf was dressed better than most. However, life wasn't always easy or pleasant for Olaf around other children. The people of Laxardal had long memories and genealogy was an obsession with them. Whenever he was around other young boys, excluding Barð of course, they would call him names, pull on his fine clothes, asking why a son of a slave could afford to have such fine things. Olaf tried hard to deflect this name calling by holding his head high, he would stick out his chest and walk away. I saw myself in the way I used to deal with Jorunn's rantings. My boy was wise beyond his years.

One fall day many people were visiting Thord's farm for a harvest feast and to celebrate his divorce. Even me. Thorbjorn and his mother, Dora were also invited so we went together. Hoskuld and his family were there as well, they were the honoured guests and sat in the high seats with Thord. After the feast Jorunn was nowhere to be seen as we gathered around the children to watch them play some sort of ball game I did not understand. I had to reassure myself that I had every right to be here but I kept looking over my shoulder, fearing her wrath even here on neutral ground.

Hoskuld was holding court making comments on how his youngest son would try to protect Olaf from the teasing from the other boys. He claimed that he was very proud of this closeness between the two brothers. He suddenly laughed out loud saying to us,

"Look at Olaf strut like a peacock, he is totally unaffected by their taunts, he really doesn't need Barð's help or anyone's help after all. Well done son."

Olaf heard his father's laugh and came over.

"What is so funny pabbi."

Melkorka

"Nothing son, my Olaf Pai."

'What did he say? He had called him Olaf the Peacock to his face -- but with such affection. Why Peacock?'

After hearing this nickname for the first time Olaf, looked quite confused and asked his father,

"What is a pai pabbi? Why do you call me that?"

Hoskuld ruffled his hair and smiled with great fondness as he explained to him.

"Son, a pai is a very striking, colourful bird. They have the most beautiful feathers, green and blue feathers, that are very iridescent and the way they walk says I am proud of who I am. The pai reminds me of you. You love your fine clothes that are brightly coloured and you walk like you are very proud to wear them and that you are very proud of who you are. I admire the attitude you have, you will be a great leader one day."

This explanation made Olaf very happy and he stuck out his chest even more as he walked away from his father to join Barð and the other boys. Hoskuld laughed heartily at this proud strut.

"I am very proud of my boys and the love they have for each other".

I felt his pride as well and quickly accepted Olaf's new nickname especially after his father's eloquent explanation.

Suddenly my skin started to crawl, a fearful sensation came over me and I quickly glanced over my shoulder. Sure enough there was Jorunn walking as fast as she could towards us. I had been standing next to Hoskuld and knew it was time to go elsewhere. Threading my arm through Dora's I whispered into her ear.

Melkorka

"Dora min, please come with me. Let's walk toward the other group as casually as possible. Jorunn is heading this way and has a thunderous look on her face."

We walked away whispering to each other as if we had not seen her and were sharing a private conversation. When we reached the other group I looked over and saw her standing next to Hoskuld with her arm through his. He had his hand on hers patting it as if to say all is okay but her eyes shot daggers at me. He could very well be in trouble but it was of no concern to me. I was here to visit my son and I was not about to let either one destroy my joy. A sense of strength flowed through my body as I bravely nodded and smiled at her then looked away as if engrossed with the children play this confusing ball game they loved so much. I had no understanding of it and I did not care but my happiness to be here was too evident to hide, so I tried to relax and just enjoy the day. Her fearful hold over me dissolved as I watched my son kick the ball over to his brother.

Chapter 30 – Love's turning point

Since Thord's harvest feast Hoskuld had taken to stopping by Melkorkastaðir more often and now he was generally alone. He would drop by on his way home from visiting a neighbour or from Thord's place. Sometimes Thorbjorn was there or close by so Hoskuld would never stay too long. Even if he wasn't there Hoskuld never stayed very long but I was always happy to see him, it felt like a long lost friend had returned. Whenever he had just come from Thord's farm with cloth for me to make clothes for Olaf he would bring news of him, relating stories of how well he was doing and how proud and happy his foster father was with him. I had long since forgiven him for his cowardice with Jorunn, I was too thankful now for giving me my freedom and this small farm. I loved my new life and no longer feared being alone. One winter day it was snowing hard and it was very cold.

Bessi barked at some commotion outside and I soon heard a loud knock on the door. Hoskuld entered claiming he had stopped by to drop off some linen from Thord to make into shirts for both Olaf and his foster father. I welcomed him in and offered him something to eat and drink. He refused saying that he needed to get home as the storm was getting worse. We chatted for a short while about Olaf and how happy he was with Thord. Later Hoskuld opened the door to leave when he saw how bad the weather had gotten, he exclaimed in astonishment.

"Freyr must be angry, the weather has become worse and very quickly too. I will have to stay the night --with your permission of course? Jorunn must never know though. You know what she can be like when it comes to you. Has Thorbjorn come by today?"

"He was here earlier to make sure I would be okay and then checked and secured all the animals for me before he left."

Melkorka

I hesitated knowing only too well what Jorunn could be like but there was no way I could or would force Hoskuld to leave in this weather, so I graciously invited him to stay the night. He struggled in the intense blowing snow just to put his horse in the shed for the night. He brought everything else in with him and shut the door tight scattering the snow that came in with him everywhere.

That night we ate by the fire with knitted wool blankets over our shoulders for extra warmth. He complimented me on my mead. "A delicious mead. You have learned much and learned it well".

Thrilled, I responded to his compliments.

"I will never be a good cook but thank you. For some reason I do seem to make a decent mead and even my skyr is pretty good."

His words made me feel warm inside and so did the mead. I sensed that a dangerous mood was developing between us.

While drinking another horn of mead together he asked me to tell him some of my Irish stories. After several stories and a few more horns of mead, he was soon snoring, sitting up on his bench. I relaxed, thinking that I had been imagining this *'dangerous mood'* I thought was hanging over us. I covered him with another blanket, before I banked the fire so it would be warm for the night. Then I made ready for bed and crawled under the covers on the other bench thinking he will be gone in the morning. There was never anything to fear, my imagination must have been playing tricks on me as I went over the evening with him in my head. I couldn't believe just how much I had enjoyed his company, it was like old times on his ship in Norway. I realized then that I still had strong feelings for this man -- if only things were different between him and Jorunn.

'Mæl, *don't be stupid, there can never be anything between you and Hoskuld. Ever!'*

Melkorka

I had to give myself a real talking to as my heart was pounding with passion and I thought that I would never get to sleep.

The wind continued to howl during the night, I could hear it even through the thick turf walls so it was a fierce storm. Suddenly I woke up to feel a body squeezing in next to me. Surprised but not disappointed by this I heard Hoskuld whisper into my ear that he could not get me out of his head. He missed me desperately he whispered. His breath wreaked of the honey mead he had drunk but his lips were soft and warm against my neck as he kissed me all over. I did not stop him - my heart throbbed - my whole body tingled for this man.

"Could we be together for just the one night for old time's sake Mæl Curaig?"

He had even pronounced my name correctly. I turned around with my arms crossed, blocking him from my body. I now knew that I had never gotten over my desire for him and NOW he admits that he still cared for me but I knew for certain that I had to stop this madness before it was too late.

"Hoskuld... your words mean everything to me. You have no idea how difficult this is for me but I must refuse your advances. I am a woman on her own. You know how much I value the freedom you have given me, this farm is my life now, but more than anything else I treasure the one gift we share together. Our son! As well as the memories of our time in Norway. You must understand -- do not get offended by my refusal. I cannot deal with any complications such as what you are suggesting. I am sorry but surely you realize what I am saying is the only way for both of us to go forward. We must remain as friends – only!"

The silence was deafening and I could feel his body stiffen as he turned his back to me. I wanted to cry out that I had changed my mind but I remained silent too. Then his body relaxed.

Melkorka

"I do understand Mæl. More than you will ever know. I just wish that things could be different between us. I suppose I want it all but I do understand how this could be very difficult for you. We will remain neighbours, Olaf's parents and of course -- friends. I would like that. We will talk no more about this. Goða nott."

My heart was pounding as I lay quietly by his side. His back was a wall of silence but a wall that radiated heat so I gradually relaxed and curled up against it. He was soon snoring. Sleep eluded me for a long time as I listened to the wind raging outside but my mind was too busy going over what had happened to hear it. Would he ever forgive me, would I ever forgive myself for refusing him? I had wanted this man like no other and now I had permanently closed the door. My mind wandered to the best friend I had, Thorbjorn. Although I was happy that Hoskuld was once again a friend, I realized I would never want to jeopardize my relationship with my neighbour, he was more important than I wanted to admit.

The next morning, all was much quieter, I could no longer hear the wind howling but when I looked outside I saw that it was still blowing enough to scatter the snow. We were very awkward with each other at first until Hoskuld looked into my eyes and apologized to me profusely saying,

"I never meant for this to happen -- I am truly sorry. I have forced you into a bad situation, my mead induced brain has once again taken control of my body. Can you ever forgive me?"

I touched his face softly, I remembered it all too well. I spoke so quietly he had to strain to hear what I said.

"Are you are asking for my forgiveness? Hoskuld... a big part of me regrets refusing you but thanks to you I am a free woman. I am able now to make my own decisions, difficult as they can be. This is very important to me to be free of any man except for the role of a mother to our son. I will remember this night for a long time to come, thank you. One thing though Hoskuld, I must know how you managed to pronounce my name correctly after all this time of mispronouncing it."

He looked at me with such care in his eyes and held my hands in his. "Mæl, I have practised saying your name over and over whenever I am alone and riding off somewhere. But in front of anyone -- if I was to speak about you -- I would make a point of pronouncing it like all Icelanders. Melkorka the thrall prinsessa. You do know that is what all Icelanders in this region call you now, don't you?"

"Some call me that to my face, so yes I do know."

I slowly pulled my hands away from his and I offered him something to eat. He refused saying,

"I must leave quickly, before Thorbjorn shows up to check on you. I do not want to compromise your reputation any further and I will never put you in this situation again, I promise. I know this will sound crazy to you but I am going to go towards the way I came from yesterday. There is not much there so no one should see me and then I will turn around and come back. If Thorbjorn comes by try and keep him here. That way he can witness my arrival with the cloth for you from Thord. After the storm we have had I am convinced he will come by to check on you. You do know that he is crazy about you, don't you?"

"Of course."

"I think I was a little jealous and just testing your relationship with him? Is it serious?"

"No, he is just a friend, but I value his friendship very highly."

"Well then, if he is here when I return and after I pass over the parcel of cloth to you, I will have some skyr and leave immediately for my farm.

Melkorka

The wind is blowing lightly so hopefully it will cover my tracks as I leave here so Thornbjorn won't suspect anything."

He left with Bessi hard on his heels. I shouted at the dog, ordering him back inside and readied myself for the day. Not long after the daymall Thornbjorn did show up and fortunately the lightly blowing snow had covered all the tracks. '

Thank God,' I thought to myself surprisingly with no guilt what so ever, *'someone is looking over us -- was it his god or mine? Mæl, why is it always about the gods when in reality we made this situation ourselves? We or rather I decided that it should not happen, god or no gods! So stop this silly nonsense.'*

Bessi sniffed the door with great excitement, he never barked when Thorbjorn came by. We both heard the soft knock and I opened the door to greet him. Bessi jumped all over him, licking his face, as he knelt to pet him.

"Thorbjorn, it is so nice of you to come by and check on me. The storm raged all night but I can see that it is all over. Would you like some skyr?"

"Let me check on everything first and I will come back in for some skyr. Come with me Bessi."

Hoskuld's plan worked. After Thorbjorn had checked on all the animals it was easy to convince him to stay awhile. I had just started telling him one of my Irish stories when Bessi announce someone's arrival. Hoskuld entered scattering snow everywhere once again, he always managed to make his entrance into a grand show but he greeted us both warmly and handed me the package of cloth from Thord. We talked together about the storm that blew through the night as we ate some skyr. We both knew this question would surface as Thorbjorn asked him where he stayed to escape from it all. Hoskuld explained that he knew of an

Melkorka

abandoned farm a few miles from here and when he mentioned the name Thorbjorn knew exactly where he had spent the night.

"I know of many people who have been forced to spend a night or two there. It is a good place to stop rather than risk riding through such a storm as we experienced last night. You may have been close to home but too far for safety. A wise decision Hoskuld."

"Yes, I agree with you Thornbjorn. When I saw the snow coming I purposely headed towards it. I built a fire to keep warm and hunkered in with my horse. He kept me warm through the cold night."

I busied myself with clearing the table so I could hide my face from them both. I was afraid I would give myself away. Then Hoskuld excused himself saying that he needed to be on his way home.

"Everyone will be worried about me so I must be off. Thord said that there was no rush for these clothes he wants, Melkorka, thrall prinsessa."

I smiled at the nickname knowing he was saying it for Thornbjorn's benefit.

"Also, thank you for the skyr, which was very good. See you soon Thornbjorn."

He left and took my heart with him but I truly felt free for the first time. True independence now looked to be a possibility.

After Thorbjorn left I threw my hands up into the air addressing God directly.

"Why am I such a fool when it comes to this man who is a very married man, when there is this wonderful man right here who loves me deeply? What kind of fool am I? Do you think he cares enough to keep my

reputation intact or was it simply to protect himself? Never mind, either way I do not care, I had him all to myself for one night, it was wonderful. BUT! My decision to be strong was a wise one, don't you think? My faith in you keeps me on the right track to live a decent life, a life without sin. Thank you for staying in my life and blocking out the devil himself. I couldn't do it without you!"

I treasured my memories of that stormy night with Hoskuld, our secret night together reassured me that he did care for me after all. Although I continue to struggle with the fact that I obviously still yearn for his love and attention - why? When I have Thorbjorn, a dear friend who proclaims his love for me with such passion?

Chapter 31 - Ulla

Life returned to normal with Bjorn's normal weekly visits to drop off the wool to weave and on the rare occasion Hoskuld would accompany him. With Olaf not here most of the time there was no need for him to visit but the respect and kindness he now accorded me in front of Bjorn put us both on a neutral path to a conciliatory friendship. This new relationship suited me just fine, along with his efforts to stay loyal to his wife restored my respect for him as a man. I turned my full attention to the running of my small holding and looked forward to every visit from my beloved son, he was always the only man in my life that could ever make my heart sing, but now Thorbjorn seemed to pop uninvited into my head.

'Hmmmm... what is happening here?'

As rare as Hoskuld's visits were, Thora's were even more so. The day she appeared with both Bjorn and Hoskuld was a surprise indeed, it was a very pleasing day for me. The men went off to complete a small chore which left her with me for the whole morning. After we had settled with our cups of chilled butter milk I asked her for all the news.

"Ahhh Melkorka, I do miss our talks but there is a very important reason I am here today. I have told you all our gossip except for one thing. My niece Ulla, my brother's daughter, has come to stay with me. My brother lives at a very large and busy farm in Hofn where he is the estate manager. It is a very important, responsible position and unfortunately his daughter is no longer welcomed there. There are not many farms in this isolated region and the silly girl has got herself in trouble with a young man my brother does not like. Rather, he does not mind him so much as he dislikes this boy's father immensely who happens to be the manager of the only other large estate. His name is Einar Thorvaldsson and my brother and this man have had a feud thriving between them for a very long time. Now my brother cannot forgive his daughter for getting involved with this man's son. The few other farms in that area are much smaller and the families that own them only manage to get by and cannot support another soul. There was nowhere for Ulla to go but here. On top of everything else my brother Ragnar and his temper managed to scare this young man, Einar, off to Norway with threats of violence so he is not around to take care of Ulla and the baby either, not that he would according to my brother. Apparently he got on a ship last spring as part of the crew that was going to the Trondheim area in northern Norway to buy timber and he never returned. Now Ulla has had his child, a young boy she has named Thorstein. My brother begrudged her presence there and since there has been an explosion of births at the farm, the goði there has sent many away as it is too expensive to feed and clothe all the extra people, including Ulla. This young lady is a hard worker, a beautiful young woman with the most magnificent red hair. She is a descendent of Thorstein the Red, as I am, and inherited his red hair as did her son, so she named him after this famous ancestor. Sadly Jorunn does not want her at Hoskuldstadir either. I fear her presence reminds her of you with your child and she cannot erase this jealousy she bears against you ever since your appearance here in Iceland".

"Some things will never change Thora, but I no longer bear her any ill will. I was but a child then and have grown up, it cannot have been easy for her to see another woman bear her husband's child. I am sure I would have been the same."

"True enough, I would not be happy either. I planned to speak to Dora and Thorbjorn to see if they would take my niece and her child in but it was Hoskuld who put another idea into my head. He has always been concerned about you living on your own and suggested that Ulla and Thorstein move in here with you. What do you think? My biggest fear was that anyone else who might take her in may want to separate her and her child. Would you be able to find it in your heart to accommodate this lost girl and her son, together? I know you enjoy your own company, but if you could it would be such a blessing to all concerned, me included. Then I would have a better excuse to visit more often, a reason even Jorunn could accept. I will help with her upkeep whenever I can spare anything."

"Well... well... well Thora. You ask much of me, I really have to think on this one."

"Please think it over while I am here as Jorunn is losing patience with me. If you cannot I will have to walk over to Thorbjornstaðir to talk to them before I return home to Jorunn. Time is off the essence Melkorka."

"Then let's go for a walk so I can think this over and if I find I cannot grant you this favour you will not be far from Dora and Thorbjorn."

I struggled with this decision, my place was quite small and felt it may not be enough space for three people. The child would soon grow and I remembered the space Olaf needed as an active child. Then I thought of the many lonely nights I have had, especially during the long dark nights of winter. Why not, she is alone like I was. She deserves a chance to raise her child herself as I did and she is not a slave.

"Thora, let's go back. I don't need to think about it... and yes... I will take them in."

"Oh my dear friend, this is such wonderful news. If you don't mind I will walk back to Hoskuldstaðir to prepare Ulla for her new home. Bjorn will bring over everything she will need later today. Thank you. Thank you. May Freya bless you and your kind heart... may all the gods bless you."

Winter was approaching and now I may never spend one alone. Olaf will be pleased I think.

Chapterr 32 – Olaf's journey

Taking them in was the best idea ever, Ulla became like a daughter. One skill she had that I still lacked and never really took to was cooking plus she did not mind the milking. She made such wonderful dairy products and from any excess goat milk she made a luxurious soap that tantalized my skin back to perfection although the old lava soap we had always used before was still useful for a scrubbing if a scrubbing was required, like after smoking the meats. That awful smoky smell would cling to our bodies, but the lava soap and a dip in the hot spring was the only thing strong enough to erase that. Then we would use the other soap to soften our skin. While growing up in Hofn she had been trained to work in the kitchen which included making soaps. Taking over some of my chores freed me to do all the knitting, weaving or embroidery I wanted and I thrilled to float from one project to the other. My creative ideas ran amok and between my extra items and any extra soap she could make we were becoming more self-sufficient. The long cold winters were busy for both of us and for her the cold was the best time for her to make her soaps. Generally the lye would cook the delicate milk so the goat's milk set better in the cold. This method produced a creamy soap infused with herbs that had a milky white colour that was much sought after.

Better still, I once again had an audience for my stories every night. Thor became as dear to me as my own child but Olaf's visit could still make my heart soar with excitement and Thor adored Olaf's attentions.

The years passed quickly my Olaf grew into a handsome young man. He continued to dress in fine colourful clothes and later he carried fine weapons with which he became very accomplished with and learned to fight like his famous Viking ancestors. Thord bought the best he could for him. Languages were another strength he had, not only was he fluent in Norse and the stories of his father's ancestors, the sagas and their poetry, he was also fluent in the Irish Gaelic language. I had taught him many Irish stories that I had learned as a child, as well as many stories about my family and my dearly beloved nursemaid, Mor. After all she was the one who had taught me the Gaelic stories that I had taught him.

One day Thora and Bjorn showed up to bring my wool and to visit Ulla and Thor. Bjorn was there to check on things for Hoskuld so he went off to do just that while Thora stayed inside with all of us. Thor was always happy to see his aunt and uncle as they often brought him a surprise, like a carved animal from Bjorn or some new clothing from Thora. Between us all this young man will be dressed as well as my Olaf was, if not better.

"Ulla, do you mind if you took Thor outside for a while to see what his uncle is up to. I need to speak privately with Melkorka. Also, I noticed that Thorbjorn was here as well and I know Thor loves to visit with him and his wonderful dogs. Maybe you would like to visit with him too?"

Surprised by Thora's comment I wondered if Ulla had expressed some desire for Thorbjorn to her. Never before had I felt jealous of anyone, but now it consumed me, I must watch and see if there was anything between them.

"Okay Thora, out with it. What news do you have for me? Does it concern Ulla and Thorbjorn?"

"No... I just said that. Thorbjorn only has eyes for you and you know that. Besides, Ulla still carries a torch for the untouchable Einar who is lost somewhere in Norway. I overheard a conversation between Jorunn and Hoskuld. He wants to find a way to relinquish the support he gives you, he feels that Olaf will soon be old enough to take care of you himself."

Melkorka

"Olaf... take care of me? I can do that myself."

"Of course you can. Both Bjorn and I are so amazed at how well you and Ulla have worked together as a family and as partners. She has blossomed into a strong, beautiful woman with your support. Woman really can survive without men!" Then she put her hand over her mouth laughing, "Maybe not... we need them in times of danger... like during feuds... as well as for hunting and fishing and for bearing children. So I suppose they come in handy!"

I chuckled along with her but dealing with this recent news I knew I had no time to lose so I went straight to Thorbjorn who had remained close by after they had left and asked if any ships were in. Ships from Norway and a few from Greenland on their way to Norway would come and go all summer so I was not surprised to hear that indeed there was a ship in from Norway and readying itself to sail off before the full moon. Olaf was due to visit me soon - I thought that it was time for him to look into going on this ship.

The day Olaf arrived Hoskuld and Barð came by with some wool to weave and to visit with him. He sent Barð and Olaf out to fix the fence Bjorn had told him needed mending and asked Ulla to take Thor outside as well. Then he confessed his plans to release his hold on the two of us. Little did he know I already had other ideas for our son's future but I required his support to make my plans a reality? While Olaf was growing up into this fine young man, I had filled his head with ideas of going abroad, to Norway and then hopefully to Ireland. So now was the time to tell Hoskuld what my plans were for him instead of accepting his goals for Olaf.

"I want Olaf to travel abroad like you did as a young man. He has every right to, don't you think?"

'No, I do not! I think that it is time for Olaf to be a man, to support you, to get some experience running your small farm until he can take over the farm and land from Thord, his foster father. Don't you be filling his head with these fancy ideas of traveling to Norway or trying to get to Ireland? He is not yet a wealthy man and he has much to learn. Besides things may have changed too much in Ireland, your father may not even be alive. It could be too dangerous for him so do not tempt him to go anywhere. I am afraid that he may never return -- don't you understand? A father has fears too."

My attempts to get his help for this venture failed miserably, *'what a selfish man!'* He stubbornly refused to help. I was angry with him and to show this anger I stamped my foot, raised my arms to the sky and yelled at him.

"*You* did!!! Why shouldn't he go if he wants?"

"That was different, I came from much wealth plus my father was still alive and well and gave me the freedom to go to mother's family who were all living in Norway. They were a very powerful and wealthy family with close connections to the royal family which could give me an inside connection to the king. My mother insisted I go to meet them and give them news of her life here in Iceland and they did introduce me to King Haakon *the good*. Olaf's situation is different. Both you and Thord must share him and as an only child he needs to realize his responsibilities come first. Not traveling off to far lands. Thord is still able to run everything so Olaf can spend some extra time with you, maybe even increase your holdings until he is ready to take over his inherited lands."

Hoskuld ignored my argument remaining firm stating once again that it was time for Olaf to take on the responsibilities of me and the farm. I knew I would never win him over to my plan for our son. He could be so stubborn, but then so could I.

I walked away angry, but determined as Hoskuld made his excuses to leave.

Melkorka

Who else could I talk to but the cat sitting on the bench -- staring at me as if I had gone crazy?

"Kisa did you hear that and don't look at me as if I am a berserker! Hoskuld continues to humiliate me, our son deserves more support than he is willing to give. I am not asking that he get a share of Hoskuld's lands, just a small stake to help him find a ship sailing to Norway. He is a rich man and can afford it. Why am I continually such a fool when it comes to Hoskuld Kollasson? Why do I always think he will come through and support my ideas? Since the sock fight he has turned against me except when he made the decision to give me my freedom, which I would never have thought to ask for. Hmmmm -- maybe blackmailing him is the answer? If I was to threatened him that I will somehow tell Jorunn about that stormy night he would do anything to stop me. Alas, I could never be that underhanded and he knows it. Now he is trying to stop his support as well. Will these disappointments never cease? I have worked with Olaf all his life to prepare him for such a journey. There has to be a way – there just has to be a way to send Olaf on this journey."

Kisa meowed at me as if she agreed and stalked off to lap up the milk I had just poured into her bowl.

"I will find a way kisa. Trust me I will find a way!"

Olaf, Ulla and Thor came inside after everyone had left. Later that day when we finally had some time alone I explained what his father's expectations were and suggested that he visits his father the next day to try and change his mind. He returned disappointed, he had given Olaf the same reasons he had given to me. Stubborn man that he was!

"As I told your mother... you need to learn to manage her farm, to manage a small holding before taking on a much larger one, not to go sailing across the ocean."

Melkorka

Olaf very sarcastically told me word for word what his father had said. He looked so disillusioned, I could see he was heartbroken by his father's refusal of help.

"Mam, in the same breath he asked me to accompany him to the Althing. He will be leaving in a couple of days and would really like my company. I'm afraid I was rather sarcastic with my comment. I told him that I had better stay home and learn to manage my mother's farm since you so desire this of me. I have to say that I am very disappointed with father."

"Me too son, me too! Talk to Thord, maybe he can help you?"

He had asked me to accompany him to Thord's farm, he thought he would need some support. Since I was able to leave everything in capable hands I joined him. Thord apologized to him and to me profusely but was unable to help. He claimed all his wealth lay in land and livestock, that he had no moveable goods to give him. He had lost all that in his divorce and had no woman managing his farm as well as Jorunn managed Hoskuldstaðir. His farm could never seem to make the extra cloth or dairy products needed to trade with, it only ever managed to feed and clothe the people living on his homestead. Thord felt very bad and said

"If I had known two years in advance maybe I could have managed it son. There is nothing I would not do for you, you know that don't you? Any silver I had I gave to Vigdis along with most of my wealth. Unfortunately she knew about my stash so there was no way of denying it, when she was my wife she was well informed of all my holdings and I had no choice but to give her my stash as well as half of my herds just so I could retain my land holdings and farmstead. Anything to be rid of her. Between us we have re-built those herds so that the farm and land are basically all I have left to give you."

Melkorka

"Yes of course I do understand Thord and I thank you for all you have done for me but I really want to leave this summer. I did not realize that this was my desire until just yesterday. That is until mother heard that a long ship was in the harbour. When I went to investigate yesterday I discovered that the ship is going to Norway shortly and I really want to be on it."

Thord fed us a nice meal then Olaf returned with me to my farm the very next day. As we journeyed back to Melkorkstaðir we discussed all our failed efforts. I was angry and mulled over this situation. Hoskuld WOULD NOT help and Thord, the foster father, was UNABLE to help. What could I do to make this a reality?

I mulled over the situation as we made our way back to my farm. What had instigated all this was the knowledge of a long ship docked at Bordeyri in Hrutafjord. When we returned from Thord's I sent Olaf back to the ship to investigate further. This time he talked to the captain and found out for sure that it would be sailing to Norway and very soon. He also found out that he could join the crew if he wanted. It was owned by an Icelander whose name was Orn, who was one of Harold Gunnhildarson's men, the King of Norway. Orn was back in Iceland on a trading mission to gain some wealth for himself but also to look for young able bodied men for the Norwegian king. Even though he is in Iceland looking for men he told Olaf that there were no guarantees that he would be taken on by the king's army and even if he was, he explained the predicament of being one of the king's men.

"It is essential to have some of your own wealth to survive. King Harold is not known for his generosity. You may need to pay for your own room and board when you first arrive and you need to have available money to return if necessary. It is important that you are prepared."

When Olaf had returned with this news I was so excited.

Melkorka

"I am so tired of these locals calling you a son of a slave woman." Holding his hands tight, "my son, my precious son, I will miss you desperately but I want you on this boat. Once you reach Norway you must find your way to Ireland and prove everyone wrong for me. My neighbours still call me the *Thrall Prinsessa*, even though Iceland has no royal titles. Yes -- I may have been born a princess but I am NOT a slave -- I am a free woman and you are NOT a son of a slave! By proving to all that I was really born a princess maybe they will finally accept that I am a free woman and not a slave."

This was a big responsibility to put on a young man shoulders, but Olaf promised me that he would definitely leave if I could get him passage on this boat. We were both disappointed that our attempts of finding support with either Hoskuld or Thord had failed. There had to be a way, then I had another thought but it was a long shot at this stage.

Thornbjorn "Pock-marked", my very good neighbour and long-time friend, may be the answer to our problem. He had asked me to marry him shortly after our arrival at this farm and on several other occasions since. I had always refused to even consider the offers. Now I was looking at these offers of marriage with different eyes. He had not declared his love for a number of years now.

'Does he still love me enough to marry me or have I become just a friend to him? Maybe he is more interested in Ulla as a wife, she has many skills and he would have a son to raise as his own?'

My decision was made then and there. Taking a deep breath for courage I went to look for Thornbjon, he was my last hope. Since Olaf planned to return to Thord's farm the next morning I asked him to stay a little longer and accompany me to Thornbjorns. As we walked I explained my plan to him on the way.

"Mother, are you sure this is what you should do. Marriage is a big commitment and it is for a long time. For life actually?"

"Yes Olaf, I am sure. Thorbjorn is a very dear friend and I care for him very much. His mother is a very dear friend as well and I know she will be very happy if we marry. I just pray that he still wants me as his wife. Having my own farm and being freed from slavery was unexpected – it was a dream come true. I do love my life but now that you are all grown up I really think that I am ready to share my life with someone and that someone is Thornbjorn. I think I have realized this for a while now and just needed the nerve to ask him. Your need has given me the courage I need, so never fret for me elskamin. Also, Ulla and Thor would love to manage my small farm. With me gone there would be more room for Thor to grow into a young man."

We did not find him at his farm, Dora, his mother said that he was up in the hills training one of his young dogs with herding the sheep.

Dora had a small chore that needed a man's attention so I asked Olaf to stay with her while I went to look for Thornbjorn. I saw him off in the distance with the new dog. His dogs were exceptional animals and farmers in Laxardal paid good money to have one of them. He waved to me as I walked up to him and told him that I had an offer to make him.

"It must be important if you walked all the way here to talk to me Mel."

I explained our plan to him about Olaf travelling to Norway. I was very open and upfront with him saying that I would marry him, if he still wanted me, on provision that he divide his property and goods with me.

"Even though you have always been my best friend, I have always desired you as a woman and will always love you. Of course I still want you as my wife."

He was squatting down beside one of his dogs but got to his feet and held my hands tightly and drew me to him. He hugged me and tried to kiss me but I turned my face so he kissed my cheek.

Melkorka

'God have I ruined this before it starts?'

"Thorbjorn, I'm so sorry for reacting like that. It is just that you have been my dear friend for so long it is hard for me to think of ever having you as a lover. Please be patient with me."

"Mel 'elskamin', you already know that I am a very patient man and now you have made me a very happy one. I can wait – forever -- if necessary."

"Thorbjorn, you really are a wonderful man, a dear friend and I do love you in my own way. I needed to live my life free from any man but now I am truly ready to have one in my life and I choose you. You will not have to wait forever, I promise. I would never do that to you but please give me a little time to get used to the idea of a husband."

He held my hands and kissed them. Leaving the dogs to watch the sheep we proceeded downhill together discussing how we would do this. When we entered his turf house we told both Dora and Olaf the good news that we were to be wed as soon as possible - Dora was ecstatic. At this point Olaf took over the negotiations. It was after all the man's duty as head of the family to negotiate a marriage contract. Once agreed we all shook hands sealing the promises made to each other. Everyone was happy and talking all at once.

I smiled to myself thinking Hoskuld was now the one who would be humiliated for a change. When he returned from the spring assembly, not only would Olaf have left to go on this voyage against his better judgment but I will be married as well. He should be happy as we would no longer require his assistance in our lives. We celebrated our pending marriage with a horn of mead then we left Thornbjorn's farm and made our plans for the voyage and for the wedding on the way back to Melkorkastaðir. Once there we told Ulla and Thor the news.

Melkorka

"That is good news Mel and I – I mean we - wish you every happiness.
Does that mean we will have to look for another place to live?"

"Good grief no! You and Thor can manage well on your own here and I
will be close by so we will continue to help one another - I want you to
be my farm manager! Men are generally chosen for such a position but
we both know that you, although a woman, are very capable. I have full
confidence in your managing it all with your son's help, he is growing
into a capable young man already. It would be like fostering him except
he gets to live with you. Although, you must swear not to tell anyone
until after we are married. Can you do that for me?"

"Of course I can."

Olaf left immediately for Thord's farm promising not to say anything to
him about our deal with Thorbjorn. He planned on traveling with
Hoskuld to the Althing and we needed to keep him in the dark,
unfortunately he must not know any of our plans in case he let anything
slip accidently to Hoskuld. Olaf hated to deceive them, he cared deeply
for them both, but realized that this was the only way for him to leave
Iceland.

Chapter 33 – The Thrall Prinsessa gets married

The planting was done, the harvest looked promising and Hoskuld was on his way to the Althing, along with Thord. Although Hoskuld had asked Olaf to join him, he did not appear disappointed by his refusal, sarcastic as it was. He had accepted Olaf's excuse that some things needed doing on his mother's farm so he would not join him this time. He told Olaf that he was very proud of him, he claimed how grown up he had become accepting this responsibility of looking after his mother's farm. Hoskuld even confessed to Olaf that the best part was that this would release him from this burden of looking after his mother. When Olaf told me this it hurt even though I had long wanted independence from him

"This must be Jorunn's doings, will she never let that poor man rest. Now we will show them just how independent we are of them, more than they will ever know."

Hoskuld would be away for some time, it was a long journey to the Althing and there were several people to visit on the way and many people to visit with during the assembly. Olaf lost no time in organizing my wedding as well as his trip abroad. He found some witnesses, Orn the captain of the ship and a couple of his men. As a captain Orn could also officiate any marriage ceremony, whether pagan or Christian. I unpacked the dress Hoskuld had given me all those years ago in Norway, it was the most beautiful dress I owned and it still fit me. Aired out, wrinkles gone and smelling fresh it looked like new, it had never been worn since arriving here in Iceland. I even had time to make a head dress which most Icelandic women wore on their wedding day and as small as the wedding would be I would not require a tall fancy head dress which was the norm.

Melkorka

Olaf and his half-brother, Barð, although very close, he decided not to tell him until after their father had left to decrease his brother's burden of secrecy. When Olaf did talk to Barð, his half-brother readily promised he would do what he could to help and agreed to keep his mother Jorunn in the dark until their father returned from the Althing. Also he promised he would be the one to ride out to Thord's along with me to help explain to him why Olaf felt he had to leave him. But I sensed that he would be all right with Olaf's decision because he would have certainly helped him if he had had the moveable wealth to give to his foster son. As for Hoskuld, Barð felt it would be best if it came from him to be the one to break the news to his father since Olaf would be gone, saying this way it would be a lesser burden for me. I was eternally grateful to this thoughtful young man.

The wedding was very small, I had no kinsman here other than my son, Ulla and Thor who were like family. My only other friend besides Thorbjorn, was his mother and she was so overjoyed with it all and could not wait until we were officially married. Then there was Barð and the few witnesses from the ship. Thornbjorn didn't care to have many people attend and neither did I. There was not much to do so the preparations went quickly, all we cared about was that we had enough people there to witness the marriage. We did not want any neighbours to attend in case the news reached Jorunn, who could still cause problems if she wanted. The wedding was a ritual pagan event, a hand fasting ceremony, where we pledged our lives together in front of our witnesses. Immediately after we were safely pledged to each other, we enjoyed a small feast prepared by Dora. The food and drink was enjoyed by all after which Olaf lost no time getting ready for the trip he had arranged with Orn.

Legally married to Thornbjorn I was now entitled to my share. Olaf, with our permission, could now choose what items to take with him for trading. The first person to pay was Orn for his passage to Norway and then he would need some valuables to live off while away. Orn thought that Olaf would more than likely find employment with King Harald but as he had told him, there were no guarantees. This king had the reputation for not always paying his men, so Olaf would need goods to trade for silver even he did join the king's troops.

For trade goods Olaf found a couple pieces of walrus ivory which would generate much silver, also, dried fish (hardfiskur), a couple ells of wool that Dora had put by. There was even some silver that Thornbjorn had been hoarding for years. Most of this silver had originally belonged to his father but he had added to it as some people were willing to pay in silver for one of his trained sheep dogs.

"I have no use for it Olaf, it is yours now."

My heart filled with love for this generous man I had just married. Why did I shy away from him all these years? I should have known he would be the one. I left the two men to themselves to finish what they had to do as I needed to get away from them before any emotions of mine spilled over and I embarrassed myself. I busied myself and filled a small wooden barrel with fish pickled in whey to eat while sailing and to share with the other men. Also, I had a small barrel of skyr made so I set that aside for him and Dora gave him a bundle of flat bread she had made for him.

The he had a short time to return to his farm and make arrangements with the workers there. When it was time to leave he came the night before to spend it with us. Then we all walked down to the ship together to see off my brave son. Once all was loaded aboard the ship including his own chest, all that was left to do was to give him my blessings and prayers for a safe journey. Thorbjorn and Halldora echoed my sentiments along with Ulla and Thorstein.

Hugging my son I reminded him to speak in Gaelic when in Ireland and to remember to use all the items that I had passed onto him the night before. Both Mor and my father would be sure to recognize them. My biggest sacrifice was marrying Thorbjorn but I was not about to lay that responsibility on my son. That was my decision and my burden only and now looking over to my new husband I knew in my heart that I had made the right decision.

Although it was sad to see him leave I was unable to stop smiling. I had succeeded, my son was leaving Iceland and hopefully he would make it to Ireland as he promised me and then make it back to Iceland with proof of my lineage. I hugged him again and wished him a safe journey, telling him that I would include him in my daily prayers asking for his safe passage to Norway and to Ireland and another safe passage back to me, here in Iceland. Then I pressed a stave into his hand, he looked very surprised that I would do such a thing. I explained that it had been carved for Thornbjorn by a pagan priest who had been an old friend of his fathers, many years ago. Now Thornbjorn my new, kind, generous husband wanted Olaf to have it. He explained its use.

"Olaf, do you understand the Norse runic alphabet? I carved your name onto this stave. It is called a Wayfinder and I willingly pass it on to you. It will help you to find your way through rough weather and storms and will also help you find your way back from unfamiliar lands."

"Mother, you surprise me. You do not believe in our ways why would you let him do this?"

"Because you believe in them as do everyone else here seeing you off. I want to keep you safe so I have no fear to appeal to your gods. Anything to keep you safe, my son and may my God bless and keep you safe as well."

Tears were flowing from my eyes but they could not erase the smile off my face. I was too overjoyed with accomplishing this feat. My new husband and mother-in-law were holding tight to my arms as we wished Olaf a safe journey and a speedy return.

Melkorka

Hoskaula

Melkorka

Chapter 34 - Deceived

The assembly was exhausting as usual, it felt good to be home, to what I thought would be peace and quiet, only to find out that Olaf had left Iceland after all. The biggest shock of all was that his mother had married. Barð had kept the wedding and Olaf's journey from his mother, not wanting to upset her and I was at first furious with him for keeping it all a big secret. Barð tried to explain everything to me, admitting that he attended the wedding and that he helped Olaf in it all.

"How could you do this? Do you have any idea how much that hurts me that my own sons went behind my back like that?"

Barð tried to calm me down asking me to listen to reason.

"Father think about this carefully. As much as you and I care for Olaf you are better off now that he is gone away and especially now that Melkorka is married", he exclaimed calmly. "They are... NO LONGER... your responsibility. Just think pabbi... before you say something you may regret. You are free from of all of your responsibilities... to both of them. Think before you allow your anger to boil over. Please pabbi, I beg of you... listen to reason."

Slowly -- I did simmer down as his words sunk in. "Yes, yes, of course you are right son. I am now free of this slave, this so called thrall prinsessa, who has been the result of much stress between me and your mother. Olaf has made his own choice in life which is a grown man's right. Your mother will be very happy about the end result, I no longer need to provide for them. Why should I let this stress me out? I will go and break the news to her. But don't *EVER* go behind my back again. Do you hear me Barð?"

Melkorka

"Yes pabbi, I promise. Now, with your permission I must ride over to Thord's with Melkorka and explain the reasons why Olaf has left, before the gossip mongers get a hold of it all and twist the reasons into something else."

"Yes, of course son, you do that while I break the news to your mother. It may be better if you are not here when I do."

As I walked away still trying to digest this news, a great sadness came over me. Mæl married! That was really unexpected news. I guess she had the right, I did give her freedom -- but to marry Thorbjorn, a younger man? I see now that there is nothing she will not do for her son. What a stubborn, determined woman she is. In spite of my anger I do hope for her sake that Olaf does return and with some good news for her. *'Is she happy with her choice of a man – now that is the big question?'*

I found Jorunn discussing something with Thora and motioned her over. "Jorunn, I have news for you. Olaf has sailed off to Norway after all, and without my permission, to seek out his fortune. The other news is that Melkorka, the thrall prinsessa, has married Thorbjorn Pockmarked. By marrying this man she has accomplished what she has always wanted for her son. I can't say that I am happy with Olaf leaving Iceland especially when I had other plans for him. As for the thrall prinsessa getting married, well that is good news, we are free of her from now on. She no longer requires our support but I need to know what you think? "

"What did you say – married?" She stood staring at me then hugged me so hard it hurt. "That is the MOST *WONDERFUL* news! She is out of our hair and you no longer need to help her out. Right? As for Olaf what does Thord have to say about his leaving?"

"I do not know what he thinks, they kept him in the dark too. Obviously he does not know that Melkorka had found a way to raise the money for Olaf to leave and this she did by marrying Thorbjorn. Although we did discuss how we were both unable to help him in this venture and we both thought that was the end of it. But do you know something elskamin, I just realized what a great relief all this is for me. I was so angry at first... mostly I think because Barð kept it a secret from you and only just informed me after I returned home. Alas, I realize now that he could not have done anything else as he did not know himself until after I had left for the Althing and why burden you with it? All I feel now is liberation... freedom from a great responsibility. My only concern was how you would accept the news, I wasn't sure if you would be happy about her getting married, her being a thrall once upon a time. You surprised me with your acceptance. Barð is off to visit Thord with Melkorka to explain how she managed to send Olaf on his way. I will go and see him myself in the next day or two to hear what he has to say about it."

"I am more than happy to get her out of our life, once and for all. Come to think of it, we should have tried to marry her off earlier. You have no idea what a great relief this news has brought me. I may even start to like this woman – maybe? Maybe not?"

I gave Jorunn another hug. Melkorka would always have a special place in my heart as the mother to one of my sons but I must accept that she is entitled to her own life. Only now have I come to realize, as I am fast becoming an old man, my wife Jorunn and our children were the most important people to me. It has taken me a long time to realize my priorities so I must release this *thrall prinsessa* from my life for once and for all.

Melkorka

Part III

Ireland

May you never forget what is

Worth remembering,

Nor ever remember what

Is best forgotten.

(Anon. An old Irish blessing)

Melkorka

Olaf Pai

"There is more in the heart of man than money can buy."

Grettir's Saga, c.47

Melkorka

Melkorka

Chapter 35 – Norway

The winds were pounding the northern waters, known to us as Aegir's sea. They were blowing furiously straight from the north and steering us southwards to our destination of Norway. Towards a country which I knew so little about other than it was my ancestor's home once upon a time. Now, after listening to Orn's stories of life in and around Norway I anticipated having many adventures and looked forward to meeting some distant relatives. Iceland was my safe haven and I was now willingly facing the dangers that lurked all around us. Aegir, the god of the sea, moved with the power and rhythm of the waves and he could change his mood in an instant from friend to foe. The waves today were crashing over our ship forcing us to continually bail out the excess water, the chore was arduous, never ending it seemed but finally Aegir's ferocity diminished and the few of us allowed some sleep literally passed out from exhaustion. I had much to learn about sailing. Occasionally there was some down time with the calmer winds and then and only then would I allow myself to dream of Ireland, of possibilities. My mother's plans continued to overwhelm me, I had no idea how I would ever manage to accomplish those promises I had made. However, the thought of this adventure had captured my imagination.

'Somehow I will find a way.'

Before I left the country, my mother gave me items of proof. A gold arm ring from her father, the gift he had given her when she had cut her first tooth. From her nursemaid there was a small knife that she had given my mother as a child and a belt that she had made for her just before she was kidnapped. It was evident to me that my mother had being planning this journey for me since the day I was born. All I could do at this point was to ask for Thor's guidance and beg Freya to weave this journey into my destiny so that one day I would fulfill my mother's dream. I promised to make the necessary sacrifices to them.

'With your blessings I will travel Aegir's sea to Ireland. May Freya's destiny for my grandfather be a long life and may she weave our lives together. It would be my greatest honour to meet this man and bring news back to Iceland, back to a mother who is desperate for a father's forgiveness and love. Much could have changed in the nineteen summers since my mother was kidnapped - what a challenge I face! Thor, I will need you to watch over me as I plan this venture. Freya I beseech you to make Ireland part of my destiny.'

The crossing was not without its' lessons of survival. As I bailed out buckets of water from our knarr, side by side with the rest of the sailors, I thought about my mother's first journey to Norway. Her words flowed through my memory from her tale of her fearful kidnapping.

"Sea sickness is a sailor's curse son and I pray that you do not inherit my weakness. I was so ill crossing the sea for the first time I prayed that I would die."

"Why would anyone want to die mama?"

As a child I could not imagine anyone being that sick that they would want to die. But she did survive! I was born and got to live a good life in Iceland and now I begin this great journey. Thank goodness I did not inherit her weakness on the sea but now I need to survive as another black cloud was looming ahead of us threatening to swamp us with seawater once more. Frigg, the wife of Odin was the goddess of the sky. She loved to sit at her loom and weave fluffy clouds but this black cloud was evident of her anger with someone or something.

Orn shouted orders constantly as well as encouraging us to continue baling the constant flood of water that flowed over into our ship. Suddenly the waves started pulsing with a deadly energy, unlike anything I had yet experienced. Is Aegir preparing for war with Frigg, pulling us into the middle of their torment with each other, Freya's destiny for me was not looking good. Orn shouted for the sails to be brought down and tied up tight, then for all of us to find a place and tie ourselves to something solid. These waves seemed to swamp the ship one minute then the next fling us over a gigantic swell landing us into the depths of hell or what looked like hell. The storm bounced our ship around for what felt like forever, but in reality it was a short-lived squall. When it broke all of us were too exhausted and too relieved to be alive to do anything but sit on the floor of the knarr. We were all soaking wet, at first too weak to stand or even voice our thanks to the gods for looking out for our safety. But thank them we did. This storm had blown us off course but our skipper had some sort of crystal that he used to view the sky through the clouds and soon had us back on the correct path.

'Yes, I do have much to learn!'

From this first journey I learned about survival -- about handling a big ship on such unfriendly waters. Not long after this second storm we arrived safely in Hordaland, Norway. There we publicly gave thanks to our gods Thor, Odin, Frigg for keeping us all safe and to Freya for her magical powers of controlling our destinies. Then I praised Orn for his masterful skills sailing the ship through such waters and asked that we remain together if the king granted me a commission in his army.

"I cannot imagine serving under a more competent man than you Orn."

Orn assured me that the king would more than likely take me on, especially since he would be the one to recommend me. He told me that I had the makings of a skilled sailor and would eventually make a good leader, because I followed orders so well and that I understood the importance of doing so. Orn put his hand on my shoulder, he confided in me that we would not be standing on this very spot, getting ready to visit the King of Norway, if all the men on the ship had not followed his demands.

"That was a fierce storm we encountered, albeit short lived. Men can fall apart with the fear of the unknown, strongly voiced orders from the captain keeps everyone busy and their minds off their plight."

So this experienced captain must have feared for all our lives -- I had the urge to cross myself like I had seen my mother do in times of stress and in thankfulness. Instead I gave my captain a salute and thanked him again for his leadership skills.

Once docked and cleared by the harbour master, Orn urged me to join him and pay his respects to the king. After King Harald heard who one of my kinsmen was, I was warmly received and he immediately offered me a place among his followers before Orn could even suggest a commission for me. Apparently my uncle Hrut, my father' brother, was well known and because of that I was well received. I was happy and relieved that there would be food and a bed while I was here in Norway. My few items of wealth were now a bonus. I felt quite rich.

The king's mother, Gunnhild, was not there on my arrival but the king said that he would pass on this information to her that one of my kinsman was Hrut Herjolfsson whom she once knew very well. I had heard some rumours about this infamous queen from the few men I had sailed here with so I was not looking forward to meeting her. Before that I knew about her reputation as a witch from pabbi who claimed she had put a curse on his brother for leaving her and according to pabbi her witch's curse worked, Hrut never did find love or have children. His first wife divorced him claiming he was not man enough for her, then on his way to marry his second wife he drowned. The river he had to cross to get to his own wedding was swollen from the spring runoff and the current was too strong for him. His body was not found until a year later. I feared Gunnhild would not be my favorite person as pabbi never had a good word for her even though he was not close to his much

younger brother - at first. Hrut was born in Norway and had only come
to Iceland to claim his share of the wealth his half-brother, Hoskuld,
held. Their mother, Thorgerd, had moved back to Norway to be with her
family after his father had died, claiming she no longer liked living in
Iceland. She was still a young woman and while in Norway she met and
married Herjolf. They had one child, Hrut, so Hoskuld never knew his
younger brother. After Herjolf died, she had moved back to Iceland to
live out her life with Hoskuld leaving her son Hrut to live his life in
Norway as he wanted. Hoskuld was by this time married with a child on
the way, while Hrut was busy fighting in the king's army. When she died
shortly after returning to her home in Iceland, Hoskuld claimed all her
wealth. Soon after, Hrut came to claim his share. There was much
animosity between the brothers until Jorunn intervened. With her wise
console she made him realize that they would be fighting over this
forever and would never move forward. He relented and gave Hrut his
share and afterwards they became more like brothers. Although there
was never much love between them, they learned to respect each
other.

A few weeks later when Orn and I were back at the king's table there
she was. She sent a kitchen thrall over to invite me to sit beside her at
the table. I got up with much apprehension and sat in the space she had
made available and she immediately asked after my uncle. Once I told
her what I knew about his short time back in Iceland I could see that she
was very upset about the loss.

"I foolishly cursed him when he left me but I honestly wished him no
harm. You may not know this but I loved him very much and did not
want him to leave. It was very selfish of me to show such anger, he had
the right to live his own life as he saw fit. This is sad news indeed. Very
sad."

*I sure wasn't about to admit to her that I knew about this famous curse
and here she was admitting to it. I suppose she had done what any love*

Melkorka

sick woman would have done in the anger of the moment, uttering curses to a man she thought she loved.'

After spending a few hours with her I arrived at a new decision, the stories about her must be an exaggeration, but I must clarify this with Orn as he seems to think quite differently about her. She proved to be an intelligent dinner mate and I enjoyed her company very much. Before the end of the evening I was regaling her with stories of growing up in Iceland and she appeared to enjoy them very much.

I left the king's court sated from a delicious meal, lots to drink and with a return invitation for another night directly from the queen herself. Orn slapped me on the back as we walked out of the room telling me that this was quite an accomplishment for a young man to become part of the Royal entourage so quickly. I confessed then just how much I had enjoyed her company.

"Do not forget all the rumours you have heard recently or the story about her from your father. Gunnhild Gormsdottir is an infamous character. Many, besides myself, think that she is a witch who can cast magical spells. Not many people like or even trust her and most take a wide berth of her when in court, just in case she will give them the evil eye and cast a spell on them. I suppose it is the fear of their unknown power when you are in the company of a witch, especially such a well-known one."

We had left the confines of the royal compound and were walking down a long narrow street on our way back to the ship.

"And here I had just changed my mind about her being a witch, you must tell me all you know about her. Her sympathy on the loss of my uncle was very convincing."

"Well", said Orn, looking over his shoulder to make sure we were alone. "She is known as the *konurgamodir* or Mother of kings. Not only is she a mother of kings, her husband was Eric Bloodaxe who was a King of Norway for a while and later was even a King of Northumbria, England, for a short time. Her own brother, King Harald Bluetooth, was once the King of England. Our King Harald was named after Harald Bluetooth, as you have probably guessed. Gunnhild is quite experienced in dealing with kings and they all respect her opinions. She is not a stupid woman but beware, she is feared, she has much influence over her sons and it is well known that she was in love with your uncle Hrut Herjolfsson."

"Yes – it is well known even back home. According to our Laxardal Saga she was enamoured with Hrut while he was in Norway as one of the king's men."

With one hand on my chest and the other held out like I was presenting the words to a full audience, I quoted verbatim what this saga had to say about this queen. After all I had heard it told many times and knew the whole saga by heart.

"Gunnhild, the Queen, loved him so much that she held there was not his equal within the guard, either in talking or in anything else. Even when men were compared, and noblemen therein were pointed to, all men easily saw that Gunnhild thought that at the bottom there must be sheer thoughtlessness, or else envy, if any man was said to be Hrut's equal." (Laxardal Saga, c19)

"Olaf, you are such an ass – what a show off! I too know this saga well, remember I am from Iceland too."

"Ha ha! I know, I know my friend, I apologize. I cannot help myself, I just love to perform. My mother told me many times that my father loved centre stage as well. I suppose it is in my blood."

After showing off to Orn I realized then that I must be on my guard, so far any advice from him had been sound advice. Even though she had chosen to befriend me, she could be a valuable ally or a dangerous foe.

Melkorka

Before I knew it we had arrived at the ship -- all too soon. Now I would have to wait for any more information, if Orn had anymore to tell me. We got on board, checked that all was good with the men and sought out our sleeping mats. I for one had had too much to drink and desperately needed a good night's sleep.

The next day I badgered Orn for more information on the royal family, making it my new mission to find out what I could about these brother kings and their mother. He went on to tell me that when Haakon the Good died he had had only one child, a daughter, so he had named the sons of Eric Bloodaxe as the next in line despite their constant waging of war against him. Iceland was not that isolated, news did reach us, but his telling brought new enlightenment.

Years before Haakon died, these sons of Eric had led a Danish armada to do battle with him at Rastarkraft. They always wanted his crown and had always felt that it was rightfully theirs. My father was at the battle of Rastarkraft, he helped King Haakon, Sigurd the Jarl and the others with their few men to defeat this Danish army. They sent the Danes and Eric's sons running out of Norway, back to Denmark. They had fooled Gunnhild's sons and the Danes into thinking their army was much larger than it was. Pabbi had played an important part in that battle and told us that story many times over. I was sure that Queen Gunnhild would have brought this up if she knew anything so I decided not tell this to Orn, it was important that nobody find out that my father was part of that group. It appeared to me to be unlikely if anyone knew unless, I told them myself. My lips remained sealed on this one, whenever I spoke of my father or my mother. In my stories I acknowledged that they had been in Norway but they never left Hordaland... they never went to South Möre.

Orn filled me in with some more information. When Queen Gunnhild's sons first came to Norway to rule together, they discovered that they only had control of the midlands of Norway and King Harold Greycloak was very displeased that he had to share such a small area with his brothers. Sigurd the Jarl, who had been a good friend of King Haakon's controlled the Tronheim area in the north, while another old friend controlled the Vik, leaving Gunnhild's sons only the midlands.

"Apparently, Queen Gunnhild was not happy about this", continued Orn. "She is a very ambitious woman who has great control over her sons. I am told that they often get together in private to discuss this unhappy circumstance of so many petty 'kings' in Norway. They like to think that they are the most 'king-like'. They are constantly planning ways to take over, but in the meantime they have to maintain their kingly lifestyle. To do this they take turns raiding out of Norway in the summer taking many Norwegians with them. Maybe even us one day, no? What would you think of that Olaf? They plunder both to the east and west to raise the money they require to maintain their lifestyle. When they return they usually claim most of the booty for themselves, so don't plan on becoming rich if you go out on a raiding mission with them. I have been once and am still looking to make my fortune. The sad part is they are losing their reputation with the Norwegian people, they are becoming known for their close-fisted methods. If I was brave enough I would approach King Harald and warn him, rather, counsel him, to change his ways or he will lose his men if they are not well rewarded".

I took note of this message from Orn and thought to myself that the only way to King Harald would be through his mother.

Orn continued on with his royal saga.

"While I was away in Iceland Gunnhild and her sons tried to have meetings with Sigurð the Jarl and his brother. Sigurð refused to meet with Gunnhild's sons so instead, they worked on Sigurð's brother, Grjotgarð. He eventually came down south to meet them. At this meeting they wined and dined him and later convinced Grjotgarð that he was treated very poorly by his older brother, Sigurð. They discovered that Grjotgarð was very envious indeed of his brother's power. It turned out that he was only a half-brother and a bastard one at that and anything Sigurð controlled would be passed onto his son and not to this unrecognized half brother. Regardless, Gunnhild's sons saw him as an opportunity and promised him much wealth and power if he agreed to spy on his brother. They gave him a bag of silver as down payment. He proved to be an easy mark -- maybe too easy? Anyways, one day not long after they had wined and dined him, word was sent secretly from Grjotgarð to King Harald that now was the best time to come for Sigurð".

We were momentarily interrupted by one of Orn's men, but he soon continued on with his story. I was anxious to hear it all and begrudged the slightest interference.

"Normally Sigurð travelled with many men and the word that King Harald received was that at that moment he was feasting in Algo with only a few men. Harald and his brothers quickly organized a few ships and they sailed during the night getting there before daybreak. They found the house where they had been feasting, lucky for them everyone was still passed out from all the excess drinking. They set fire to it killing Sigurð the Jarl and all his men and the few that managed to escape were quickly killed by Harald and his brothers as they were waiting by the door. It was not an honourable battle. Haakon, Sigurð's son, soon got word of this and raised a large army. He never came after Gunnhild's sons but he quickly managed to secure his control over all the areas in Tronheim that his father had previously ruled. Soon after securing his power he killed his bastard uncle, Grjotgarð for treason. Apparently, it was not difficult to discover who had deceived the family. Right after Sigurð the Jarl's death, they uncovered his treason, his meeting with Harold and his brothers. It was not difficult to put two and two together since Grjotgarð had suddenly come into an unknown inheritance. I heard that they tortured him into a confession and they confiscated his small fortune. Harald Greycloak and his brothers were unable to raise a big enough army, so they did not go after Haakon, Sigurð's son, and still Haakon showed no signs of coming after them, so now everyone was at a standstill. In reality nothing had changed at all. Harald and his brothers remained in their own area, the midlands with their mother Gunnhild as their advisor, while Haakon, Sigurð's son, maintained control of his father's region. He had built up mightier defenses than before, so apparently Tronheim is now an impenetrable fortress. Gunnhild and her sons in their haste to conquer had failed in the end. This was the situation I came back to when we had arrived from Iceland. King Harald was very happy to see that I had returned and had brought help. He probably plans to do battle one day if he can ever raise a large enough army but I personally hold no hope for their success."

I mulled over all this information for several days while waiting for our next mission. It turned out Harald had a special assignment for Orn and his men which included me. There were areas that were constantly threatened but he kept us busy battling to maintain authority over trade routes along the Norwegian coasts. These taxes we collected from the areas he controlled were also very crucial to his coffers. In the meantime he or his brothers went raiding in other countries to find the wealth to maintain their lifestyle.

We were gone for long periods of time working to maintain the coastal trading routes. This kept us employed and fed, so life was good. We did not go raiding with any of the brothers, at least we were not yet asked to go. Over the summer months when in Hordaland, we often visited the king's household and enjoyed many wonderful evenings of good food and entertainment. Sometimes I was the entertainment as everyone loved to listen to the Icelandic sagas and their poetry. I was quite the bard and loved all the attention. I even regaled them with Irish stories. One story that fascinated them was my mother's own story. Here I had to be very careful not to tell too much, they must never know that my mother was near their site of battle with Haakon the Good.

Melkorka

At one of these meals I was sitting with Queen Gunnhild as usual when she asked me to tell her how I had obtained the nickname "Peacock" (Pai in Icelandic).

"That is a rather strange nickname, is it not," I replied to the queen. "I am not surprised you are curious. As you know, my mother claims to be an Irish princess kidnapped by some Vikings and that my father bought her as a slave while in Hordaland and brought her back to Iceland. We are not children, you and I, so we both know that they must have had a relationship while together in Norway. It is not uncommon in Iceland, or Norway I believe, to be born out of wedlock although in Iceland all children are cherished. I am not familiar with how they are accepted here in Norway but my father acknowledged me as his son the day I was born and has always been a true father to me. As much as Icelanders cherish children they also love scandal. With the encouragement of Jorunn, my father's wife, she would not accept my mother's claim that she was a princess, so she very sarcastically nicknamed my mother "The Thrall Prinsessa." My mother is very gifted with embroidery and made beautiful clothes. I always had the best and our neighbours had a difficult time understanding how a child of a slave could have such beautiful things. As a result, I was bullied and teased all my life about having a mother who was a slave – even though she has been a free woman since I was about three years old. Icelanders are a stubborn lot and they have long memories. They are obsessive with their genealogy and like to think that a true Icelander is only descended from the Norwegian or other Scandinavian ancestors. Most of the powerful leaders in Iceland all claim to be descended from the kings and queens of Norway as is my father's family. We may even be related to you, Queen Gunnhild? We must try to figure it out one day."

Boldly I smiled at her, looked her right in the eyes and said, "Well, my mother's father is also a king and I intend to prove it one day."

After quenching my thirst I continued.

Melkorka

"I guess, in a way, my mother's claim went to my head a bit and I felt very protective of her. Whenever I was teased or bullied, I would think to myself that I am the son of a princess and my father, Hoskuld, is descended from many kings of Norway. I would walk away ignoring their taunts but I did not realize that I would stick my chest out as well. Also, I happen to like nice clothes, as you can see.'

I pulled my cloak forward to show off some of my mother's work.

"My mother creates magical symbols with the embroidery needle and has sewed many beautiful clothes for me. My father and foster father Thord provide, rather provided, past tense, I provide for myself now. They provided me with beautiful, colourful, cloth so I was always well dressed. To any Icelander a sure sign of wealth is to be well attired. Many children had a hard time accepting that I could own such fine clothing and at the same time be the son of a thrall. One day my foster father had a big harvest feast and had invited the whole region. Many children were there and as usual were teasing and pulling on my clothes and as usual I ignored them and walked away. My father witnessed the teasing claiming that my walk was more like a strut and that made him think of a peacock. When my father was a young man he had travelled to many countries and even to a country that had peacocks which he admired greatly. He said that their walk was very stately and that their rich colours reminded him of my choices for my clothes. I know that he loves me and meant this nickname in a very kind way. I am quite used to it now and rather like it. Nobody else has such a nickname."

Queen Gunnhild held my hand and said that now, she too liked my nickname and yes we must work out our family trees, maybe we could be related. In the beginning she had always sought out my company to tell me stories about my uncle. Lately she was asking more about me, maybe I should be concerned, this may not be a good thing? I had heard she had a voracious appetite for men of all ages. I could not and would not want to be one of her lovers. The very thought of making love to her repelled me. There were many beautiful woman here and I was slowly getting to know a couple of them who were willing to introduce me to the world of love making. They were both safely married but their husbands were never around and they were bored, so chose me to entertain them. The older of the two woman loved to tease me, telling me that I was her inexperienced country farmer while the other one was younger. The things I learned from the older one kept the younger woman star struck with my sexual prowess. She was very good for my ego. Orn could always tell when I had been with one of the woman. Apparently my "peacock strut" was more pronounced than ever.

The more Queen Gunnhild asked me about my mother, for some reason, I tended to put my father down. Why I did that I don't know because I love and respect him very much. I suppose I was still angry with him for not supporting this venture of mine, especially since his mother, Thorgerd's, relatives still had some power here. I even had the audacity to say that I was against slavery and that my father empowered these slave traders when he bought my mother. That was either brave or very stupid of me as Hordaland was a big trading centre for slaves which brought the Royal family much wealth. She chose to ignore my remark. I had confided to her just how cruel Jorunn had been to my mother and her lack of compassion towards her had always bothered me even though I knew this same woman cared deeply for me. I never understood that but under the influence of too much mead, I confided much about my family to this woman. I couldn't seem to stop myself and even dared to say that the only reason my father gave mother her freedom was because he couldn't handle the two women bickering. Well that was really a stupid thing to say, mother would still be a slave if they hadn't always bickered with each other and I certainly would not be welcomed at the queen's table if she was still a slave. I quickly stressed my mother's royal lineage to cover my *'faux pas.'*

"My mother's lineage is very royal indeed and I intend to prove this to my father and his wife Jorunn. It may sound childish, even cruel but, they need to humbled, just a little. Maybe they even need to ask my mother for forgiveness. What do you think as a woman and as a mother?"

"I can see you have a mission and if you were my son I would be very proud of you. I have enjoyed your company very much and look forward to another evening talking and drinking with you but as an aging woman I need my rest. Good night my dear Olaf – until we meet again!

Gunnhild had dismissed me from her table, had I said too much? Bowing to her highness, I said goodnight then stumbled over to Orn. We left for the evening to return to our ship.

Life in Norway had turned out to be better than I had expected but I was getting restless and feared that it was time for me to get far away from the queen mother. When together, she manipulated me with drink and I knew I talked too much. She was much too cunning for me to handle. Plus it was time to distance myself from my two paramours before their husbands discovered who I was.

Towards the end of that summer, Harald and one of his brothers had returned with much booty from the last of their raids and with all that wealth to show off they had a great feast. Orn and I happened to be in town and we were formally asked to attend. At this feast the king made a few presentations of gifts taken from their hoard and given out to some of their men, including Orn and myself. When our names were announced he could not praise us enough for our work collecting his taxes along the coastal area, it was all rather embarrassing. He presented me with a glorious gold helmet which I proudly wore on the coastal missions over the winter months and fortunately Orn was presented with a glorious sword for increasing their wealth with more silver than expected. This was a very generous gift from a man not known for his generosity, but Gunnhild had much influence over her sons. I knew she liked me, as for Orn she did not have much to do with him but I was greatly pleased that he was included.

Orn and I kept busy over the whole summer and now this would continue into the fall with occasional stays back in Hordaland. We were doing something right as we were always assigned to fight the coastal battles for Harold and his brothers as well as collect all the taxes from these coastal villages. From these taxes collected there was a constant stream of silver now coming in for the brother's coffers – something that had been very erratic before. Their greed was boundless.

The winter solstice was a special time with many feasts all over Hordaland where the drink flowed freely. They referred to it as the Yuletide where they honoured our pagan gods and the few Christians of Norway honoured their god and the birth of his son Jesus. This was all started by King Haakon the Good in Norway and we now celebrated at the same time in Iceland due to his encouragement. All in all it was a joyous time. Since we were expected to be in Hordaland at that time we were invited to one of the many Royal feasts. In the meantime my restlessness was growing and I was getting disenchanted fighting King Harald's endless... useless... battles and collecting his taxes. I was beginning to feel like the king's bully boy forcing these men to pay his unreasonable tax demands. One evening, after the feasting, I was off to the side discussing with Orn my need to leave, telling him about my desire to go west to Ireland when the Queen mother happened to walk by. Gunnhild overheard Orn telling me that he knew of no ships going in that direction at this time of year and I knew she would approach me about it so I was prepared.

Later she did ask me to explain what he meant by this comment and why did I want to leave. She appeared displeased with me so I apologized profusely, hoping that I had not offended her and her son's hospitality. I quickly reminded her about the story of my mother being an Irish princess and about the promise I had made to her. The promise that one day I would make my way to Ireland. Bowing before the queen I confessed that the time had come for me to fulfill this promise stating with an apologetic tone,

"I have enjoyed my time here in Norway immensely your highness, especially my visits with you, but as a mother yourself, you must understand my obligation to my mother, as well as my need to honour the promise I had made to her".

Gunnhild nodded, saying she liked that I had so much respect for my mother and claimed that she too wanted my mother's tale verified. Once again I stressed just how important it was to me and hoped that she would not take offense with my departure. I asked if she knew of any ship that was going to Ireland. I began to feel like I was groveling too much and needed to stop this conversation when Gunnhild offered her full support. Her offered stunned me into silence. She not only promised her full support, but that she would organize it all and asked me how many men I would need.

Astonished -- I stood tall and automatically stuck my chest out just like I would have done as a child – just like a peacock --and said to her,

"It is very important that Orn accompany me and that I have sixty men -- not merchants -- but soldiers".

My bravery did not last long. Groveling again, I explained as I sat down that I realized that I was quite young to captain such a group of soldiers but much to my surprise the Queen mother agreed to my demands.

"Your request will be fulfilled and I think you have learned much and will be a strong and fair captain."

The relief and joy that washed over me as I walked away from her made me feel like I was walking on air. I was going to go to Ireland and with my own army of men.

Melkorka

'If only my mother could see me now.'

Orn, the skipper who was now my closest friend agreed to go with me but would have to clear it with King Harald. Since I needed to speak to him too we went together, only to find out that the king's mother had already spoke to him about our plans. Harald gave both Orn and myself permission to leave, providing we came back to Norway to rejoin his army after my so called odyssey. Orn later confided to me that he suspected Harald was a little jealous of me from all the attention I was getting from his own mother. If that was true it was definitely time to leave and the king most likely agreed for the same reason.

Queen Gunnhild had her own stipulation. All she asked of us was to wait until spring and to continue to support her son Harald until that time. We both knew that that would make him happier about our leaving and we readily agreed. I was ecstatic that we had her full support, the men we needed and a long ship to make this odyssey of mine a reality.

"We had better remain as the king's bully boys and continue to do a good job for him or she might change her mind Orn."

"I agree Olaf, but this should not be too difficult as King Harold understands that control of the coastline changes continually, our work is never ending, and the taxes we collect helps to maintain their lavish lifestyle."

"In the meantime Orn talk to anybody you know who has sailing knowledge of the Irish seas. My mother tells me that my grandfather's kingdom is in Leinster just south of Dublin. If we can make our way to Dublin it shouldn't be difficult to find the Leinster region. The Killcullan Monastery would be an ideal marker for us."

True to his word, King Harald did keep us busy while we remained in his army and a few times he even accompanied us on our missions along the coastline himself. He told us that he needed to show his men that

Melkorka

he was still the commander of us all but I secretly thought he was not only checking up on us but trying to figure out who best to leave in command. Spring finally arrived and it couldn't have come fast enough for me. It was even early that year and Ireland was waiting for us.

Chapter 36 – Queen Gunnhild's support

One stormy evening while we were docked in Hordaland, I got word that Queen Gunnhild wanted to see me. Worried that she had changed her mind to support my trip to Ireland I cleaned myself up and dressed in my best clothes and wore the gold helmet to help me brave this meeting with her.

I arrived at the castle and told the guards that the queen mother was expecting me. They were not surprised, they were also expecting me and led me directly to her suite.

'Hellavitas Thor… I may be in trouble here and may need your help.' I knocked on her door and when I heard her say enter I did, but very slowly and with much apprehension. There she was lying on her bed on luxurious skins. It appeared that she was ready for bed. It must be time to pay for her generosity but I didn't think I would be able to pretend to like making love to this old woman. Sweating profusely I sat down on a chair as far away from her as possible.

"Olaf…. How good to see you back from your assignment. Pour yourself some wine, then tell me all you know about the Battle of Rastarkalf?"

"Ahhhh… did you say Rastarkalf?"

"Yes… I did and I think you know all about it. Correct? Your father was there when my sons challenged Haakon to a battle just before you were born. Somehow they tricked my sons and the Danish army into thinking King Haakon had a much larger army than he actually did. I have a feeling your father told you about this battle and many times over. Correct?"

Melkorka

"AAAH…"

"Come now Olaf…. are you sweating?"

"Well it is very hot in here you majesty. Your fire is banked very high and there is much heat radiating from it."

"You look uncomfortable young man? That is to my advantage -- is it not? Honesty now is the key – so be careful what you say."

"Well… yes… you are correct. I did know about it but did not feel that it was my place to bring it up. Have you always known?"

"We are being truthful here --so yes -- I have. We found out not long after the battle from an Icelandic skald at one of our Danish feasts. He was provoked into reciting the famous poem about the Battle of Rastarkalf and in it your father's contribution was well documented. Unfortunately that Icelandic skald lost his head after reciting it for us all."

'I am in trouble here. What do I say to her now Thor? I think honesty is the only way now.'

"Forgive my ignorance you gracious queen… but what does this mean for me? That battle had nothing to do with me, it was before my time." I really was sweating but felt at this point I had nothing to lose.

"Why… nothing dear boy. Nothing at all. I just wanted to clear the air. We got our revenge on Sigurd the Jarl, he lost his life. Haakon's other advisor Egil Wool Sark was already an old man and died in battle as he wanted. He is in Valhalla celebrating his long life of battles. Now -- my revenge on your father is to support your Irish voyage. I -- like your mother -- want you to prove that she really is a princess and then for you to return to Iceland and tell everyone. I am hoping that this will really humiliate your father and set things right for your mother. Your mother and I are royal women, we are women of power and must never let our menfolk step on us or put us down."

"I don't know what to say Queen Gunnhild. I do value your support and although I love my father and I know he loves me I really do want my mother to be able to hold her head high."

"King Haakon named my sons as his heirs -- so I was able to forgive him. This king and Sigurd the Jarl were the main characters in all this beside Egil Wool Sark. As I explained before, we got our revenge on Sigurd. Your father may have helped them win the battle but he was not the one who planned the battle strategy. Just tell him to never come to Norway while my sons are in control -- I cannot promise him a safe entry into our country. You must understand that this is just business between leaders. Your father will understand so do not worry -- you still have my support. Now be honest – did you think I wanted something else from you? "

"No, my queen. I was just worried that I had offended you somehow and that you were pulling your support for my Irish voyage."

"Go home – rest assured that you will be sailing to Ireland and very soon."

"Goodnight your majesty. Thank you once again."

"As for being related – you and your father are distant cousins of my husband Eric Bloodaxe. I, on the other hand, have no lines to you or your father. Family trees are one of my many passions. Now go to bed and get some rest. You leave soon."

I was out of there as fast as my feet could take me. My clothes were soaking wet from sweating. The Queen mother was no fool and I must never forget this. Who was I to think I could pull the wool over her eyes. I think that this was a strong message, that she is and always will be smarter than me. Obviously that move to kill Sigurd the Jarl wasn't about taking over Tronheim but simple revenge. Queen Gunnhild really can be a dangerous adversary and I must never forget it!

Within days the news was brought to me by the queen's own guard that the long ship she had promised me was sitting at the dock awaiting my inspection. As Orn and I walked towards it we couldn't help but be impressed by the beauty and slickness of the design. It was an incredible long ship with a beautiful carved dragon head at both the bow and the stern. These dragon heads were there to frighten people. Normally there be would a carving only at the bow now there were two heads, this should really frighten those who came near us. The queen's own banner flew from the mast and the sixty soldiers along with their weapons and shields were already onboard awaiting our orders. It didn't take us long to inspect the ship or to transfer our chests with our few belongings and our necessary leather sleeping sack called a huðfat.

Queen Gunnhild even saw to it that there was plenty of food on board, pickled fish, hardfiskur (dried fish), several barrels of meat stored in whey, there were even hard boiled eggs stored in whey along with some hard cheese and flat bread. Barrels of drinking water and two of mead. We would eat well on this journey.

All was set and I was anxious to leave but before we could, we had to wait for the king and his mother. I was informed earlier by one of the soldiers to wait for their arrival. He claimed that they were on their way. Of course they were late but never would I offend my benefactor, as anxious as we were to leave we waited patiently. Finally they arrived at the dock -- the king was dressed in all his finery as well as his mother along with their royal guards. They made quite a royal procession and took up most of the harbour space but we were all very impressed by such a send-off.

King Harald told me in front of my crew that I was a fine young man and that I had proven myself to be as worthy a soldier as my uncle Hrut.

Melkorka

Gunnhild of course had her own message. She told me to stay safe and to come back intact and that she wanted the full story of this expedition. She was reminding me who was really in charge. Thanking them both profusely, I held my hand on my heart making my solemn pledge to return if I survived the trip. The king waved to the tower and the harbour guards blew their horn giving us permission to leave. Orn and I stood at the helm while the sixty soldiers sat on their chests and rowed away from the dock. Once in the open fjord the sail was hoisted and we all prayed to Frigg for a good wind and to Freya that all our destinies would be woven together with a safe and eventful journey.

Chapter 37 – Ireland bound

With a good wind blowing we were soon on the open sea and then we set off in a westerly direction where we made headway for the first two days. Suddenly the weather changed. It was no longer favourable for sailing. Lacklustre winds came in from the wrong direction and to make matters worse, a heavy dense fog rolled in. Loki, Odin's blood brother was playing tricks on us, we were stuck in the middle of nowhere, with basically no wind, not knowing which way to row. It was a very eerie situation and soon patience ran thin. There was much discussion among all the men, even as seasoned sailors, none had ever experienced such a strange situation. They were all fearful that our Gods were sending us to hell and before long everyone was giving advice -- all at once. Orn the skipper was trying to shout his opinion over all the noisy chatter but the haunting conditions had terrified the men and they were not listening. Realizing how quickly things could get out of hand, it was time to remind them who their captain was so I stood tall and shouted as loud as possible over all the noise the sixty men made arguing amongst themselves.

"IN ODIN'S NAME – I COMMAND YOU ALL TO STOP THIS RACKET!"

Silence – good! I lowered the tone of my voice now that they were listening.

"The Gods are having a rest, they cloaked the seas with this mist only to have some peace and quiet now they are covering their ears with the pain of all this noise. It's to no one's advantage to have so many opinions all at once. You need only one captain and that will be me and only me – UNDERSTOOD! I know you all think that I am very young to be commanding such a group of fine soldiers but you must remember that it was King Harald as well as Queen Gunnhild who gave me the right to be your leader and I demand that you all obey my commands. Orn is an accomplished skipper with more experience than all of us put together, so he will be the skipper and he will decide when to raise or lower the sail, or when to row, not any one of you. Orn, now you take the lead, you are the skipper, after all."

The men all cheered obviously feeling better that their leader took control and they all agreed that Orn was the skipper and that I was their captain with a loud chant that all Vikings are famous for. Surely the gods heard this loud support and they would lift this awful mist.

"Alright men – this fog is too heavy – it is blocking my crystal's ability to view the sky to help direct us so we all need to be patient. I know this is very difficult to do but we need to be thankful we are not at the mercy of any strong winds blowing us off course. Once we have visibility we will set sail and since there are no winds we will not be much off our course. Patience is in order for now, which of you men can play an instrument. We, as well as the gods, need some entertainment while we wait for Frigg to lift this shield of mist."

A voice from the back of the ship called out.

"I have my lur with me."

Soon other a voice was heard, "me also' then another, "me too."

"Now we have entertainment! The first one who spoke up can you play us your favorite, then the others can take a turn."

This went on for some time then our music faded to silence. I suspect some of the men nodded off, at least they were no longer frightened.

"What was that?" Someone shouted out.

"What was what?"

Melkorka

"It sounds like something fell in. There it is again... do you hear that?"

"Orn get the men ready – ICE flow ahead! What side did the sound come from?"

Someone shouted back, "Port-side."

Orn commanded the men to man the oars and for the port-side only to row to turn away from that sound.

Banging his sword on his shield he got them into a rhythm. "1-2-3-row; 1-2-3-row; 1-2-3-row now all men- oars in the water. 1-2-3-row; 1-2-3-row."

Fear engulfed the ship which fueled the men's energy level to the maximum and we flew over the calm waters.

"Oars out – now stand guard for oars back in."

We listened for any sounds – nothing – then a crack resounded through the fog followed by splashing sounds.

"Which side?"

"Still port-side!"

Orn ordered the oars back in and once again for port-side only to row first - then all to row. With the fog so dense we had no idea just how large it was. To me it felt like we heading back towards Norway but this fog had disorientated us all. It was better to be way off course then to run into one of these ice flows, we had all heard stories about these giant killers. Are we destined not to arrive in Ireland - instead are we meant to all drown together? If it was breaking apart chances are it can become top heavy and flip on us creating a massive wave that could swamp us and pull the ship down under.

Melkorka

We glided over the water, every now and then stopping to listen until the cracking was no longer heard.

"We are heading in the right direction men, now we can slow down to save some energy. Starting from the front every second row put your oars in to row. We will take turns so all of you can get some needed rest."

He beat a slower rhythm out as we continued to flee this killer and flee we did right out of the dense part of the fog. Breathing a sigh of relief that the fog was starting to lift, we felt the soft breeze but I feared we were not totally out of danger. Although still cloudy, Orn was able to use his sun stone to determine where the sun actually was and set us on a course that would hopefully bypass the ice flow.

Hours later one of the men shouted, "I see land over there!"

Impossible I thought but then spotted what he was pointing at. It was our ice flow off in the far distance and it did look like a small island, it that massive. We were still in danger if it was ever to break apart so Orn re-adjusted his route taking us further away until we could no longer see it. The soldiers began talking amongst themselves and decided that their journey had been blessed after all by our gods, especially after this perilous experience. Those ice flows were called silent killers but Thor's hammer had called out a dire warning and we took heed.

With a stronger wind the sun finally came through, Orn gave the men a much needed break from rowing and set the sail to capture its power, then steered our ship west towards Ireland once again. My heart soared with excitement and gratefulness, I could not believe my good fortune. Here I was, with the long ship and the men I needed, we had avoided a hazardous situation and were back on route towards Ireland. I tried hard to look like the commander they expected as I slowly walked past my men to the front of the long ship. The sun was setting soon but the moon would continue to guide us westwards. I had my *'Wayfinder'* stave in my hand, then silently made a request to gods, that if my grandfather was still alive to keep him safe and to direct us both to a common meeting place. Could my good fortune hold out for this too? I promised Oðin, the wisest and the father of all gods, that I would make a grand sacrifice if I was to find my grandfather alive and well.

Our journey continued westwards without a squabble from any of the crew and I began to feel more confident in my leadership abilities. The Gods appeared to be still with us as the weather held for a couple of days, clear with a good wind before it changed to a hard rain and a stronger wind. My soldiers were able to cope with great skill and managed to keep the sail up through it all, then the weather reverted back to clear sailing weather.

During the rainy squalls Orn had changed his direction south, southwest and now that the weather had cleared we could see land in the distance. The coastline was definately Ireland's Orn said as we all anxiously watched for the great centre of Dublin. We did not want to be too close to it in case we were forced to enter their longphort so we remained further out in the open sea. Finally we saw all the lights and knew it had to be Dublin itself so we slipped into the River Liffey under the safety of the darkening skies. Killcullan Monastery would be our next marker, once there we could ask for information about my grandfather. Surely someone would be willing to find him if the price was right but it was getting too dark to see properly. Making sure no ships were sailing after us we headed further into the river's throat before finding a secluded bay where we anchored our boat and decided to wait till morning to find the monastery. The bays into Ireland were notorious for sandbars and rocky outcrops and the sun had set and with an overcast sky there was no moon to guide us safely. Darkness created too many dangers, so before we settled in for the night I organized a lookout schedule to watch for any approaching danger and directed one of the men, the smallest and most nimble, to climb the mast to remove the Queen's banner and replace it with a plain white banner that meant we were a peaceful ship. I was afraid that the queen's banner might give the wrong message to any Irishman that would see it. Then I carefully folded it up and packed it in my personal chest so it was ready to fly on our return to Norway.

Morning arrived with the sun shining brightly through some scattered clouds. We discovered to our dismay that we were stuck in an outcrop of rocks. The darkness the night before had hidden their shadows and we had become stuck in the shallow water of the low morning tide. This left us in a dangerous situation if anyone should came by on shore or even by ship. We were not familiar with these waters and had no choice but to wait for the high tide. Preparations were in order in case of attack.

Not long after discussing battle preparations with the men, a group of peasants came running out of the forest and waded out into the low tide. We were ready for them but fortunately they did not get far. Suddenly they could go no further, they had run into a deeper area or appeared to be sinking in some quagmire. Thankfully whatever it was it was too deep for them to get any closer. They raised their bows and started firing arrows but none reached our long boat. The soldiers had lined up in a row along the side of the ship facing the shoreline just in case of an attack and they quickly interlocked their shields forming an impenetrable wall. The peasant's crude arrows did not hurt us because none even reached us. It was very difficult to aim while trying to keep your balance in waist high water. To get any closer the peasants, who all appeared to be rather short, would have been under water. The Irish went back to shore but made several more attempts using a slightly different direction each time to our ship but hit deeper water each time. In most countries, by law, any foreign ship that was stranded in their water was theirs for the taking so they were not giving up just yet. The poor peasants were running out of arrows and the tide was rising, albeit too slowly for us and too quickly for these unskilled attackers. We would have massacred them if they ever reached us, I did not want to have to do battle with these men.

Each attempt they made I tried to explain in their language that we were on a peaceful mission looking to speak with King Murchertach. I even tried calling him as the Norse do, King Myrkjartan. They ignored me. All these men could see was an opportunity for what they thought was a rich booty or maybe my Gaelic was not good enough? We easily warded off several more attempts from these unaccomplished peasant warriors and soon enough it would be safe to sail away from this area.

Suddenly, out of nowhere, another group of men appeared. On horseback this time and with weapons that looked more professional. They looked like soldiers with a proper leader, nothing like the bunch of peasants we were previously dealing with. Maybe the peasants were smarter than I thought and sent a runner for help. These men were not afraid of us and came into the sea with their mounts and readied their bows. Although we prepared to do battle once more, I felt confident that we could win this but desperately wanted to avoid it. I did not want to have to explain dead men to my grandfather if I ever found him. Once again I called out in their language that I was here on a peaceful mission and that I needed to reach a man called King Muirchertach.

Astonishingly, the leader responded.

"I am Muirchertach, King of Allech. And pray tell -- just who are you? "

Dumbfounded by this response I had to take a moment to digest it. I decided to tread carefully as this could be a trick just so we would give in to these soldiers but I was determined to find my grandfather and did not want to throw away this opportunity because of a possible ruse. I decided to put myself in the hands of the Gods. *'Odin, the wise one, are you there? If I could just have a conversation maybe I would be able to figure out if it was a trick or not.'* I explained to the king, in Irish, who I was and why I was here in his country. I shouted as loudly as possible,

Melkorka

"I am the son of Mæl Curcaig, your daughter. She was kidnapped when she was fifteen during a Viking invasion at the Killcullan Monastery almost nineteen years ago. She has sent me here to tell you that she is alive and well and living in Iceland. I have gifts for you from her that you will recognize."

The king was silent, he did not respond for several minutes. He turned to his men to converse with them. I could just hear enough to understand what they were saying as their voices floated over the water towards me. His men, apparently, did not believe me. It is a ruse they said, they are Vikings come here to invade and steal from us. The king acknowledged that that was a possibility but their leader looked like a high born man and he spoke Irish more fluently than most Irish. No Viking he ever knew could speak such good Irish so this man was brought up speaking our language. It is very possible that he is speaking the truth. I held my breath, it looked too good to be true. The king told his men that he would give this Viking a chance to tell his story and he turned back to us and promised us safe passage into his country.

"I will give you the benefit of the doubt... for now. As to your kinship with me, we will have to discuss this more fully before I can give you any answer" the king stated. "Lower your weapons and come ashore, I promise you all safe passage."

I turned to my men and ordered them to lower their shields and spears. "We need to show these men that we do not intend any force." They did so, but not without some disagreement, some felt it could be a trick to capture them all. I stood firm in this command telling them that a king had made them a promise of safe passage and I believed him. I explained to the men that they all knew why we were here and that this man could very well be the grandfather I was searching for. Now I needed them to comply and lay down their weapons and shields. I had a good feeling in my gut about this encounter, but did not tell my men that this order was based on such a flimsy decision. Once the men laid down their shields and weapons I turned back to my grandfather.

"We have complied with your demands. Now it is your turn to keep your promise of safe passage. "

Melkorka

Chapter 38 – King Myrkjartan

Once the tide rose higher we managed to get out of the area we were stuck in and slowly but carefully sailed over the rocks hiding below. We were able to manoeuvre safely through those outcrops and got as close as possible to the beach to anchor the boat. Orn and most of the soldiers stayed onboard while I climbed overboard with two of my men into the low water. We inspected the long boat to make sure no damage had been done to the hull while stranded in that shallow water bouncing on the rocks. There were some scratches but the boat was well made. We had a barrel of tar onboard so with some minor sanding repairs could be made quickly. Fortune was on our side once again.

Slowly with a man on each side of me we walked through the water and approached the king. I showed my respect, I kneeled down in front of him. As I did so I removed my gold helmet given to me by King Harold of Norway. Then I handed it over to one of my men so I could remove the gold arm ring from my purse hanging on my girdle. I handed the arm ring to my grandfather saying,

"This you gave to my mother when she cut her first tooth".

A look of amazement crossed his face as he inspected the gold arm ring. He declared to everyone around him that this was indeed the ring he gave his daughter as a young child. "It has my own mark on it." He also said loudly so all could hear.

"I would have known this man was my daughter's son with no evidence. My eyes see the truth." He put his hand on my shoulder and asked me to rise. "You look just like my daughter Mæl Curcaig. You have brought me great news. We assumed that she was dead, never to return to us. Now she has returned through you, her son. Her old nursemaid is still alive but just barely. She can now go to her grave a much happier woman."

Relieved that the king had acknowledged our kinship, I stood up and donned my helmet. But first I had to ask.

"How is it you happened to be close by lord?"

"This is the time of year for our spring fest and my household always come and stay at Dun Ailinne Castle to celebrate with the High King, father-in-law who refuses to die. As I am sure you know from your mother's story it is close by to Killcullen Monastery where she was kidnapped on the very day of the fest. This year's has come and gone but only a few days ago. We were just preparing to return to my seat at Mullaghat Castle. Coincidence or did you plan this timely trip here?"

"I feel blessed that the gods have been with me on this journey."

"Hmmm... I see you are a pagan. My daughter obviously does not have much control over you."

With that comment he turned his back on me and organized horses for me and two of my men to accompany him to Dun Ailinne. I left Orn in charge of the remaining men and the king left a small army of men on shore to protect the ship from the peasants who were still hanging around. Before we left I ordered my men to make the necessary repairs and also to make the necessary sacrifice to each god or goddess, Oðin, Frigg, Thor, Freyr and to Freya for a safe passage and for directing me to my grandfather. A special sacrifice to Freya alone for fulfilling my destiny was in order. That I would do myself later, when I had more time. I began to think that my nickname should be changed to Olaf "*the Lucky*" as everything was turning out so well for me. I could not believe that such good luck was possible.

Melkorka

The king pointed out Killcullan Monastery on the way to castle, we were so close. My original plan had been to connect with the abbot of that monastery and have him find someone, whom I would have paid, to contact my grandfather, but in the end it had all worked out. Once we arrived at the castle I was taken directly to my mother's nursemaid who was now old and feeble. She approached me very slowly. She was indeed close to her death time, I thought to myself. I am very lucky to have arrived in time. When she was finally beside me I handed her the knife and belt. She became overcome with emotions when she had the items in her shaking hands. She recognized both at once and held them to her lips then to her heart. She staggered slightly from the excitement. Being so small I picked her up and sat her down carefully on a bench nearby. Then I kneeled at her knees as I told her that my mother was well.

"Her life is in Iceland now. I promise I will tell you her story as soon as you feel ready to hear it. My mother has missed you very much and speaks of you often, you have never left her heart."

I managed this all in fluent Gaelic. The old nursemaid looked up with obvious adoration at me, she too thought I looked like my mother, except for my reddish hair, which she continued to stroke. Then she put her hand on my face and with tears in her eyes tried to tell me how much she missed her.

"Mel 'astor', I thought that she was gone forever. She was like my own child. I loved her dearly and I thought my heart would break with sadness when we discovered that she was so brutally taken from us. We missed her so much -- she had brought us all so much joy. Do you realize just how much you are like her? You not only look like her but I can see that you are as kind and thoughtful as she was. The only difference is your hair colour. Did you know that your grandmother Flann was a red head"?

I nodded.

Melkorka

"Oh, I know all about my mother's family, at least all that mother knew up to her kidnapping. Mother is well looked after and has enjoyed her life as a free woman in Iceland since I was two years old. You need to rest and later I will tell you more. I too have some questions."

Mor handed mother's treasure back to me.

"Take them back to her with my blessing and with my love."

Over time I told Mor all I could about mother starting with her kidnapping which brought tears to us both. Later how my father had bought her as a slave, not knowing who she was. I explained how mother pretended to be mute, how she found strength in this muteness. I left out the animosity between mother and Jorunn, there was no need to upset her with all that. I explained how father had given her freedom once she found her voice and told him that she was a princess. I skimmed over a few things in my mother's life to spare her any more pain. I described the farm, Melkorkastaðir, and how she loved her life as a free woman farming her own land. About Ulla and her son, how mother generously took them in and now loves them like family.

"Just recently she married her best friend and together they work both her farm and his. As a couple they have a much larger holding so she has done very well. Even though mother is married she has achieved her independence from father, something she has desired since she realized her freedom."

The old nursemaid looked so much heathier after hearing all about mother. Her cheeks became rosy, she began to look like she would live forever. Also, she answered my most pressing questions. What did the O'Neil clan do after mother disappeared? What happened to cook and did Niall die at Kilcullen monastery?

Melkorka

The king, my grandfather, invited me and my men to spend the summer with him. He stated that no honour would come my way until I passed the test stating that I had yet to prove I was a man worthy of his kinship.

I told him, "I have no problem with that and will not hold it against you."

The king took a step backwards when I made that response about not holding it against him. He looked surprised with what I said, then smiled and nodded his head in agreement.

"Pagan or not, you really are my daughter's son. Now prove your worth!"

We made our way to Mullaghat Castle along with grandfather's household. His sons and other relatives continued to eye me suspiciously so I kept my distance. The king was a very busy man fending off attacks from disgruntled Irishmen as well as a few Viking invaders trying to rob from his land. He was always on the move. My men and I fought with him side by side on these attacks even the few, but by midsummer the king called an urgent assembly. He was having many problems with some local chieftains who were trying to take control of a part of his holdings just outside of Leinster. There was a strong leader called James McAlpine and with his leadership, grandfather's spies told him, they were banding together to raise a larger army. This rebellion was turning into a major battle.

"This James McAlpine has been a big thorn in my side ever since I married Siobahn. Her land became mine after her father's death, now he claims this land as his. This land was part of our marriage contract so it legally belongs to me. Siobahn's father's sister, her aunt, married a cruel hard man but died shortly after giving birth to their son James. My father-in-law never forgave this man and blamed him for his sister's death so he swore no child of McAlpine would inherit this land. Instead he made an agreement with me if I married his daughter it would pass to me alone. Now this James fellow thinks it should be his and not mine.

Melkorka

I need suggestions from everyone gathered here today. Since this McAlpine is one of our own and is taking his men from our clans how do you propose we find the extra men we need?"

He desperately needed ideas from his family and his loyal followers but there were no suggestions forthcoming. Slowly an idea was forming in my head but I was not sure how it would go over with everyone, especially grandfather as he appeared to despise all Vikings. He was especially upset that the Vikings, under the leadership of Olaf Sigtryggson, had re-captured Dublin and had once again made it into an impenetrable fortress.

"Your highness I have an idea but I need to work out the logistics of it. Well, you may figure that out yourself, if you like my suggestion, so please hear me out with an open mind. Norway's King Harald Grey Cloak, I have told you much about him. He and his brothers, who share the rule, often go raiding in the spring and summer for booty. They are brave, strong men and have a great army but he needs wealth to maintain his army and his life as a king. Right now in Norway, as I had previously explained to you, there are several rulers so King Harald does not have full power to collect all of the taxes from all of his countrymen. I think he would leap at this opportunity to fill his coffers if we were to promise him much silver to become our mercenaries and ask them to join us on this one mission -- to stop this impending invasion. With his army behind us I truly think we could put an end to these chieftains who are against you. Especially this James McAlpine. What do you think?"

King Murchertach asked for a moment to think about it then he strut back and forth with his hands clutched behind his back. His sons all had an opinion, they all claimed it was a very bad idea but he shushed them all. They glared at me when he asked me if these men could be trusted to keep their word and return to Norway after the battle had been fought.

Melkorka

"I am confident your highness, they are only interested in silver to maintain their lifestyle. They are not interested in taking over any part of Ireland. Besides they would not want to challenge one of their own, a man like Olaf Sigtryggson, and I am confident that they would not cross you if they were to become your mercenaries. Gold and silver are their gods."

Grandfather then asked me. "Tell me, how would you get word to King Harald?"

"Orn can take my boat along with half of the men that came with me. Together they can sail to Norway and make the offer to King Harald and his brothers. He must make sure that their mother, Queen Gunnhild is included in this decision as she has much power over her sons. Harald and his brothers as well as their mother are desperate for silver and will not be able to resist it."

Grandfather talked privately with his advisors and when they returned he announced his decision.

"We have agreed that this may just work but they have to be here before the next full moon or it will not work. When they are here, then and only then, can I go after these rebels or even challenge them to a full fledge battle. You must understand that in the meantime Olaf, we will all be warding off many skirmishes while we wait for these men that you have recommended. The rebels are getting braver through the leadership of Siobahn's cousin and if they manage to get more men then us, we may be in deep trouble. So -- Olaf—yes--- organize your men and Orn together for the trip back to Norway as soon as possible. They must return with King Harald and his army as soon as possible. Do you really think they will come?"

I assured him once again that the reward of much silver and some gold would be irresistible to them, assuring grandfather that when a Viking agrees on a deal that they are very honourable and will stick to what is agreed. But I had to ask.

"Just how much gold or silver are you willing to give them? I must know in order to entice them to come to Ireland."

There was an audible gasp from the assembly when he stated the quantity of silver he was willing to part with and he even had a few gold pieces he was willing to throw in with the hoard. One of his sons asked "and just where is this vast treasure trove?" I could see that he was flummoxed by his father's decision but he managed to send a deadly look my way.

"Never mind where, I have had a secret stash hidden for many years. As for the gold pieces they may as well have them. The abbot has been coveting them for years now - those monks can't fight my wars with me but these mercenaries can. Meanwhile we must work at building up our forces just in case this does not work out as planned."

Then I asked grandfather where in Ireland should Harald and his army land if they agreed. He took me aside and explained in great detail exactly which bay to enter, where there were no sand bars or rocky outcrops to hinder them coming ashore which I later related to Orn. Then at the last minute he produced one of his men who was willing to sail with Orn, a man who could direct him to the right bay when they returned. They set off the very next day with half of the men and that one Irishman, along with the queen's banner neatly folded but ready to fly.

Melkorka

Chapter 39 – The final battle

Grandfather was right, we had many skirmishes and were beginning to feel that these rebels would break through our weakened defenses. Every day I begged the gods to convince Harold Greycloak to agree to this plan. Time was slipping by and I began to think that Ireland was to be my end but just before the full moon the lookout men came racing into our camp. The leader excitedly told them that a great armada of imposing long ships had just arrived.

"The ships are beautiful with dragon heads on each end and there are fifteen ships in all. It is a huge army of men."

Grandfather ordered his man to bring his horse and a horse for me. His man saddled them up and we headed to the shore. Only King Harald's long ship came forward and set out a plank as it edged near to the land. Grandfather and I waited as King Harald walked towards us through the little bit of water uncovered by the plank.

I bowed before the Norwegian king, immediately thanked him for coming, then stood up and introduced my grandfather.

"King Harald may I introduce my grandfather, Murchertach, King of Allech, known to most of us as King Myrkjartan."

I could not help but feel proud that my mother's story was true and I could see that King Harald was impressed that this Irish king was indeed my grandfather and that he was obviously a very wealthy king able to offer such a prize.

Melkorka

Later the two kings talked over the deal, with me as their translator. Grandfather knew some Norse but felt more comfortable in Gaelic. They each spit on their hand and shook on the deal -- it was sealed.

Grandfather immediately sent word to the chieftains who were opposed to his rule and challenged them to a battle not far from his current camp telling them all that he would be there in two days' time. He told them that this rebellion of theirs needed to be resolved once and for all and he was only giving them this short time to ready themselves. He challenged them to fight for what they believed was theirs to claim, or to leave him in peace. He sent out his trustworthy spies to spread the rumour that the king's army was weak from all the battles they had had with them. They fell for it. Anxious that an enemy may have seen the strange ships, grandfather did not want to waste any more time, he needed the element of surprise on his side.

Wasting no time myself, before grandfather could assign any mission for me, I took him aside and explained that I should go with King Harald aboard his long ship.

"King Harald trusts me and will feel more secure with me along. Also, this way he will have a hostage if needed to get the booty you promised."

Grandfather hesitated but finally agreed when I assured him I would be in no danger.

The long ships sailed to the small desolate bay near the battlefield. We tied the ships together and anchored them, leaving a small force to guard them. Then we hid in the forest overlooking the designated battlefield. We saw grandfather's army arrive and soon his enemies charged towards them on the battle field. Their advance showed their confidence of victory, there appeared to be more of them than there was of grandfather's men. Once the fighting began in intensity it looked like the rebels had the upper hand. Grandfather's army showed signs of weakening, then they began to fall back while some other smaller groups of rebels swarmed through them and around them. It looked to this rebel army that they would win but the fall back was a ruse we had planned. When they started to surround grandfather's army we came running down the hill and managed to surround many of the rebels. Now they were caught between two armies. Grandfather's enemies were so taken by surprise they either fled right into our path or into grandfathers. Any that got away we gave chase slaying them as they fled. Many just fell to their knees with their hands in the air, they gave themselves up rather than be killed.

Then I saw him, James McAlpine. He was yelling at everyone to stand their ground telling them that they could win this battle if they stayed together. Some stayed and backed him but many more fled. My group went forward to challenge them and I personally challenged this James who was such a thorn in grandfather's side.

My challenge turned into quite the battle. This James was a large man, a determined man and I thought for sure that he would slice through me if I faltered just once. He called me and my grandfather names to rile me up so I would not stay focused. I had to admire his brave stand to fight me. Even if he managed to kill or maim me the Viking mercenaries would shred him to pieces and he knew it.

"Muirchertech is nothing but a villainous thief, may he rot in HELL. He stole my rightful inheritance and YOU! YOU are nothing but a bastard, his bastard grandson who brings our enemies to fight his battles. The mighty King of Allech cannot even raise a proper army of his own."

He spat at me.

"My grandfather, King Muirchertech inherited that land legally – you were never meant to have it and you know this to be true! Your father was a cruel, heartless man who killed his wife, your mother. You are just as heartless as he was. Neither one of you – your murderous father or you - ever had the right of inheritance! You are a liar and a thief spreading falsehoods to make yourself powerful."

We continued in this manner but my advantage was that I was younger, better trained with the sword and more nimble on my feet, I was able to dance around him. He was an ox of a man and this dance of mine drove him crazy which undid his focus, his defence finally fell. I had him then and pushed my sword through his throat. He died instantly.

Along with his death most of the other rebel leaders were killed so they could no longer cause problems for grandfather. This battle proved to be short skirmish, it was a resounding success with the help of these north men. Grandfather had not only exterminated all the leaders but had put the fear of god into any who had opposed him. The remaining rebels soon came forward, heads hanging, and pledged their loyalty to King Murchertach if he would spare their life. The rebelling counties were left in shambles and without leadership. King Murchertach took immediate command and put his faithful men in charge of the leaderless counties, each with a small army of men to back them up. Grandfather, once more, had complete control of both Leinster and Munster. He was very grateful.

King Harald received the promised silver as well as some gold. Happy with all his new found wealth which was soon loaded onto his ships he declared that he was leaving immediately before Olaf Sigtryggson of Dublin discovered they were in Ireland. Since there was no more need for their services they planned to return directly to Norway to spend the rest of the summer in the lavish style of kings. The life they felt they deserved since there was no more kingly men than them. Grandfather also made them promise to avoid the shores of Ireland in future raids which they agreed as they were in a rush to leave but King Harald made me promise to return as soon as possible. Grandfather was quick to cut in.

Melkorka

"My grandson has promised to spend the winter with us. We will discuss his leaving or not leaving in the spring, so the queen's boat and her men will be returned to Norway then."

Surprisingly Harald agreed but I felt corned by my grandfather.

Later after grandfather's loyal men were in place and once they had established control he had a big feast. Even the High King of Tara, my great grandfather, who was still alive, although very old and feeble came to the feast. He was very impressed with the outcome. Grandfather, I knew, still coveted the Kingship of Tara, but even he was beginning to think that the old man would live forever, that he would outlive him, denying him that powerful crown. I felt for him, somehow it did not seem fair that the *'old man'*, as grandfather called him, should live to such an old age and not relinquish power. When we were all assembled and before the feasting began, he made a statement about his victory.

"What a glorious victory and we have our Olaf to thank for it. Thank you grandson, son of Mæl Curcaig, our beloved daughter. You are a very accomplished young man with great ideas, great visions. We now accept that you come from a good family in Iceland and we all know you come from a very prominent one here in Ireland."

He motioned for me to come to him. I wondered what he was up to as I walked slowly through the crowd of people to stand by his side.

"You have proven yourself to be a greater leader then even my own sons. In England the crown is passed on to the oldest son, here in Ireland our system is different. It is called Tanis try which means chosen and now I choose you. I wish to make you the heir to my crown. If you accept my offer your mother and her husband would be welcomed here too. Your mother could eventually become the Queen mother, she would like that don't you think?"

Melkorka

My heart sank, this was not good. What was I to do? Not only could I feel the glares of hatred from my uncles and cousins, how do I tell this man that I had no interest in his crown. What have I learned about dealing with a difficult situation?

'Be honest!' I told myself.

"What a great honour you bestow on me but in truth I cannot accept. My place, my destiny is in Iceland where I was born. The country is relatively young and in need of strong leaders and I hope to become a someone of note someday like my father. I sincerely hope that you understand my position your highness. My mother depends on me to return to her. She has made a good life for herself in Iceland and has accepted that she will never return to her home in Ireland, she loves her adopted country. Besides, sailing on open waters make her very ill and since she is now a free woman and has a choice she has vowed never to cross a large body of water ever again. So I beg of you to respect her wishes."

I quickly scanned the crowd hoping that my Irish relatives knew I was sincere and addressed them directly.

"Everyone here knows that your sons are very competent leaders, as I do. I have much respect for all of you and I am proud to call you kin but I have no desire to be a king. Kings are not something we have in Iceland and I have been raised not to expect such high titles. Although there is a good chance I could become a chieftain or goði as we say in Icelandic. We are all farmers there and one day soon I will inherit a very good estate as well as mother's smaller farm. I have learned so much about leadership from you, all of you and I most graciously thank you."

I bowed towards my relatives then turned to face the king.

"Grandfather, I sincerely thank you for such a gracious offer but I MUST politely refuse."

Melkorka

This was the first time I had addressed him as *'grandfather'* in front of him and everyone else -- I hoped that it would soften the blow of my refusal. It would be impossible to be the ruler in Ireland after grandfather had passed. My uncles and cousins would watch my every move, waiting for an opportunity to get rid of me. They would feel that it was very unfair to give such an honour to such an unknown, to someone so young, to someone who had not even grown up in their country. Mother would not be safe here either once her father was gone. I wanted no part of it and I prayed that my speech was eloquent enough to talk my way out of this offer.

Grandfather did not speak right away, I thought he looked sad.

"Olaf, grandson, you are a good man and a good son. I knew that you would have to leave one day and I think - I hoped - this offer would keep you here with us but you are right. My oldest son deserves to be king one day as I deserve to be High King of Tara one day."

He directed his focus on his father-in-law who sat in the high place of honour. Although old and feeble looking his brain was still sharp. He stood to speak.

"Young Olaf has made the right decision to return to his own country even though we remain in his debt. There is no doubt in my mind that your son Niall will make a good king when you are gone from this world, but you have many years left and he still has much to learn. I am an old man, I can feel life leaving my body and know that God is waiting for me. Soon enough you will become the High King of Tara, a title you have coveted for many years. Who would have thought that I would live to such an old age, I am more surprised than any of you here that I can still walk this earth."

He sat down as a huge cheer erupted from everyone in the room. My cousins were smiling and clapping each other's backs. What a relief this was to me, I was free once more. Grandfather was smiling.

Melkorka

'The crafty old dog planned this, it was never about me – he used me. He wanted to put the old man on the spot and get him to commit to passing on the crown to him publicly.'

A few days after the feast I asked permission from my grandfather to leave.

"Now that summer is half over and all the counties appear to be calm and reorganized to suit your needs, it is time for me to leave. I really must return to Norway for the winter so I can prepare for my journey back to Iceland in the spring. Please give me leave to go grandfather. I may never return but you will be held in my heart forever."

If granted permission to leave, I also asked if mother's nursemaid could come with me knowing full well that the answer would be no. Grandfather hesitated for what felt like ages but finally permission was granted to leave but not to take the nursemaid. The reason given was that she was too old and feeble and grandfather was afraid she would not survive the trip first to Norway and then another long journey to Iceland.

"What would be the point of her going with you if she does not survive? She deserves to die here in her own land and in her own bed."

"Of course grandfather, you are right and mother will fully understand I am sure."

Upon leaving, grandfather saw me off where he presented me with a beautifully decorated spear with gold inlay. He also brought a cart full of gifts for both me and mother. One of the gifts was the Kilcullen Psaltery, the Book of Palsm, that grandfather had requisitioned the scribes to make for her as a wedding present all those years ago. He also returned the gold arm band saying it was always hers, never his to keep.

Melkorka

'I agree that the arm band is hers but will she want this Book of Palsm - would it not haunt her? She had been kidnapped and was now living in Iceland all because of this book -- BUT -- it is not my place to refuse it. She needs to see it and make her own decision whether to keep it or not.'

I accepted the book as graciously as I could and kept my fears to myself. I left Ireland a more mature man but with much more wealth than before. We parted good friends.

Chapter 40 – Olaf returns to Norway

The winds blew favourably, we encountered no storms or flat winds, just constant rain. Aegir was obviously at peace with the other gods as the rhythm of the northern sea as powerful as ever but constant. We arrived back in Hordaland flying the Queen's banner sooner than planned but everyone was cold and wet through. We all looked forward to a hot meal, a hot bath and a dry bed after docking our ship but I needed to release the sixty soldiers so they could return our long ship to the Queen first. The news that I was really descended from a king had preceded me because when King Harald had returned he had spread the news himself. We discovered this as we tried to pay our taxes to the harbour master. He and his men told us all that they had heard, plus no taxes were necessary. They were expecting us and apparently since this ship and all in it belonged to Queen Gunnhild we were exempt. Once cleared, the sixty men sailed off to the king's private harbour. Next Orn and I moved our belongings over to a small inn where we had rented rooms until our old ship was back in harbour, then went to find a bath house. Once cleaned up, fed and dressed in clean warm clothes, we finally went to report to King Harald and to Queen Gunnhild.

The king welcomed us back with open arms and thanked us for giving him the opportunity to earn so much silver and gold from such a famous Irish king. Queen Gunnhild's welcome was even warmer than before. She was pleased to hear that all sixty soldiers and her ship were still intact, they had already reported in. According to her, I had more than proved my great leadership abilities. She loudly claimed that she had missed my company and made much of my return. She compared my accomplishments with those of my famous uncle Hrut, whom she had loved so dearly. This was somewhat disconcerting. What plans did she have for me? Later I realized that I was safe from her advances, at least for now. Her interest appeared solely to be for my stories of our adventure so I soon relaxed in her company, but I must always remain vigilant with her. She was a wily old lady, cunning and devious, she always had a hidden agenda. It also helped to ally my fears when I heard that she was having a hot romance with a young Swedish man who was a distant heir to the throne there. She claimed that she was training him to be the best king they ever had.

'What a woman!'

We were feasting with the Royal family when King Harold asked Orn and myself for a private audience.

"Men, it is good to have you both back. As you are two of my best I want you to sail farther north than usual. Collect the normal coastal taxes in my name and see what kind of reception you get from the people there. I want to find out if Haakon, Sigurd the Jarl's son, has any control over this area. Rumours have it that he is trying to advance his power on the west coast. It is outside of his domain of Tronheim and if he is stretching his power hold then we have to find a way to stop him."

"We will do as you ask but at the first sign of trouble we ask permission to withdraw. We have men behind us in other ships but I suspect it will not be enough backup."

"Yes, of course withdraw. Return to me as soon as possible with any news and we will go from there. I will send more men and long ships out with you so Haakon will get the message. The west coast is my domain – not his!"

"Your majesty." We bowed and withdrew from his presence.

Once out of his sight I groaned loudly. "In the name of Thor what have we got ourselves into Orn?"

Melkorka

"I don't like it one bit Olaf but we have our orders so we will see what happens."

We set off on our normal duties the very next day and all went as normal. As we inched farther north we did get some resistance but we flew the king's standard and every ship we stopped paid their share of tax. There were more of us than them but some bravely asked why they should have to pay when King Harald does nothing to protect them. We assured them that the king will hear of this and that we would see that more ships came out their way to watch over them.

After inching our way more northwards each day we finally got the message. Something was definately happening here as more and more ships were resisting payment of tax. At the village of Molde we met with definite resistance. It was time to head south to report to the king but the first night on our journey south a terrible storm blew up and Orn's ship, mine and one other got separated from the others. We were holding up the rear of our flotilla of ships but were forced to pull into a small bay to wait out the storm. Once the worst of the storm blew over we ordered the men to start rowing, we were still too far north and were vulnerable here on our own. Before we knew it five long boats had surrounded us and they all had many men aboard outnumbering us. They locked onto one side of each of our long boats, laid planks over to walk onto our ship. My luck had finally ran out, we were outnumbered so we laid down our weapons.

Orn explained who we were. "You men have no right to take King Harald's ships or his men."

"Really. Your King Harald had no right to murder my father, Sigurd the Jarl either. I want to send him a strong message. We are ready to fight him whenever he has the guts to meet us. Now tell me your name."

Melkorka

"I am the skipper and my name is Orn son of Halldor the Easterner, my captain's name is Olaf. We are both Icelanders but in the service of King Harold Graycloak."

I saw my chance to explain who I was. "My name is Olaf son of Hoskuld. My father fought along with your father, Sigurd the Jarl, Egil Wool Sark, and King Haakon the Good at Rastarkalf about twenty years ago where they tricked the Danes along with Harald and his brothers into thinking their army was larger than theirs."

Orn swung around to look over at me standing at the stern of my long ship. "Whatever are you saying Olaf?"

"I am sorry Orn. I thought it would be safer for you not to know this information. As it turns out I have since discovered that the death of Sigurd the Jarl, this man's father, was a revenge killing. Rest assured Haakon Sigurdsson, Queen Gunhild and her sons are not trying to take power over Tronheim. They have also warned me because of my father's involvement, to tell him not to sail to Norway while they have rule here. I expect he would not survive for long if he dared to come. But as for you, Haakon son of Jar Sigurd, it is our sworn duty to warn you and your men that you are encroaching on King Harald's territory."

"Well well well! Olaf Hoskuldsson you are outnumbered but you sound very bold and sure of yourself. This is indeed a strange turn of events. Hoskuld Kollasson, your father, was a man my father spoke very highly of and it is indeed a pleasure to meet his son. Unfortunately I need a hostage in order to negotiate with your king. Better still, hostages, but one of them must be one of you leaders. Which one shall it be?"

Orn spoke before I had a chance. "Take me along with some of the men. Olaf has more influence over the queen and it is really her who controls the king and his brothers. Beside he has had more experience dealing with kings as his grandfather is the King of Leinster in Ireland."

"Really? This just gets more interesting all the time. What do you think of this arrangement Olaf Hoskuldsson?"

"It would appear that I have no choice in this matter. How many of the men do you expect to hold hostage with Orn and what are your demands?"

We discussed his demands and where we would next meet. When we would next meet was something I had no control over, it all depended on King Harald, his mother and brothers. Later after we concluded with Haakon's demands, Orn and five of the crew walked across the plank onto his ship while I and the rest of the crew got ready to row away to catch up with the other long ships.

What a predicament I was in. I was not sure if Harald would ever agree to any of his demands or care if he lost a few of his men, but I cared. Orn was my best friend and mentor.

It wasn't difficult to catch up with the others as they were waiting for us. We sailed to them and hooked all the ships together where I was able to explain our quandary, our very embarrassing situation. Then we all sailed off to Hordaland where I would have no choice but to approach King Harald, his mother Queen Gunnhild and his brothers. It had been King Harald's idea to venture further north and now we were in a hostage situation.

'Was it his constant greed or was it actually his fear of Haakon's growing power that decided this plan? Would he care enough to agree to Haakon's demands to get the release of Orn and the crew members? Thor I need you now more than ever!'

Melkorka

Chapter 41 – A hostage calamity

"Your majesties, as you can see I have returned minus Orn and five of our crew. Haakon Sigurdsson has indeed extended his power over the north end of the west coast as far south as Möre and Romsdal. We especially got resistance once we hit the village of Molde which is about midway between these two areas. He is demanding that he control the coastline of both Möre and Romsdal with the border between you and him at Nordfjord. Some of the local people confessed that they had no choice but to pay Haakon the shipping taxes as you have not been around to collect or protect them for some time."

King Harald jumped to his feet, threw his hands in the air.

"How dare he challenge me? Leave me now to discuss this with my family. I will send for you when you are needed."

This did not sound promising they left me with no choice but to leave. It wasn't until the next evening when I was summoned back to court. A guard took me into the dining area and Queen Gunnhild waved me over to sit by her.

"We will eat first and then all of us will talk later."

"Thank you your highness. I am very troubled for Orn and his men. They have all been very loyal to King Harald and I fear he may be willing to sacrifice them, all of them."

"I understand your concerns but be patient. We will work this out."

I had more faith in her than in Harald so I agreed. As we ate and drank for several hours, I feared my mind would not be sharp enough for any discussions. I tried very hard not to drink any more wine but with Queen Gunnhild's company that proved to be very difficult.

Eventually King Harald summoned us all to his private rooms where more wine was poured.

"We have discussed this extensively. We have avoided those regions coastlines for far too long and fear we are at fault for not pursuing them. By this lack of attention to them we have allowed Haakon Sigurdsson to move south. What we have decided since Molde was where you received the most resistance that the border should be at Molde and Moldefjorden and not further south at Nordfjord. You are to return to your meeting place tomorrow and do not agree to Nordfjord ONLY to Moldefjorden. See what you can do for us as we need to maintain some control up there. Then once we have the control maintained maybe we can gradually get back the northern part of that region even though there is little there to protect. It is a barren coastline with sparse populations but this blatant takeover must never happen again. We will increase our armed forces for strong coastal management and now I have the funds to do so, thanks to your grandfather."

"Yes your highness'" My gut feeling was that Haakon Sigurdsson would not agree but at least I had approval to go back and hopefully attain their release. I dearly wished at this point that I was back in Iceland where sanity reigned.

Our convoy of long ships was larger than normal, twelve instead of the usual six. It felt good to have the extra backup but I had no idea how large Haakon's fleet really was. We were soon back near the bay where we sought protection from that storm that separated us from our original convoy. Haakon was already there waiting and with more than his five ships that had accosted us that dreadful night. I ordered just my ship to slowly sail forward then stopped and waited to see what he would do. One ship came forward and I assumed it would be Haakon's.

Melkorka

We met halfway and hooked our ships together. He invited me to his side but I declined saying,

"We can talk standing on this plank just fine."

"Olaf Hoskuldsson I have a feeling that you do not trust me. Why don't just the two of us take my small row boat and row away from all our men, that way nobody can hear what we have to discuss."

It felt like a strange request but I was curious to hear what he had to say.

Once we stopped rowing the small boat we stared at each other for what felt like a long time. Finally Haakon broke the silence.

"I have heard much about you from Orn. You are a fortunate young man to have such a loyal friend. Now what did your King Harald have to say."

I told him what the king's offer was. Haakon took his helmet off, bowed his head and ran his hand back and forth over his bald head for some time. Then he looked up and smiled broadly. I wanted to ask him if he was bald because he had rubbed off all his hair but I knew it was such a childish question, he may not find it funny.

"I am going to be honest with you Olaf. Do you know the border of Molde and Moldefjordon was going to be my final offer so let us agree here and now -- that will be the border -- do you agree? Your King Harald must be advised that he needs to watch over that village. We sometimes get pirates all the way up here and they come ashore to steal their cattle and pigs. They generally don't come much farther north as we are diligent in protecting the Tronheim coastline. It is quite barren north of Molde but it is the trees I want from there. Timber is a lucrative business for us in Tronheim and lately we have much need of it, for houses as well as charcoal, as our population is growing. Tar and boat building go hand in hand and our ships are the best in the country and are in greater demand than ever. All of these things are making myself and my people very wealthy men and that is the only reason we have ventured south of Tronheim so rest assured I have no desire to challenge your king for his crown. I like how the Icelanders govern their country with no need for kings or Jarls. It is more important to me for my people to have a good quality of life living in warm and secure houses. If Harald ever got power over us he would tax us to death, probably even tax us for dying. That is why I work so hard to keep him out of Tronheim. Now we should stay out here a little longer to let the men think the negotiations are not easily reached. What should we talk about?"

I couldn't help myself, I laughed out loud. This was just too easy and I told him so but was careful not to agree with his analysis of King Harald.

"Well young Olaf, my father had such respect for your father so I do not plan to make things difficult for you. That is why I requested to row away from everyone. They need not know I came to this decision so quickly. Now if King Harald himself had come I would have been very difficult, just to spite him. Do you plan on staying with him forever?"

"No, no. Of course not. I plan to return to Iceland soon where we do not have kings, queens, princes, or princesses. Not even Jarls like your father was. My farm awaits me and one day I hope to be elected a chieftain where I can go to the Althing to argue for the rights of my people, to protect their assets just as you are doing for your people. Even our slaves have rights. Did you know that? My mother was born a princess but came to Iceland as a slave. After only two years my father gave her freedom but there is a story to that freedom if you are willing to listen?"

"Ahh, I remember now -- Orn said your grandfather was an Irish king. Go ahead, we have time."

Melkorka

I proceeded to tell him my mother's story leaving nothing out including why I journeyed to Ireland.

"That is quite the story. Now I am really sorry you did not get to meet my father. He told me that your father was quite the story teller and I see that you have inherited his talent. He would have liked you as well as he liked and respected your father. Now let us spit in our hand and shake for all to see that we have reached an agreement."

We rowed back and once Haakon boarded his ship he waved and another smaller one came forward with the hostages. Orn slapped my back and shook my hand thanking me for his release.

"They treated us all very well Olaf but I have to say I am very happy to be returning to Hordaland. But I must tell you something though… it is a small world. There was a fellow Icelander who is in the employ of Haakon of Trondheim called Einar Einarson from the Hofn area. When he told me where he was from I asked if he knew of a red head named Ulla from Hofn. What do you think he said?"

"I don't know – what do I think he said Orn?"

"He does – not only does he know her - he was involved with her before leaving and did not know she was expecting his child. I assumed it would be his if he had had a relationship with her and especially with the name Ulla gave her son, Thorstein Einarsson. That tells it all and he was very excited to hear he had a son. He claimed he had to leave Iceland in fear of his life and that he later settled here where he married a Norwegian woman who gave him three daughters but died after giving birth to the third one. He said he may just venture to Iceland on one of the timber ships and see is Ulla and her son won't join him here in Norway and help him raise his daughters. What do you think of that?"

"Well I can't see Ulla running off to Norway but maybe he will stay with her in Iceland? But whatever makes her happy – it will be her choice not ours to make or my mothers. You are right – it really is a small world. Who would have thought that the first person I would run into in Ireland would be my grandfather? This world really is smaller than we think"

Chapter 42 – A hero's return

King Harald, his mother and brothers rejoiced in our return. They bragged to each other how tough their offer was then patted me on the back for my negotiating skill. Little did they know I had nothing to do with it but that secret was going with me to the grave? They had a big feast for us all and we drank ourselves into oblivion.

Orn and I remained in the king's company of men for the remainder of that fall and over the winter fighting any opposition to Harald where necessary. Fortunately Haakon kept his promise as we had no run in with either him or any of his men. Securing the trade routes along the Norwegian coastline was an arduous, continuous task and I saw no end to these constant battles with the Viking pirates from other Scandinavian countries. Although, one day I feared the Norwegians would gather together in strength and rid themselves of these *'kingly'* men and their mother, they were getting tired of paying his increasing taxes.

Iceland and my mother were constantly in my mind and I was getting more anxious each day to return to a way of life that I understood. There was nothing here for me and I felt that my luck had ran its course. Also Queen Gunnhild's lover had returned to Sweden and rumour had it that she was looking for a new lover and that frightened me more than anything. I just prayed that she would let me leave without putting a curse on me.

Luckily, I managed to stay out of her clutches because King Harald had ordered us to sail all the way north to Molde now, so we spent less time in Hordaland. Less time with the royal household. Once spring arrived, I truly felt that I had been gone from Iceland long enough, two winters had gone by. I asked for permission to leave but I could see that the king was not happy to let me go. Queen Gunnhild was there as well and I appealed to her good graces as a mother to help me explain to King Harald how important it was for me to return, to complete my promise to my mother and to bring her the news of her family.

"Queen Gunnhild, you once told me that your greatest desire was for me to return to Iceland so I could proclaim my mother's story as the truth and to humble my father and Jorunn. How did you say it? Woman, especially women of equal backgrounds must band together to show their power?"

"Olaf, you do have a good memory. Yes, my goal was equal to yours. That is why I supported you with men and a ship. I do want Iceland to know that your mother was born into a royal family and that she deserves her freedom along with the respect of her neighbours. It is a pity you people don't honour such titles of royal power. But truth be told, I am getting rather attached to you and don't want you to go."

My heart skipped a beat -- then she gave me that devilish smile of hers.

'Thank the gods -- she was only teasing me -- once again! Would I never understand this woman? She has had too much enjoyment at my emotional expense -- it is definitely time to leave!'

She was true to her word and gave me permission to leave. With her backing the king finally succumbed granting me permission even though he would have preferred that I stayed with him.

"I would have granted you anything if you would stay, but my mother has convinced me that you must return to your mother. You have brought me much favour and for that I am grateful."

Relieved. I bowed in thanks to my king and silently thanked Thor as well as all the Norse gods that Queen Gunnhild had granted my request and did not expect anything else from me as a man. My mother was always in our conversations and I firmly believe that kept her amorous needs at a distance besides the fact I had spent so little time here all winter.

A few days before it became time for me to leave, the king asked me to walk with him to the harbour. I had just found a small ship that was soon returning home to Iceland and planned to secure passage for myself. He pointed to a knarr, a merchant's ship full of timber along with other goods, ready to sail. He claimed proudly that I would not have to buy passage home with anyone else. It was now my boat as well as all the goods aboard and it was ready for me to sail back to Iceland whenever I was ready to leave. All I had to do was secure passage for his men to return to Norway as soon as possible after we reached Iceland.

The king had given me much honour by this and we parted good friends. Orn remained in Norway claiming there was nothing in Iceland for him to return to but I left, a much wiser man as well as a very wealthy one.

Part IV
Iceland

A Toast to Iceland

Our land of lakes forever fair
below blue mountain summits,
of swans, of salmon leaping where
the silver water plummets,
of glaciers swelling broad and bare
above earth's fiery sinews —
the Lord pour out his largess there
as long as earth continues!

by Jonas Hallgrimsson (1807 – 1845)

Melkorka

Olaf Pai

Melkorka

Chapter 43 – A father's welcome

Other than lashing rain some days and every day those mighty north winds we had to fight against, the passage back to Iceland was uneventful. My *'Wayfinder'* stave had indeed been blessed and Aegir continued to be at peace with the other gods.

'I really should have been nicknamed Olaf the Lucky' – no--- I rather like "Peacock" the nickname my father gave me. Nobody else has such a name or probably ever will have.'

I watched with pride as we came closer to the south of Iceland. We sailed into Hrutafjord and landed at Bordeyri, the very same place I had left from.

My father was waiting for me as I came ashore. He must have heard of our arrival and came to welcome me home. He offered me his hospitality for the winter which I gladly accepted. If anyone would have the storage space for my goods he would, so I asked him if he had anything available for me. He was proud to tell me that he had recently built several large warehouses and that I could use one of them. I immediately organized the men to beach the ship and to build a shed to protect it. Then I sent all the goods in smaller boats along the Laxa River to the waiting warehouse. The warehouse was enormous, there was even plenty of room for all the timber. I was indeed set to get on with my life back in Iceland. It felt so good to be back in my own country, with a culture I understood and respected.

Father and I rowed one of the smaller boats laden down with goods and while together on this boat as we carried some of the goods to this warehouse I managed to tell him much about my trip to Ireland

Melkorka

"Besides finding out that your mother is truly a princess what lessons on life did you discover son?"

"There were two very important lessons I have learned pabbi. The first being, greed destroys a man and second, friends and family are all that count. For instance your friendship with Sigurd the Jarl may have saved my life but I will tell you all about it later when we have time to drink a toast to them all."

"Let us go inside and get Barð to help us, he is very anxious to see you."

We entered the long house at Hoskuldstaðir to a warm welcome from my half-brother and little sister. I could tell that Barð was especially pleased to see that I had returned safely. Even Jorunn was happy to see me and welcomed me with open arms. With Barð 's help we soon unloaded the small boat. Then I sent word off to mother telling her that I would be coming to Thorbjornstaðir shortly. Although difficult but I finally got away from everyone. Anxious to see my mother I rode off on my borrowed horse carrying my sack of gifts for her and the rest of the family. She was already at the gate prancing back and forth anxiously waiting for me. With a huge hug from such a small woman she asked me for all the news of her family.

I told her some of the news as we walked from the gate to their farm house. When inside I proceeded to hand out the many gifts from her family and from me. It was bedlam as everyone was excited to see me and to receive so many gifts. As expected, she was very disappointed that her old nursemaid did not come back with me. I explained that her father did not want to send her because she was old and feeble, he was too afraid she would not survive the tough journeys. The presents were a good distraction for her especially the Book of Psalms so she never got overly upset.

"I really did not expect to hear that Mor or even my father were still alive and I do understand father wanting to keep her in Ireland.

Although, I would have given anything to look after her myself in her failing years."

She held the book in one hand and caressed the cover.

"I thought you may not want this gift as it would be a reminder of why you went to the monastery."

"Oh no – no son. I want very much to keep it. Olaf you cannot imagine how wonderful it is to read and write, what a sense of power it gives you to have this knowledge. I never told you but I can read! Just think of all the stories this country has, if the people could write, it would be possible to preserve them so that they would never be forgotten. This is a nation of storytellers -- we must find a way to protect them."

She paused here hugging the book tightly.

"No maybe not -- maybe these stubborn Icelanders are not ready? For now they must retain their oral traditions but we ourselves, must teach our children to read and write. It would give them much power. Can't you see this? In Ireland we use this very book, the Book of Psalms, to teach our children to read. Now that I have another son, Lambi is his name, I will not only tell him our stories, both Irish and Icelandic, but I will teach him to read and write. When you have children, I can teach them too."

"Another son! Congratulations! Where is he?" Olaf rushed over to shake Thorbjorn's hand in congratulations and hugged Dora a second time.

"He is sleeping right now but you will get to meet him very soon."

"Mother - there are not enough words to tell you how thankful I am for all you have done for me. This journey would not have happened without your faith in me accomplishing it or without you pushing me to go for that matter. Also, thank you for teaching me your tongue – I don't think your father would have listened to me if I could not have conversed in his language. He is a very tough warrior and probably would have fought with us first and asked questions later but I think I shocked him when I spoke Gaelic to him. He later told me that he would have recognized me right away because according to him I look like you. It was so great to be with him for that short time. I will tell you much more later, I will tell you all that happened while I was in Ireland -- when we have more time. But yes, I think I do understand how powerful it would be to read and write. I see changes coming with this new religion which is spreading all over Europe. It is here already in Skaholt and Holar and soon it will spread, then they will push this ability to read and write. The ones that can already read will be the ones in control. That I can see, so we must be prepared but I would not go around telling everyone that you plan to teach your son Lambi. Is that agreed mother?"

"Of course I understand son - I am not stupid! Oh, elskamin, it is so good to have you home, safe and sound."

I put my hands on her shoulders and gave them a gentle squeeze.

"The most important thing now is that you can hold your head high, you are a p-r-i-n-c-e-s-s mother. You really are a royal princess. I sincerely hope you are happy and just so you know, I think you are an extremely clever independent woman."

The tears flowed down her face and I could feel the tears of emotion sting my eyes. "Oh my son, I have always known what I was, but now, finally, so does everyone else. But first I must know – what happened to cook and Niall?"

"Well I am sorry to say Niall did die in the Kilcullen raid as you suspected. As for Cook, your father was livid with her for being part of your masquerade. She was thrown into the dungeon for some months where she barely survived. Your father eventually released her as nobody could cook like her and he missed her good food as did your brothers. I think your brothers were the ones who really convinced your father to let her go. Unfortunately she was a broken woman and did not last many years but not before she trained another cook who is almost as good as her. She would have been so happy to hear you were well and happy living in another land. As for the O'Neills, of course they were angry too, but not with your father, with the invading Vikings. They went back to the north with a broken marriage contract but more resolved than ever to kick out these Northmen. But guess what, the Vikings have retaken Dublin – soon after you were kidnapped and it wasn't long before your Liam was contracted in marriage to a Viking woman from a royal Norwegian family. If you cannot beat them you may as well join them. There is strength in alliances with the enemy. Right mother?"

Mother agreed laughing, "How strange life can be – Liam O'Neil in bed with the enemy."

"Also, I have some news for Ulla. Her son's father is alive and well and living in Throndheim Norway."

"That is old news son – he is here already and is trying to convince Ulla to move to Norway. He plans to spend the winter with her and I suspect she will weaken and eventually go back with him unless I can persuade them to stay and manage my farm."

I did not linger long at Thornbjornstaðir, promising that I would return soon to meet my new brother. She had sacrificed her freedom to marry Thornbjorn but she appeared to be happy and content with her choice. It also felt good to know that she was so elated that I had had a safe and eventful journey. She stood by the gate waving at me proudly holding her head up high shouting both to the sky and to my back.

"I was a princess once upon a time -- but no longer! I was a slave once upon a time – but no longer! My son's journey will become known all over the land – I want everyone to accept me as who I am -- a free and independent woman! Thank you son!"

I had proven this for her. Her mission was accomplished, her marriage, I hope, was well worth the sacrifice.

Chapter 44 – The family reunions

Much of my winter was spent at Hoskuldstaðir with father and part of it with Thord at his farm. I could see that they were both slowing down but Thord was older than pabbi and while I was away he had been very ill, plus he was slowly losing his sight. He was overjoyed to have me back and I was thankful that he was not angry with me going like I did. Between him and pabbi we talked much about my future and naturally marriage was brought up in our conversations. In Iceland, like many other countries, marriages were arranged in prominent families. It was part of the social economics to make sure prestigious families were joined together through marriage contracts, extending their power and thus expanding their wealth and the respect of their peers.

Pabbi recommended that I take a wife as soon as possible as we could see that I would have to take over the running of my foster father's farm and let Thord retire. I agreed that it was time to settle but asked him to choose a wife for me so I was not surprised that he had someone in mind. Pabbi told me that this woman he chose would make me a good wife, that she was a beautiful, intelligent woman from a very well respected family. Her name was Thorgerður but was called Thogerd and her father was Egil Skallagrimsson, they lived at Borg in Borgarfjord. Everyone knew who Egil Skallagrimson was, stories were told and retold about all his exploits as a young man. There was a long saga just about him and even as a young child I wondered how all of his exploits could have possibly been true. Regardless, I asked father to make the arrangements and told him that I would be annoyed if I was turned down. He said that it would be worth the risk so I did agreed to the gamble.

"I am depending on you pabbi, to make the correct choice for me. I know of this man's reputation and I am not sure how much of it is true but I have to say that I will be very disappointed if nothing comes of it. It will be like a slap in our face if we are turned down."

Our conversations continued throughout the winter with Barð joining in on many especially on the ones pertaining to the running of the farm. Both he and father had much experience on this subject and good advice to pass onto me but there was another important person in my life whose advice I craved.

Time was passing faster than I thought possible, the winter solstice would be upon us soon enough along with the celebration of the Jolablot. The Danish King, Hakkon the Good, a strong Christian, insisted that all Icelanders celebrate it. Although mainly pagans, we embraced this Christian celebration as it meant days of feasting and drinking of which we as a nation are quite fond of. Many a fight broke out during this time from overindulging but overall it was a glorious time of the year. Especially enjoyed by all children, including most adults, were the thirteen Yule lads and their daily exploits. I had not seen my mother since arriving back so one morning - crisp from the heavy frost that covered the land – I decided it was time for that visit. Making my excuses to pabbi and Barð I packed a few gifs for my new half brother Lambi and rode off to visit for a few days. It is important that I get to know this child for I may have to foster him one day was one of my reasons I had given to pabbi.

Mother was waiting for me by the gate.

"How did you know it was me?"

With her arms crossed tightly over her winter shawl, a beaming smile on her face, she retorted, „the dogs always let us know when we are about to have company but how could I not recognize our visitor as my charming, brave son. Besides, you have kept us waiting far too long... it was time you came for a visit.... I have been expecting you would arrive any day now."

Melkorka

"You are right mother, as always. Thord and pabbi have kept me busy traveling between their farms, but I am here now and have a few gifts for Lambi and I finally managed to unpack that large stash of threads I had purchased for you." Smiling down at me, „you will never run out of such luxuries if I have my way!"

Everyone fussed over me, it felt good to be near my mother once more. Dora too, she presented a magnificent feast for us all to enjoy, something my mother would have struggled to prepare. I often wondered how mother and I survived at all as she was never and would never be a great cook. At least Lambi would be spared her cooking. He was a busy little boy who soon overcame his shyness of me and hung onto my tunic, constantly under foot. I was frightened I would tumble over him and crush him.

Darkness descended quickly in winter but on a clear, cold night the sky would often light up with the brillant colours we took for granted. This night was no exception thus giving me the opportunity to get my mother alone.

"Mother, come take a walk with me. We must give thanks to the gods and enjoy those northern lights, all those brillant colours bouncing off Freya's chariot as she transports the dead warriors to Valhalla."

Donning her winter cloak and a fur hat she linked my arm as soon as we were outside.

"I noticed on my first visit that you have several new people living with you here. It was too noisy and busy so it there never seemed to be a good time to ask about them. How are Ulla and Thor managing with Einar here?

"Let me tell you about our household first - the old cripple was seeking a place to live and although he isn't capable of doing hard labour he can knit and carves the most entertaining toy animals from bones. Lambi has an arsenal of playthings, thanks to Ollie. He has also taken over the milking which relieves me and Dora from such tasks so he earns his keep. The young lad's name is Guðjon, but we all call him Jonni and he is a distant cousin of Thorbjorns. Sadly his family has fallen on hard times but my dear husband is a very kind, caring man although he does not let Einar live here for nothing, he makes him work. Jonni spends much time with the sheep in the summer and at the same time Thorbjorn is training him to work with the dogs but nobody understands these animals like he does, not even The young lad. Did you know that Thorbjorn is becoming known all over the country for his sheep dogs, they are probably the best trained dogs in Iceland. They take a long time to train properly, so farmers are lining up for them, some even pay him in silver so our fortunes are looking better each year. But this is not why you are here... is it son? So tell me the reason first then we will move onto any news I have of Ulla and Einar."

"Ahhh... you never fail to amaze me mother... you know me well, do you not? Yes... I am here not just to visit but to seek your advice. Pabbi suggests I should marry and soon. He even has someone in mind."

"But you are still young, why the rush?"

"Well, Thord 's sight is failing fast. He, as well as pabbi, want me to take over his holdings and the sooner the better. Thord will be there to advise me but thinks his eyesight, what little he has, will not last much longer. Pabbi thinks it would be benefical all round to have a woman working alongside me. As you know, Jorunn is the back bone of pabbi's holdings, he couldn't manage as well without her. I know she is not well liked by you or by many people for that matter but you have to admit she is a very efficent woman, everything is well organized by her?"

"Hmmmmm... yes I suppose you are right. Who does he have in mind?"

"Thorgerd Egilsdottir."

Melkorka

"Egil Skallagrimsson? Dear lord, he is a very powerful man and has the most notorious reputation! A dangerous man indeed! What is your father thinking?"

"Pabbi is ambitious, I will give you that. He is seeking a powerful alliance with this man. I have heard that there were several offers for her hand and all have been refused. Can you give me any advice mother?"

"Well son, all I can tell you is this. Thorbjorn asked me to marry several times and each time my answer was that I wanted to be independent and was not ready to marry any man, that I wanted time alone with you. As you have discovered, I had plans for you, although this I did not confide to Thorbjorn. With hindsight maybe I should have revealed my secret ambitions to him instead those plans were dependent on your father's support so I lived alone all those years on a dream, on a fantasy. When your father's support for your journey was not forthcoming I had to re-think my situation... but then you know the outcome. I had to be brave and ask Thorbjorn to marry me. Because of all my refusals I was not sure he would have me as his wife. Thinking back now, I wish he had been stronger, not so shy and had not given in so easy to my whimsical excuse of independence. You must know that your father's refusal of support made me very angry for several years but I now understand. He was a doting father, afraid of losing you. To me that is a cowardly way of thinking... we must free our hold on our children... give them their own wings. This will make them strong and you are just that. This lesson was drilled into me when I had to let you go to your foster father. It was the most difficult thing I ever did but look at you! You are a force to be reckoned with... a young man who has had adventures and now has much to look forward to. I am so proud of you. My only advice to you is simply do not be shy with this woman, do not give up, be strong and tell her all about the virtues of a good marriage to a man such as yourself. Tell her that her father will not always be there for her. With the right man she will not only be a wife, she will be an influential, powerful woman, in her own right."

Melkorka

"But I am a coward... what if she refuses me?"

"Have faith."

Then she proceeded to tell me about Ulla's life.

Melkorka

Chapter 45 – Olaf's marriage contract

Spring arrived, the crops were seeded and the time for the Althing was fast approaching. Pabbi asked me to join him on this trip, he thought that while at the assembly it would be a good time to approach Egil with this proposal, he was sure that he would be there. Barð was left in control of Hoskuldstaðir. Thord was not well enough otherwise he too would have come, besides he needed to remain to oversee the running of our farm. We journeyed across land and rivers to attend the assembly visiting old friends and relatives along the way. Not long after arriving, the opportunity showed itself so father approached Egil with the proposal.

"I am not surprised that a man like Olaf, from such a famous and respected family like yours, would ask for my daughter's hand in marriage. She is held in the highest esteem by many suitors and has had several good offers. So far she has refused them all."

Apparently I was famous now in Iceland since my journey to Norway and Ireland. Many stories exaggerated my exploits and some understated my accomplishments. Much like the stories about Egil as a dangerous young man I was sure. What Egil did know was that I had much wealth to offer and he told father that he would not object but that the final decision would have to be Thorgerds. He said that Thorgerd had come to the Althing with him so he went back to his booth to tell her about the proposal.

Father later boasted Egil's words to me, he was so sure that it was a done deal.

Melkorka

The next morning Egil returned to our booth and told father about the outcome. Shortly after Egil had departed, I walked into father's booth and asked if there was any news. He told me how things stood.

"Olaf, I am very disappointed but there was nothing more I could do but accept her refusal."

There were no words to explain how upset I was with father because she was his choice and he was so sure of himself. The humiliation was more than I could stand, I turned around and left the booth stating that I planned to talk to Egil himself. Father threw his hands in the air, running after me saying,

"You do what you have to, but I plan to come with you to make sure you do not say something that you will regret. Egil and his family are too important to be rude to and we all know what he is capable of, so do not insult him or his daughter!"

"Father," I promised. "I would never do such a thing, I would never go out of my way to embarrass you. Give me some credit. I have learned to deal with strong willed women, my mother for one. Also there was Queen Gunnhild. Remember her?"

"Don't I know it son, you inherited your mother's stubborn attitude to life."

Father and I walked together to Egil's booth. I was dressed in my fine clothes and wore the gold helmet given to me by King Harald. I carried the jeweled sword by my side given to me by my Irish grandfather, King Myrkjartan. I could see that many heads turned in admiration as we walked together through the alley of booths. When we arrived at Egil's booth father entered first with me following close behind him. Egil welcomed us as he pointed to a bench for us to sit on. Instead of sitting down I noticed an attractive woman sitting on another bench at the back of the booth. I strolled over and sat down beside her, greeting her politely. She quietly asked who I was and I told her my name and my father's.

Smiling at her I stated with some sarcasm, "Since my mother was a thrall, as the gossip mongers feed everyone, you must think it very courageous of me to sit down and talk to you."

Overlooking this sarcasm she was quick to answer me back with her own element of sarcasm, "Not at all, I am sure that you have faced more danger than trying to talk to me, a simple woman."

"Oh I fear there is nothing simple about you. Your intelligence and your beauty precede you so I feel like I know you well."

"Now you are telling me that I obviously do not know you. Correct?"

"Let me tell you about myself and then you can decide. Then you can tell me all there is to know about yourself. Is that a fair deal?"

"I accept but first let me tell you why I responded as I did. Father encouraged me to accept stating that it was a good match but that the final decision was mine and that he would respect that. I told father that I have heard all the gossip about this slave-woman's son and that I thought that I was his favorite daughter and told him that I was shocked that he would even consider such an offer. Does that offend you?"

"Not at all but I am surprised that you have not heard that my mother has been a free woman for many years now. Agreed, she was kidnapped and came to Iceland as a thrall, as a gift to my father's wife, but he gave her freedom a very long time ago when he realized that she was not meant to be one. It is very important that you know that Hoskuld, my father, always acknowledged me as his child. Once freed my mother embraced this new challenge and raised me on her own land. She taught me many things, most importantly the Irish language and the story of her life as a princess. I journeyed to Norway then on to Ireland to find my grandfather and to prove that she was a real princess. Knowing his language was extremely useful to get through to him but he claimed he would have known me since I looked just like my mother, his daughter. This sword I carry was given to me from my grandfather, King Mykjartan. Something else you must know is that although my mother is a princess she does not want to be one. This is her home now and she values the culture she has come to live in and likes that there are no kings, queens, princes or even princesses. She just wants to be known as Melkorka, the mother of Olaf 'Pai' and Lambi, as well as the wife of Thornbjorn Pockmarked. I will tell you later how he came to have this nickname, as well as how I got my nickname, Pai, if you are interested to hear more? What I do want you to know is that my mother is an independent woman, fiercely proud of being free, of being born Irish and of her royal lineage. Most importantly she loves her adopted country and does NOT want to be called a princess. Even though she is a wife she claims she is more independent than most women and is her own person because she married the right man. My father and Jorunn will surely state the same claim to their marriage. Both of their marriages are an alliance, neither has more power over the other. My marriage would be built on the same premise if I found the right woman. I think you are that right woman."

"Father did accuse me of listening only to the negative gossip about you. He tried to explain that you came from a more prominent family than I did. He tried to convince me that your mother was not a slave but a real princess, an Irish princess and that you were the grandson of a king. I wasn't convinced. People I have met from all over Iceland claimed that your mother was a slave and was still a slave of sorts married to a lowly farmer. I had no interest to be connected to such a man. That was when father gave up."

"Well – now you know that is not true and Thornbjorn is not a lowly farmer. He has quite a large holding and is known all over Laxardal and very likely all over the country, as being the best sheep dog trainer in the country. Maybe his nickname puts people off, he was very ill as a child and is lucky to be alive. Icelanders have such a penchant for nicknaming everyone and yes he does have many scars, a constant reminder of just how ill he was, hence the nickname "Pockmarked", but he is a very good man. I owe him everything, I could not have gone on my journey without his backing.

Also, like I told you, I have met my grandfather who really is King Mykjartan, Muirchertech in Gaelic. I even got to meet my great grandfather, longafi, who is the High King of Tara. His daughter was my mother's mother so she too was a princess. My mother truly is a princess and comes from a long line of royalty but she likes her life here in Iceland more than being a princess. My own father had enough respect for my mother to give her freedom as well as a small holding on which to farm and to raise me many years ago. Thornbjorn has always wanted to marry my mother but she always refused, she liked being free, or was it because she was a stubborn woman like yourself? In the end she was the one to decide to marry only if he shared half of his holdings with her so I could raise the capital I needed to sail to Norway and Ireland. It turns out she is very happy with her decision to marry. She even claims she is sorry she waited so long to marry Thorbjorn and wishes he would have been more assertive with his proposals."

"I had heard that you were handsome, wealthy even, but mostly the news we heard of you was that your mother was a slave. I can see that I was rash in my judgment of you. I respect your mother's choice now. Maybe it is not so difficult here in Iceland to be an independent woman after all. And married?"

"Thorgerd, I respect a strong woman with a mind of her own and I can see that you are not only beautiful and intelligent but that you truly have a mind of your own as well. The woman I chose for my wife must fit all these categories. I would never treat my wife as anything other than a partner. Also, how do you feel about stories?"

Melkorka

"Stories? Why on earth do you ask that? I love a good story."

"Well, I have many to tell. Not just Icelandic stories but Irish and Norwegian stories as well so I promise you will never be bored."

We continued to get to know each other as our fathers were into a friendly debate over some of the legal issues presented at this year's assembly, thus leaving us alone. It was a good thing that they had something else to dwell on as I had a chance to convince Thorgerd that I was a good choice for a husband and I learned much about her as well. About an hour later she went over to her father. She bowed her head towards both men, apologized saying,

"Please excuse my interruption but may I have a quick word with you pabbi min."

Egil made his apologies to father, took his daughter's elbow in his hand and walked her just outside his booth. They soon returned and he asked to speak privately with father. Thorgerd returned to sit beside me on the bench, winked, then smiled at me. My heart lurched. Father had definitely made the perfect choice of a wife for me. My previous anger with him quickly dissipated as I returned her smile. Father and Egil took their turn outside but returned shortly after.

Father congratulated us both on a wise decision to join the families in marriage.

"Egil explained to me that you, Thorgerd, had asked him to reopen the discussion of my marriage proposal stating you would now accept his decision."

Egil cut in. "I apologize for the delay," he stated with a smile towards me, "I am proud to have you as my son-in-law and can see that you will be very good for my daughter. She can be very stubborn when she thinks she is right."

Melkorka

"Pabbi!"

The two fathers spit into their right hands and then shook them to seal the marriage agreement. What did surprise me was that Egil and Thorgerd, out of respect for father and his family, agreed to the wedding taking place at Hoskuldstaðir in early fall right after harvest. Pabbi had convinced them that Jorunn had the organizing skills to pull off such a large celebration. A date was set there and then.

For the rest of the assembly we were inseparable walking around the booths together, sharing the nattmalls either in father's booth or in Egil's. We reveled in the realization that we were fated to be together. News spread quickly about our engagement and many people came out to offer their congratulations. Many asked us in for a drink of wine or mead to celebrate the good news. Both father and Egil were well known and well respected and many people there wanted to gain our friendship. It was the most wonderful time, I truly pranced around like a peacock, full of myself.

After the assembly was finished, we left for our respective farms. We would not see each other until the wedding. No expense would be spared for the wedding festivities as we were a prosperous family marrying into another prominent, wealthy family. Kinsmen and friends from both sides would be invited from all over the country to celebrate this union.

Melkorka

Melkorka

Melkorka

Chapter 46 – The wedding of the century

People came from all over Iceland to attend the wedding of the year. Tents and booths were scattered all along the river giving everyone access to good drinking water. Not that a lot of water was drunk, there was a barrel of mead or beer sitting outside every booth or tent. Everyone carried around their own drinking horns or wooden cups as they walked around visiting and sharing their drink. Wherever you looked people were mingling with each other, including me, Thorbjorn, little Lambi and Dora. After so many years banned from Hoskuldsaðir, here I was, an honoured guest. When Hoskuld and Jorunn greeted us personally it sent a strong message to all my neighbours.

'Was this all a dream? No, Olaf assured me that we would be welcomed guests, and we were, but still I could not believe this was happening, after so many years of being shunned by Jorunn. Finally, thanks to her, I was accepted. I felt like I belonged here.'

Thorgerður was a beautiful bride and Olaf looked very handsome standing next to her in his embroidered dark blue suit of clothes which I had made for him. The last set of clothes that I would ever need to make for my son. Her wedding dress was exquisite and beautifully embroidered by herself. She too was very good with the needle so I had no fear of Olaf or his children ever been under dressed. The bride's dress was made with imported silk, in a blue colour that matched her eyes exactly. It must have cost a fortune but then Thorgerd was from a very wealthy family and they spared no expense for her special day. Her head dress was very high, another sign of wealth. Her dress made a crinkling sound as she walked and the fine white silk that hung from the head dress flowed like angel wings behind her. None could compare to her beauty. Even the weather cooperated so the Gods continued to look over my son. He truly was blessed. I was blessed.

Melkorka

Our wedding present was well received. I had started this bed cover
after Olaf had left Iceland to convince myself of his safe return. First I
wove the cream coloured wool myself, then covered it with embroidery,
both Celtic and Icelandic symbols in blazing colours but with only an
outline of the Big cross in the centre -- that I had left for last to fill in
waiting for my son's safe return. Each corner now displayed Celtic love
knots done in black silk and outlined in gold in honour of their nuptials
and in the centre the big old Kilcullen cross was filled with my own
designed messages. The most important message was created in the big
circle, the centre of the cross, which according to the pagan Irish
signified the sun and the beginning of life. The wrens, done in black silk,
were flying to the gods and intertwined with a geometric pattern done
in gold thread representing Gods love shining over us all. These birds
carried messages of love and forgiveness not just to my god but to the
pagan gods as both Olaf and Thorgerð were still pagans. In my mind the
wrens represented the blending of cultures, the Norse and Celtic pagan
cultures with the Irish Christian culture and the beginning of new life. I
could never forget that that cross was the beginning of my unexpected
journey to this land of "ice and fire" -- this land that I have come to love
and now accept as my home. I cannot imagine living anywhere else, I
was fated to live out my life here. Now it would cover and protect my
son and his new wife as they began their life together.

*'Maybe Freya does exist after all? According to Norse beliefs she is the
one who controls our fate. Father Michael would be horrified if he could
read my mind right now!'*

I couldn't help but giggle out loud after envisioning the old abbot's
shocked face with such a pagan confession.

Hoskuld and Jorunn seemed to be everywhere and gracious to all.
Whenever we crossed paths with either of them they were rather
formal but treated us with respect. For all the feasts they had tables and
benches set up in rows with the head table at the top end. There all

Melkorka

family members were seated together and we were always included. I could not ask for more. The celebrations went on for three days and two nights, but now it was time for us all to leave. Our tent was bundled and packed onto one of our Icelandic ponies. Two other ponies were waiting for us to ride or walk them home. It was not far. Before we could leave we searched for Olaf and Thorgerd as well as the hosts to say our goodbyes. The newly married couple hugged us and thanked me again for the bed cover.

"We will love that cover always," Thorgerd told me as she hugged me. "We promise you many grandchildren to keep you busy sewing and I understand I owe you much thanks for the sound advice you gave your son."

My heart swelled with pride, Olaf beamed. He was very much in love and he looked so proud of her.

Olaf gave Thorbjorn a big hug and thanked him for such a valuable gift. "The two dogs you gave us will add such value to our holdings. We will start to breed them as soon as possible, but I ask that you foster any pups so they get the proper training - which of course I will pay you for!"

Thorbjorn and I wandered over to Hoskuld and Jorunn who were with a small group of people saying their farewells. We hung back so as not to disturb them but Jorunn had spotted us and took Hoskuld's arm to direct him towards us. She waved off her guests and said a final farewell. Then instead of saying goodbye to us, she took my arm and led me towards a warehouse nearby.

"Come with me, I have a special gift for you Melkorka."

It was a common tradition in Iceland for the family hosting the celebrations to give out gifts to all the guests so I thought nothing of this. The silence between us was rather deafening as the two husbands trailed behind us chatting about their farms. Walking arm and arm with my old archenemy felt surreal, bizarre even.

"I made this especially for you."

She handed me a parcel wrapped in a coarsely woven fabric. I untied it to see what it was. Surprised at the generosity of her gift, in this parcel was a large piece of cashmere fabric so finely woven it felt like air in my hands. I was stunned by her generosity. This fabric had been dyed with the rare purple lichen. So rare was this colour that it made this piece of fabric extremely valuable, something only royalty could afford. I rubbed my hand over it again and thanked her so quietly I was afraid she had not heard me. I was a mute once again -- my voice had disappeared stifled by the emotions bubbling up my throat.

"It is a rare colour fit only for royalty. Not for a 'thrall prinsessa' but for a real prinsessa who is also a member of our family. Thank you for sharing your son with me. You and Thorbjorn are welcome here any time."

Jorunn gave me one of her rare smiles, she was actually very beautiful when she smiled. Now I could understand why Hoskuld fell for her if she always smiled at him like that.

Jorunn turned to her husband, "Hoskuld what do you have to say?"

"Yes, Jorunn is right Mæl Curcaig. Did I say it correctly?"

I could only nod, emotions were choking me into this muted silence – this long forgotten silence still had a strange hold over me.

"Both of you are welcome anytime but I do hope you will forgive us Icelanders if we continue to call you Melkorka. That is how we all know you but we will make sure no one uses your old nickname, 'thrall prinsessa,' at least in front of us. Here is another gift, this one is from me. It is skins from several white foxes that I caught myself. It would make a warm liner for a cloak if that is what you would like to make from the wool Jorunn made you. Your choice, do with them as you please, I know whatever you make will be outstanding. All of us have had three wonderful days to witness the bonding of Olaf and Thorgerður, may they give us many grandchildren. Excuse us now as we must say our farewells to the rest of our guests but as our neighbours we expect to see you both in the very near future. I want to talk to you soon Thorbjorn about buying one of your famous sheep dogs."

With those final words he handed Thorbjorn the second parcel as they turned and left us alone in the warehouse staring after their receding backs. I was stunned not only by their generosity but by Jorunn's obvious forgiveness. I was that mute Irish girl silenced once again by her emotions but this time not from fear but from their acceptance of me. Their accepting of who I was and of who I am now, was more than I could contend with at the moment, it was time for me to forgive and to get on with my life. Tears of joy threaten to flow so with shaking hands I re-wrapped the valuable gift and handed it to Thorbjorn. He tucked both of them under one arm while I slipped my arm through his free one. He hugged my arm tightly and patted my hand with a tenderness that spoke volumes of love. I smiled up at him, my heart was so full of emotion but I managed to whisper.

"Eg þu elska."

'Eg þu elska! I love you! Good God!! What has come over me -- this is the first time I had ever uttered those words to him – and -- it was about time I did. Thorbjorn beamed down at me as we headed towards our waiting horses, my man strutting like a proud peacock. Life at this very moment was perfect.'

"Let's go home elskamin."

The End

Melkorka

Melkorka

Acknowledgments

Thanks to all the people who read my manuscript in its many stages, but especially to Sandy from Utah who was the first to read my attempt at a short documentary on Olaf the Peacock, which had some reference to his mother, the Irish princess and to his father, Hoskuld. Since I was able to trace my ancestry back to Hoskuld and Olaf, I decided to introduce the Icelandic Sagas, through this character, *Olaf the Peacock,* to my two young granddaughters, thinking his strange nickname would spur on their interest. Sandy proof-read my first couple of attempts, and always wanted more, so after extensive research the need to give this Irish princess, Mæl Curaig, a voice took over my story. I was consumed not just by her life as a princess, but also as a slave *(thrall)* and then as a free woman living in this strange land, far, far from home. There is a place name that exists in Iceland to this day called Melkorkastaðir, so she obviously lived there, but what happened to her, I wondered. As a free woman, why did she not return to Ireland, her son was obviously rich enough and capable of sending her home? Was she happy or miserable? The Icelandic Sagas tell us about many of the original settlers and about the things that happened to them but they give them no voice. Sandy's need became my passion to give these few characters that voice. The manuscript went from only thirty pages to this fictionalized version, without you Sandy this book would not have been written.

Thanks to my husband for his unwavering support and for his spelling skills, I call him my wordsmith. Our son Kevin, who never ceases to amaze me, took my manuscript and formatted it the way it should read. Thank you son, this process just became too daunting for me to handle. To our dear friend Jean, who claims she is not a reader but could not put it down. Her excitement for this story inspired me through to completion. You have no idea how much that means to me Jean, thank you for your enthusiasm. Thanks to my brother Larry for some great suggestions and his wife Karen, my sister Alice, and niece Robin, for

Melkorka

taking time out of their busy lives to read it. Linda and Sandy, both friends from Calgary and to the rest of the Arizona crowd, Emer, Sandra, Jane, Loyola, Bev, Michelle and Pam, each one of you took the time out of your very active lives to read the manuscript. I did not want anyone to do any editing, all I asked of them was to tell me "truthfully" whether they liked the story or not. Their responses inspired me to persevere, thank you all. Sandra's response was that it should be made into a movie and I have to agree with her. I had already thought about that and can still envision Jenna Coleman playing the role of Melkorka. The only person I asked for advice in the beginning was my long-time friend Elaine, who is an accomplished writer and a published author, very grateful for your time and comments, thank you. Recently I asked Ian, a young man I have known since he was a toddler for advice on making this book available, for advice on copyright, on printing and even on publishing. What a knowledgeable man he is. Soon after the first few copies were printed we were in Cork, Ireland, visiting our friends Ger and Icair where I got to see a printed copy for the first time. Icair gave me such value advice on reducing the printing costs.

Finally and most importantly, I must acknowledge the Icelandic Roots Genealogy database, to which I very happily subscribe to. This database gives me access to so much information with only a few keystrokes. What an incredible resource for anyone wanting to research their Icelandic heritage or interesting people from the sagas or just people in general connected to the "Land of Ice and Fire."

To all of you and to anyone I may have missed –
takk fyrir!

Bibliography

The Far Traveller: Voyages of a Viking woman / by Nancy Marie Brown. Harcourt, Inc. 1st Harvest ed., 2008, Orlando, FL

http://freya.theladyofthelabyrinth.com/?page_id=397

https://guidetoiceland.is/history-culture/a-guide-to-icelandic-runes?utm_source=Facebook&utm_medium=Social&utm_campaign=Explore&utm_content=a-guide-to-icelandic-runes&fbclid=IwAR290S3Dx2cRLllNuwm035ERkFGOErFj3XgEX3OLboamC1EbXJD3F8MDuNc

http://www.hurstwic.org/history/articles/daily_living/text/longhouse.htm

http://www.hurstwic.com/history/articles/daily_living/text/Turf_Houses.htm

http://www.hurstwic.com/history/articles/mythology/religion/text/practices.htm#foil

http://www.icelandicrootsdatabase.com/genealogy/

https://www.irish-genealogy-toolkit.com/Celtic-high-cross.html

Johnson, Peter. "The Greatest saga never told." Winnipeg, Lögberg Heimskringla, 1 August 2017, pp.12-14.

http://livingartsoriginals.com/symbols-celtic.html

The Sagas of Icelanders: a selection / preface by Jane Smiley, introduction by Robert Kellogg, "The Saga of the people of Laxardal", pp. 270-421, translated by Keneva Kunz, Penguin Putnam Inc, New York, NY, c2000

https://www.naqt.com/you-gotta-know/norse-gods.html

https://www.smithsonianmag.com/smart-news/vikings-secret-weapon-was-industrial-scale-tar-180970651/?fbclid=IwAR1jRrUVb32iLjQbtWTyqBd8Nq3_jLyxFtdak-NCoV1ZMeMEx9vvm0DpNVk

The Song of the Vikings: Snorri and the making of Norse myths / by Nancy Marie Brown. Palgrave McMillan, New York, NY, c2012

http://www.vikinganswerlady.com

https://en.wikipedia.org/wiki/Olaf_the_Peacock

Author biography

I am a first time writer, married and live in Calgary, Alberta, Canada. Alfreda Jonsdottir is a pseudonym, my legal name is Alfreda Duffy. Why use this pen-name? I can trace my ancestry back on both my paternal and maternal side directly to Iceland and since this is a story about this country why not adopt their method of naming? Most Scandinavian countries, with the exception maybe of Finland, used to have the same naming system. Today, Iceland is the only one that continues to honour this ancient method of a patronymic system of naming (and on occasion matronymic). My father's name was Gudjon John, but went by his second name of John (Jon in Icelandic), so I really am the daughter of John, ie. Jonsdottir.

Contact info: alfredajonsdottir@gmail.com

Made in the USA
Middletown, DE
27 July 2019